Parang

To Cynthia

with very best wishes

Gareth Ellis

19* October 2006

Parang

Gareth Ellis

y Lolfa

First impression: 2006

© Gareth Ellis and Y Lolfa Cyf., 2006

This book is subject to copyright and may not be reproduced by any means except for review purposes without the prior written consent of the publishers

Cover design: Pat Moffet

ISBN: 0 86243 926 4

Printed on acid-free and partly recycled paper
and published and bound in Wales by
Y Lolfa Cyf., Talybont, Ceredigion SY24 5AP
e-mail ylolfa@ylolfa.com
website www.ylolfa.com
tel 01970 832 304
fax 832 782

For Marina

One

Singapore

Seletar Airfield — 6.25 a.m. local time, 20 December 1941

THE PILOT SENSED an arm coming out of the darkness; he rose to meet it. The hand, holding a mug, was rough and strong.

"Your call, sir."

The pilot grunted an acknowledgement and swung out from under the mosquito netting. The man placed the mug on the small table next to the bunk. The mug gave off an unfamiliar odour. The pilot smelt and then tasted the contents: tea — hot, milky, strong, and over-sweet. He'd been told about 'Limeys', that they had to have tea, never honest to God coffee. He replaced the mug, slid into his trousers and shoes, gathered up soap, razor and towel, and left for the makeshift toilets and washing station. The air was cool; the sourness of sleep was still in his mouth and throat.

He washed and shaved quickly, without fuss, and then returned to the tent and finished dressing. His uniform, once clean and pressed, was now crumpled and creased. He drank reluctantly from the mug of now almost cold tea, and walked out to the plane; his plane, the plane flown by Jake Spano, 1ˢᵗ Lieutenant United States Marine Corps. The squadron markings were faintly visible in the morning darkness. The plane was a low wing monoplane, a Vought–Sikorsky SB2u–1 Vindicator, known, with not much affection, by its marine crews as 'the

Vibrator', almost, but not quite, obsolete. Its maximum speed was 255mph; range just over 700 miles, defensive armament a .5 calibre machine-gun mounted in the semi-enclosed rear cockpit, and the plane carried a bomb load of 500lbs. This dive-bomber, carrier-borne, had a two-man crew, and was already outclassed by the new American carrier planes coming into service.

Jake Spano knew all about the Vindicator's vices and good points. The plane was just three years old, having entered Marine Corps fighter squadrons in 1938. In the coming months Vindicators were to see action in the milling, ferocious, air battles at the Battle of Midway.

Jake Spano, the son of an Italian father and a Dutch mother, was twenty-five years of age, five foot nine inches tall, and 160lbs in weight. He had inherited his father's dark, good looks and, surprisingly, his mother's dimpled chin. His father owned and ran a small delicatessen in New Jersey. His mother was an unqualified nurse; she babysat and child-minded for some of their more affluent neighbours. Jake was brought up in his father's faith and grew up as a Roman Catholic. When he was nine, Jake's life changed forever. His father, always smiling, never in a bad mood, was murdered, it was whispered, by gangsters because he had refused to pay protection money. Jake's mother cried a lot, then, by agreement with Jake's grandparents, she went to Atlantic City, to work as a waitress. Jake was brought to live in his grandparents' brownstone apartment in Brooklyn, New York. They were not wealthy but the boy was well looked after. One day, he was sent on an errand to the Brooklyn navy yard. It was here, in all the noise and bustle, where he saw, in close-up detail, his first aeroplane, when a small biplane with floats passed over his head. The little plane turned and, to Jake's excitement, started to descend. The floats landed on the wind-whipped water, bounced and came down again. The plane sidled up alongside a moored barge. The propeller feathered, the cockpit hood slid back, and a man climbed down onto the bottom wing, stepped onto the barge, tied up, turned to the boy, waved and moved along the quay, his helmet swinging in his hand.

Jake decided, there and then, that the only thing he wanted was to be a pilot. He was incredulous that he, an eleven-year-old boy, had seen a plane fly, land, and a 'god' appear – not only appear but wave to him. In the years that followed, in the warm rough and tumble of the Italian community, he studied hard in school and worked out of it, driving, illegally because of his age, delivering fruit and vegetables in lorries and vans. He shared the earned dollars, dimes and cents with his grandparents, who were both surprised and grateful.

At eighteen, Jake had a good academic record, and a Catholic priest used his influence, pulled a few strings and called in favours on his behalf. As a result, a delighted Jake Spano was accepted as a student for aircrew training at the Marine Air Station at Cherry Hill. He proved to be an excellent student and transferred to pilot training at Pensacola, Florida. He was rated as 'Above average. Commission recommended.' He was duly commissioned as a 2nd Lieutenant, just after his twentieth birthday. In his Marine Corps uniform, Jake was a very proud man.

In July 1937, he met Margaret, a law student from Atlanta, small and neat. One of the things she said that first attracted her to him was his dimpled jaw. With her parents' less than ecstatic consent, they were married in May 1938. There was already talk of a European war, but public opinion was massively in favour of non-intervention.

"Let them sort it out amongst themselves," was the man-in-the-street's opinion. "America will never be attacked, never have to fight other countries' wars," predicted a senator publicly.

Their baby was born in August 1940. Margaret's parents, from a cool beginning, had proved themselves to be loving and caring in-laws, and, then, delighted grandparents. As a gesture of his appreciation, Jake named the boy David, after Margaret's father. Jake entered what was to be the happiest and most fulfilling time of his short life; flying every day and spending the evenings with his wife and son.

On a sunny but chilly day in early December 1941, Jake, in company with his squadron's pilots, waved goodbye to a tearful Margaret and bemused David, who stood forlornly on the quayside, waiting for the civilian liner with Jake aboard to sail. The liner was full of American Army Air Corps pilots, Army officers, Navy personnel and the Marine pilots. A lot of the other passengers were civilians, going on vacation to Hawaii, the majority of whom, Jake noted, seemed to be women. The liner was to take them to Pearl Harbour. From there, with the rest of his fellow pilots, they were to be flown in the new Army bomber, the B-17, 'Flying Fortress', to join a fleet aircraft carrier in Luzon, in the Philippines. The liner was due to dock in Pearl on 9th December.

The news of the Japanese attack on Pearl Harbour, the sinking and damaging of America's capital ships, anchored in 'battleship row', the destruction of almost 70% of the American fighters and bombers at Clark's Field – the planes huddled together on the ground as a prevention against sabotage – was transmitted live on the liner's radios and was heard in a stunned, horrified silence. The broadcasts from Pearl, the screamed words, the roar of the attacking planes, explosions, and the hammering of machine-guns remained for ever in the memory of all who heard them. Jake, along with a lot of servicemen, felt an impotence and rage that he was unable to contain.

When Jake and the other pilots disembarked at Pearl, battleships were still burning and whole rows of American planes were smashed and burnt. There was confusion amongst servicemen, invasion scares, and the civilians were terrified.

The Flying Fortress had gone. Some had actually landed at one of Pearl Harbour's airfields as the Japanese attack came in. The B-17s were refuelled and flown to Manila, supposedly out of harm's way. The Marine pilots were flown in civilian aircraft to the Philippines, and then staged onto Batavia in Java, Dutch East Indies. They had to while away two days, until their Vindicators, which had been transferred to merchant ships, arrived.

Jake found himself up before the squadron commander, the Major, who had slept for only four hours during the last twenty-four. He was brief to the point of rudeness.

"Take your crate to Palembang in Sumatra. You'll be met by an American Embassy official and you'll be given your orders."

The Major held his hand up, palm outward.

"Don't ask, Spano! I don't know what your orders will be. All I know is that I'll be one pilot short. Leave your crewman here. This is a solo mission."

Spano spent an hour checking and testing his Vindicator, which had been crated from the Philippines, and then he flew to the Royal Netherlands Air Force field at Palembang, where an ageing Ford saloon car was waiting for him. He was shown into a small, dusty, airless room, which he guessed, quite rightly, had recently been a storeroom. An American, the Embassy man, looked tired. There were sweat stains on a shirt that hadn't been changed for two days, and he wore no tie. The American Naval officer, by comparison, was immaculate in a crisp white uniform. The Embassy man spoke.

"Today's the 17th. Fly to Seletar airfield in Singapore. The British will modify your plane; stores will be loaded, and immediately you receive clearance, you fly back here. Your plane will be unloaded, and then you high-tail it back to Batavia. Rejoin your squadron."

He looked up. "Any questions?"

Jake wondered why he'd been briefed by a civilian, when a Navy Lieutenant Commander had been present, but he gave no reply. The orders were crystal clear. He saluted; his salute was returned by the Navy Officer.

Jake walked out of the room and into the stifling heat. The Royal Netherlands flag and the air sock hung limp and motionless in the sun-drenched air. Nobody seemed to be moving with any urgency or purpose, and with a nagging, persistent apprehension, he wondered what his duties involved. Margaret and David seemed a long, long time and place away.

★ ★ ★

He flew to Singapore. Seletar airport was under major construction. Gun pits were being dug, hangars covered in concrete. When he had taxied in, he was met by a Royal Air Force Flight Lieutenant with a quiet voice and a pronounced limp. Then he was driven to a place called Fort Canning. Singapore's streets seemed to be a jumble of frightened Chinese, with groups of sullen soldiers moving with dumb insolence reluctantly out of the way of the one-ton army truck. On several street corners, mobs of obviously drunk troops spilled out onto the roadways. Jake was conscious of a blanket of sourness and a cloying sense of despair and defeat. He shrugged. With his albeit limited knowledge of this part of the world, he had heard that Singapore was impregnable — a fortress able to resist any attack from the land, sea or air.

Fort Canning was a seething mass of service personnel, of shouted orders, stamping feet and hurrying clerks. He waited until his name was called. The British officer's belt gleamed; his tunic and shorts had been impeccably ironed.

"Your flight plan. Follow it to the letter. Your cargo will be loaded tomorrow."

As the officer's eyes took in the unfamiliar uniform and the American's unresponsive expression, he extended his arm and said, "Good Luck!"

Jake touched the proffered hand in a brief, friendless exchange.

The lorry driver started the engine and asked, "Where to now, sir?"

Jake slid the envelope containing the flight plan into his breast pocket.

"I could do with a drink," he replied.

The driver let out the clutch.

"Not in town; the place is full of Australians. They have the dollars and the tempers." He manoeuvred the nose of the lorry past two trishaws, the furiously pedalling Chinese not looking up. "And," he spat expertly through the open window, "there's sailors. You've heard about the *Repulse* and the *Prince of Wales?*"

Jake shook his head, unwilling to show his knowledge of the sinking of these ships.

"They've gone; both sunk! The Jap Air Force swarmed all over them – dive bombers, torpedo bombers, over eight hundred matelots lost." He saw the blank look on the American's face, and continued, "matelots, sailors, Royal Navy dead. Where were our planes? Nobody knows where they were; only they weren't where they were bloody needed. There were only rumours, and this place is full of them."

The lorry turned off the main road and into a quieter, residential avenue. The driver spoke again, the bitterness in his voice evident.

"It's just as bad up country. The Japs landed less than a

13

fortnight ago. They've gone through us like a knife through a bloody block of butter. We can't stop them, nor the Aussies, the Ghurkhas, or the Indians. From what I've heard, the battalions have been bled white, with drafts going to the Middle East, being replaced with conscripts, and some of them can't seem to hold a rifle, let alone fire the bloody thing!"

The lorry bounced over a manhole, and the driver changed gear. "I reckon I've come to my death," and he nodded to Jake's uniform. "You're a Yank, it's not your fault we're up the creek, but you're wearing wings, and that would be good enough for some of the sailors. I've seen enough to know you'll be safer in some bar out of town. There's one just outside the airfield. I'll take you there."

The bar, a bare two hundred yards from the airfield, was chaotic. Air Force personnel mixed with civilians dressed incongruously, so Jake thought, in white shirts and shorts. Some were carrying briefcases and umbrellas. There were a lot of drunks. The Chinese barman was curt.

"What do you want?"

Jake returned the gaze. "I want service. Whisky."

"A large scotch?"

"No, I want the bottle." Jake handed over a fist full of dollars, took the bottle and stepped back into the heat and dust outside. With a deafening roar, a flight of three planes flew overhead. The American felt uneasy. The dejection of the troops he'd seen, the truculence of some of the civilians, it was as if a new order was coming; the old order being allowed to slip away in bitterness and ignominy. Bad as he felt, and with a certainty that was almost physical, he accepted that things were to get worse – a lot worse. Jake reached his hut and tried to empty his mind of the turmoil he had witnessed. The whisky helped, but it was an uneasy, fitful sleep he slept.

Jake ditched the tea-leaves from the bottom of the mug. Two British mechanics were working on the Vindicator. He ignored them and their singsong accents and watched in disbelief as they started to remove the machine-gun from the rear cockpit.

"What are you doing?" he demanded.

One of the mechanics looked up. "Orders, sir; just obeying orders."

Jake was conscious of the man's eyes focusing on someone behind him. He turned and saw a right arm come up in a ridiculously wide arc as the salute ended.

"Good morning."

It was the Flight Lieutenant who had met him three days earlier. The American merely nodded, ignoring the elaborate salute. He wished this man would state his business and leave. He had little time for 'Limeys', the derisive nickname in common use in the American armed forces, standing for all things British, snobbish and weak. A salute from outer space, an army that had been kicked out of Norway, Belgium, France, Greece and Crete, proof they couldn't fight their way out of a paper bag. Always on the run, usually backwards, and it was happening now in the Western Desert and Malaya.

"What are you doing with my armament?"

The RAF man answered evenly, "We were given specific weight allowances. The gun and ammo have to go. I have orders, just like you and everyone else. Your crate will be loaded in twenty minutes." He nodded confirmation to the two mechanics, who continued with their task.

A British Army lorry reversed up to Jake's plane, the tyres swishing in the dewy grass. Half a dozen Japanese soldiers jumped out from underneath the tarpaulin, revealing olive faces, slant eyes, small neat men. The marine was incredulous.

"Japs?"

The RAF man smiled. "Hardly. We've not been overrun yet. These are Ghurkhas."

Despite himself, Jake felt himself flushing, his ignorance of this part of the world all too obvious. The RAF man limped away. Jake nodded at the retreating figure and spoke to the mechanics. "He trip over a dog?"

The taller of the mechanics turned to face him.

"He did, actually. It was a German dog. He's a Battle of Britain pilot. Three confirmed kills and two probables. It was one of the probables that gave him the limp. You have any kills, – sir?" The sir took a long time to come, the mechanic's voice implying that he already knew the answer.

Furious, Jake spun on his heel, passed the Ghurkhas, who were loading sack-covered boxes, very heavy boxes if their strained expressions were anything to judge by, into the fuselage of the Vindicator. Jake returned to the sweltering heat of his hut, pulled on his flying jacket, hung his belt on his hip, the Smith & Wesson revolver heavy against his thigh, gathered up his field dressing and maps, stuffed the memorised flight plan into his top pocket, and went to the shabby toilets, to relieve himself. On his return, he picked up the photographs of Margaret and David, kissed them both – a ritual he observed every time he flew – crossed himself and went back out into the grudging daylight. He wanted to be away from this place and back with his squadron, where all things were American, not some crumbling, class-ridden bastion of the British Empire.

The RAF man was waiting for him.

"Your crate's loaded. I'm not allowed to tell you about, or discuss, your cargo, other than to say that we have neither exceeded your bomb-load weight, or maximum take-off weight."

The man's accent was not familiar to Jake's ears.

"You Scotch?"

"Scotch is whisky. Scots, with an *s*, is people. I'm Welsh."

Jake's mounting irritation turned into naked aggression, which showed in his voice. "You're speaking English. What's Welsh?"

The RAF man was facing him, the pain from his leg etched around his eyes. "There are England, Scotland, Ireland and Wales – collectively we're called British."

Jake's ignorance of European geography surfaced into a near snarl. "So where the hell is Wales?"

The man was turning away as if a schoolmaster were dismissing a stupid pupil. "Turn left at London, and it's where I'd like to be right now!"

Jake's temper was clouding his mind in a black mist. "Oh!"

The RAF man had stopped. "Where is your flight plan?"

"I don't have to produce it to you," Jake snapped.

The man turned full face and Jake noticed the green eyes had acquired a glint. "Your flight plan...?"

Jake balled his fits and took a step forward. The man spoke rapidly in a language Jake had not heard before. The two mechanics immediately picked up long rifles, with medieval-looking bayonets already fixed. The RAF man spoke in a flat, even voice. "Give me your flight plan, or I'll kill you."

The very starkness of the words sent a stab of coldness into Jake's chest. It came with the realisation that his life was in immediate danger, however improbable the reason, and was about to be terminated.

The mechanics had adopted a bayonet-fighting stance, right

legs bent at the knee, left legs fully stretched to the rear. Both men seemed to be on the balls of their feet. The steel was less than a foot from Jake's chest and throat. Lieutenant Jake Spano, USMC, took a decision. He slowly raised his left hand palm outwards, in a gesture of surrender, slid his right hand into his pocket, retrieved the flight plan and handed it to the officer.

"Wait here."

The Ghurkhas, who had witnessed the spectacle, were dismissed. The Flight Lieutenant limped back to the orderly tent that served as an office. The mechanics did not relax or move out of the bayonet stance.

"You are having an escort?"

Jake's response came in a vehement spurt. "I want no escort from your Royal Air Force." He accentuated the languid drawl he had heard in the bar at Seletar. "I hear you get shot out of the sky. The Japs are too good for you."

"As a matter of fact, you're right," the smaller of the men replied. "Our lot, the Aussies and New Zealanders fly Brewster Buffaloes. You know them? Not good enough for the Yankee navy, but good enough for Singapore."

Jake was conscious of the steel inching forward.

"I don't know who you are, Yank, or what you're doing here – don't really care. What I do know, and so does he," his head jerked to the other mechanic, "is that we've been fighting for over two years with obsolete ships, guns, tanks and planes, and with some generals and admirals without the sense God gave to a duck. And we are still fighting! Then, you lot get attacked, and suddenly it's all so different. You and your country will learn the hard way, and it is hard. The Blitz – women and kids blown to hell. You want to pray it doesn't happen to your family. So, Yank, don't be so stinking cocky. This will be no Hollywood war, so wherever you are flying to, piss off!"

The bayonets were now an inch from his throat and eye. Jake's breathing was laboured, and what felt like a river of sweat ran down his back as he forced himself to return their stare. Out of the corner of his eye, he saw the limping officer returning. As he expelled his breath, a long forgotten moment of his life was recalled, when an old, Italian doctor had lanced a carbuncle on his back; he had known the relief of the pain subsiding as the poison was released. The realisation that he would not die at the hands of these men was like that moment.

"At ease."

The rifles were returned to the men's sides. The envelope was returned.

"You've memorised it? Very well, you are cleared for takeoff. Tune into the tower for your vector, and note also the emergency frequency, if you need it. It's been added to your flight plan."

The RAF man took a pace backwards and gave again a huge, sweeping salute.

Jake accepted the envelope, ignored the salute and the silent disdain of the mechanics, climbed aboard the Vindicator, flipped through the pre-flight checks, started the Pratt & Whitney engine, and taxied gently out onto the tar macadam strip. The aircraft accelerated, roared down the runway, clawed itself into the morning sky, climbed, banked and flew into the rising sun. It was 7.58am, on the 20th December 1941.

* * *

The mess had put up Christmas decorations, which hung forlornly over pelmets, doors and the small bar, and a minute palm tree masqueraded as a Christmas tree. The building and grass strip belonged to the local flying club, requisitioned urgently by the Royal Air Force and now home to a Royal Australian Air Force squadron.

The Squadron Leader looked tired, his cotton uniform jacket was open wide, and sweat glistened on his face. He motioned to the two similarly dishevelled sergeant pilots.

"Sit down," he ordered; they pulled up chairs. "You've drawn a cushy number."

The taller of the two pilots pulled a cigarette packet from his jacket and lit up, his fingers not quite steady as the match ignited the tobacco.

"Take off in twenty minutes. Are you fuelled and armoured?" He received affirmative nods. "You are top cover for a...," he checked the flimsy, "...a Yankee Vindicator. Form up over Seremban, at 12,000 feet; escort him to Palembang in Sumatra; and don't leave him until he lands here." His finger tapped the open map. "At Buitenzorg. It's a Royal Netherlands Air Force strip. Refuel, and, this is the cushy number, wait there until you receive further orders from me." He turned the paper over and his voice lost some of its tiredness. "Royal Air Force Headquarters Singapore, no less."

"Why do we have to wet-nurse the Yank?"

The younger of the two sergeants was drumming his fingers on the table. In the dusty stillness of the room, the sound was loud.

"Not a clue. I'm a Squadron Leader, not an Air Vice-Marshal. Do you need anything? Okay. You rendezvous over Seremban in...," he glanced at his watch, "in thirty minutes."

Both sergeants rose. They were young men but their limbs seemed heavy, slow and awkward. The events of the last twelve days, which had seen an almost unbelievable series of disasters, were taking their toll.

The Squadron Leader, an accomplished fighter pilot, was four years older than the sergeants. He was also human.

"Look, I know what we've been through. It's nothing short of a full-blown nightmare. The Japs invaded twelve days ago, and we've lost control of virtually every airfield north of Kuala Lumpur. We've been clobbered with just about every bit of bad luck there is, and some of it's on two legs."

Both pilots nodded. The word was that a traitor was calling in Japanese strikes when Allied planes were landing and taking off, and were at their most vulnerable. This, in time, turned out to be true. A Captain Patrick Heenan, an Air Liaison Officer of the 3/16th Punjab's Regiment was arrested, tried, found guilty and executed.

"I repeat: is there anything you want?"

The older of the two sergeants exhaled cigarette smoke. "A couple of Spitfires would be nice."

The Squadron Leader's laugh came out as a barely concealed snort. "The Brewster Buffalo is all I've got to offer."

The small, tubby, under-powered fighter, with a top speed of 313mph, was no match for the Japanese Navy and Army Zeros. The fact that Buffaloes and Blenheims offered no effective opposition to the Japanese was compounded by awareness that the Zeros were flown by skilled pilots, something which had come as a painful and shocking surprise to the British, Australian and New Zealand aircrews. The Japanese pilots were good, very good; many had gained experience from years of combat flying in Manchuria and China, where they'd all but wiped out the fledgling Chinese Air Force. The Buffaloes went up every day, often unable to defend themselves. The pilots earned themselves grudging praise; brave but baffled was a common thread in the servicemen's messes throughout Malaya.

Both Japanese Zero and 97 type fighters cut swathes through the British air defence of airfields in Northern Malaya, with the result that the British Army was all but helpless, bereft of air cover. The soldiers were made to move at night, to avoid the daylight skies seemingly swarming with Japanese planes. The British, Australian, Ghurkha and Indian soldiers had to make suicidal retreats against road blocks; the Japanese infantry moving with stealth and skill through jungle that was thought by the British High Command to be too dense for European soldiers to operate in. The war was turning into one long retreat, in some cases it was a rout.

Both young sergeants nodded. It was an uncomfortable but accurate assessment. The Squadron Leader spoke again. "Remember when we were stationed at Alor Star, and we had a mess night with officers of that Jock regiment? Well, I asked this Major, a company commander, whether we, the British, could hold Malaya. He was emphatic in his opinion. With the old battalion, we could hold it till the cows come home; with three drafts of regulars being sent to the Middle East and replaced with conscripts, he shook his head. Nearly all the reinforcements we have been sent so far are untrained in jungle warfare. As I see it, within these walls, the best we can hope for is to get back to Singapore and await further reinforcements, ships and, crucially, aircraft carriers, Hurricanes and Spitfires. Then, we should be alright and able to give the Japs some of their own medicine."

The sergeants nodded.

"Roll on Singapore. At least that's defensible. Some Singapore gin slings a nice plump 'pinkie'."

'Pinkie' was the term servicemen gave to European women. It was the servicemen's belief, a widely held one, that all European women wore pink silk knickers. All three men smiled. The universal soldiers' creed: beer and women – for some, it was the only thing worth fighting for.

The Buffaloes took off from the dusty grass strip, and came back low over the field, waggling their wings. The airmen on the ground, toiling at digging trenches, gave a brief glance upwards, a hasty thumbs-up, and the Buffaloes were gone. The Squadron Leader watched them go. Riding shotgun for a Yank! What was he carrying that was so special? The tiredness was closing in. He walked away, to check the field.

★ ★ ★

The flight leader was experienced; his Zero was the complete fighter aircraft, with its two 7.7mm machine-guns, two 20mm cannon, maximum speed 351mph, exceptional manoeuvrability and excellent climb rate. In 1941, it was widely and rightly regarded as King of the Far East skies. As the leader brought his flight of four Zeros up through the cloud base, at 7,000 feet, his goggled eyes caught movement to his right. The wingman waggled the Zero's wing and pointed upwards, 9 o'clock high. He had spotted two Buffaloes struggling to gain height. The leader nodded an acknowledgement, pulled back the joystick and the flight surged upwards, to close on the as yet unsuspecting Royal Australian Air Force pilots. Closing to 300 feet below the Buffaloes, all four Japanese fighters opened fire. The machine-gun and cannon hits were instantaneous and deadly. The port Buffalo staggered, and yawed to the left, smoke and flames streaming from the engine. In a bright, blinding flash, the plane exploded. The left-hand Zero sustained fuselage and wing damage as debris from the Buffalo impacted. The surviving Buffalo dropped like a stone in a near vertical dive, running for its life. Two Zeros peeled away and chased the diving Buffalo. The hood of the tubby little plane flew backwards and a figure struggled to bale out. The Zeros' cannon shells slammed into the airframe. The figure slumped back in the cockpit; the stricken plane, streaming black smoke, started a shallow glide into the approaching jungle. Both Japanese pilots saw the Buffalo slide in a splintering crash into the yielding greenness. They did victory rolls; the whole attack had taken just eighty-five seconds.

The patrol was from the Loyal Lancashire Regiment battalion. The Buffalo had passed over their heads with a loud, stuttering roar, invisible through the green canopy above them. Next, there was a deafening crash, leaves and branches flying down to the jungle floor, a bare fifty yards away. There was no explosion, no fire, just an eerie silence as the jungle closed in around the downed plane. The patrol was led by a corporal, a regular soldier. Six of his companions were conscripts, or recalled Territorials. When the patrol found him, the Australian pilot was still alive – just. The soldiers clambered up onto the one intact wing and looked into the cockpit. The unfortunate pilot had lost an arm, and both his legs were smashed. As quickly as they could, the soldiers gently lifted him out, two pausing to vomit as the blood-splashed cockpit released his body. He asked for a cigarette, but died as it was being lit. The corporal took the dead pilot's identification tags, wallet and revolver, and covered his body with the shredded parachute. The patrol left, leaving the pilot's body and the wrecked plane to the jungle.

Above, the two Zeros climbed to rejoin their flight. In their mess tonight there would be rice wine and toasts to be drunk, but neither of the Japanese pilots had seen a low wing monoplane disappear into the shielding clouds.

Two

Malaya

Negri Sembilan – 15 February 1957

IF THE GODS OF WAR were looking down they would have been impressed. The patrol, comprising four men, moved easily, smoothly, even silkily through the greenness. The leading scout was armed with a Bren gun carried on a sling. A corporal, a fusilier, was the second man, and he carried a short Lee Enfield rifle. The third man had an Australian Owens Gun; he was a 2nd Lieutenant. The rear man, with an American semi-automatic carbine, was another fusilier. They were three days into a seven-day operation, their base camp 800 yards and one hour away. The jungle had long since lost its terror for the men. They moved with a confidence that only familiarity with the jungle can give.

The patrol was from 14 Platoon, D Company, 1st Battalion, The South Wales Fusiliers. The jungle teemed with sounds, and there was always the smell, a unique, strange mixture of rotting vegetation and primeval animal smells. The very air seemed like a warm, wet blanket, covering everything in a relentless film of moisture. The sun was seldom visible through the green canopy above them; the occasional sounds of unseen animals and the rustling and sway of greenness seemed always to be moving away from the men. There were still tigers in the Malayan jungle, and elephants, and crocodiles in large rivers, though none of the men had seen any, and there were snakes, of which they had seen plenty. Every platoon could tell tales of cobras and snakes like the Krait, a small black snake, nicknamed 'the bootlace snake'. It was said that the Malayan jungle was home to 133 varieties of snake, 127 of which were poisonous. Four months earlier, a fusilier on a night ambush had died of snakebite. None of the men spoke, their eyes moved restlessly, trying to penetrate the gloom, seeking any movement, any sign that did not fit into the chaotic jumble all around them.

Four days earlier, three of the men had sprawled in unselfconsciousness laziness in the platoon basha in Gemas. No. 14 Platoon was nominally twenty-seven strong: eighteen fusiliers, three corporals, three lance corporals, a fusilier signaller, a platoon sergeant and an officer, but five members of the platoon had left. Four national servicemen were on demob to Britain, a regular had been posted to Hong Kong, a lance corporal was in the venereal disease ward at the British Military hospital at Kuala Lumpur, and one was in jail, his temporary home for the next twenty-eight days. The Sergeant was on temporary attachment to the demonstration platoon at Kota Tinggi.

"Who's taking us out? Quivering chins?" Tucker was a regular with six years service; next to the sergeant, he was the oldest in the platoon, an acknowledged hard man, quick with his fists. Griffiths, the senior corporal, answered.

"No, he's on a course."

"Is he on his honeymoon?"

All three men grinned. Second Lieutenant Neville Lloyd Jones, also known, but not to his face, as 'quivering chins', had been unwise enough to leave a half finished letter to his girlfriend, complete with address, in the drawer of the company office. The night guards had found it and given the letter to Griffiths, the accepted wordsmith of the platoon. In a very creditable imitation of the officer's handwriting, he had composed a letter of love, desire and straight forward lust, with graphic details of what their wedding night would be, ending with, *My very own Darling, I want and love you so much since being in this green hell. I yearn for you every moment of the day. Darling, will you marry me?*

Neville Lloyd Jones, despite his nickname, was no fool. He pulled the platoon sergeant aside. "Sergeant, there's something wrong with the platoon. I sense they're hiding something from me?"

The sergeant, who knew nothing of the letter, replied honestly, "I dunno, sir. They're an evil lot."

Eleven days later, by return of post, from a rectory in Suffolk, a delighted letter of acceptance was received.

My very own darling, what a beautiful surprise. Of course I'll marry you. Mummy and Daddy are over the moon. And darling, I can't wait for our wedding night.

Thoroughly alarmed, 2nd Lieutenant Lloyd Jones sought urgent advice from the Company Commander and a reluctant padre. There followed a flurry of telegrams and long distance phone calls, culminating in an icy final letter from the outraged rector and his wife, threatening, amongst other things, a possible Breach of Promise action.

In the officers' mess, Lloyd Jones found no comfort at all. The other 2nd Lieutenants universally sang Don Cherry's hit record, 'Band of Gold', every time he set foot in the place. Someone must have felt sorry for him because he found himself on a seemingly endless round of courses, all well away from the battalion headquarters, which rendered the poor man hard to locate. He hid willingly, losing himself in various training courses and regimental messes.

"Who'll it be, then?" Tucker spoke for the fusilier, Parry, as well as himself. With a good officer, sensible, clued up, operations usually went well, no nasty surprises. The terrorists hunted with a cold skill. If it was some Gung Ho officer and gentleman of the

'Fix your bayonets, men, and follow me,' type, anything could happen and, on occasions, it had.

Griffith took his time to reply, lighting up a cigarette before he answered. "It'll probably be Grievous Bodily Harm." It was another nickname, the initials GBH standing for Gethin Barringon Hughes. GBH was a popular officer.

"Pancakes for tea," Tucker said gleefully. 2nd Lieutenant Hughes was a known pancake fan. It was something he always ordered in the mess.

"Corporal Rhys and I have an O Group at 14.00 hours. If it is him he'll be there for the briefing. We'll be operating a two-section platoon."

Cigarette smoke hung like a grey cloud over their heads. With a free issue of fifty cigarettes every week, even the one-time non-smokers had caught the habit.

"When do you reckon we'll go back to Blighty?"

This was increasingly the platoon's major topic of conversation. The battalion was on a three-year tour and had arrived in Malaya in August 1954. The question most frequently asked was, "Would the battalion leave for home to be back in Britain by August, or leave in August?" With the Suez Canal closed, a five-week voyage around South Africa was the only alternative.

"No idea," was the equally frequent reply.

The little group enjoyed an easy, close-knit companionship, an everyday occurrence in most armies, but very rare in civilian life.

"You still stuffing that schoolteacher?" Parry was engagingly honest in his approach to matters sexual.

Griffiths smiled at Parry's directness. "Not from out here, anyhow."

Griffiths had met the schoolteacher whilst undergoing basic training at the Fusiliers' depot at Cardiff. He was the object of some envy. The teacher was several years his senior and, most important, had her own flat in Cathedral Row, a quiet residential district. No fumbling or groping in doorways or at the back of pubs for her. Two years older than most recruits, because he was an indentured, apprentice electrician, Griffiths had settled into the, at times, very, very rigorous and physical part of basic training. He had been made up to corporal in order to take a fifty-strong draft to Malaya, been returned to the rank of fusilier for jungle training, and then quickly made up to corporal again. The reference to the schoolteacher caused him pain. They still wrote, but the letters were increasingly empty of any romance or tenderness. She was always giving him news of local people and events, but Griffiths sensed that the letters would soon stop.

"I suspect a 'Dear John' could be on its way," he said ruefully.

"What was she like? You know what I mean." Parry made an obscene and unmistakable gesture.

Tucker intervened. "Don't be so bloody nosey," but smiled and nodded at Griffiths. "Come on, Griff, was she any good?"

"You're never going to know."

Their initial meeting had been outside a cinema in Cardiff. The feature film had been *The Man from Laramie*, a western. Griffiths had thought it overrated but it had a hit soundtrack. Afterwards, they had walked back to the end of Cathedral Row, he dressed in uniform, a little shy, she very smart. He thought she oozed sophistication. They had arranged another date; he had suggested Friday, the day recruits were paid. They had enjoyed a meal at the only Italian restaurant in Cardiff, the motherly waitress giving large helpings, and clucking approvingly. They had walked back hand-in-hand in near silence, he hesitant and unsure of himself. She had put on the light in the small, neat lounge, then knelt and lit the gas fire. She rose and moved to him, her arms going around his shoulders.

The kiss was gentle, the sweetness of her lips on his; he felt her body tremble. As they continued he felt his nervousness slipping away. The words came easily.

"You're beautiful."

She moved her hand to the back of his neck, the kiss was stronger, urgent; his hands went down to her hips, pulling her into him. She stepped away, holding his hand, and led him to the yielding sofa. The embrace was all embracing. They undressed eagerly and left their clothes in an untidy trail across the carpeted floor. The bedroom was dark, the bed and sheets delicious in their smoothness. They had made love with a sense of wonder. They lay together afterwards, her cheek soft and cool against his.

"You've done this before?" he asked, his voice quiet.

"I was engaged for two years," she admitted. The unspoken implication rested easily on him. "You have?" she enquired, and he sensed a tease in her voice. They kissed before he answered.

"I have, a few times," he said.

"That's all in the past for you and me," her voice was firm. "No regrets. What matters is now."

They moved into each other, seeking the warmth and comfort of each other bodies. They'd talked and loved until the early hours, sharing all their dreams, hopes and ambitions in a loving, warm sense of belonging to each other. Griffith had never felt so tender towards another human being; he was exhilarated, excited and amazed that a woman could love with the desire she had shown. In the darkness of the room, with the warmth of her body next to him, he felt, and now he knew, that he was

30

different from the man, or, more truthfully, the boy that he had been a few hours before.

The remaining weeks of his training were spent with her, the evenings stretching into a kaleidoscope of laughter, drinks at the pub at the end of the road and lovemaking. He'd asked her about the school teaching.

"The kids are fine, but some of the parents…"

She spoke of her ambition to leave teaching and find a job with the BBC, in television, which was increasingly superseding radio.

The end of his basic training was looming, and then the posting either to Libya or Malaya started to figure largely in their thoughts. When the recruits' postings were announced, Griffiths' intuition told him it would be Malaya. She had cried; he felt helpless, not knowing how to stop the tears.

"It'll only be for twenty months." It sounded pathetic, the time stretching into the interminable. Their last night together was a miserable affair of forced cheerfulness, the gloom of a cold November all around them. They had kissed and said their goodbyes, and he walked away without glancing back at the forlorn girl who stood at the end of the road.

★ ★ ★

Tucker pulled on his cigarette. Parry fiddled with his ammunition pouches.

"What's the book, Griff?"

Griffiths held out the book to show the cover. "*Singapore 1942,*" he said.

"What's it about?" Parry asked, curiosity evident in his voice.

Griffiths shook his head as he withdrew the book.

"It's about the biggest cock-up ever to happen to the British army. What could go wrong did go wrong – out-thought, out-fought, a complete shambles."

Tucker and Parry were listening. "Well, go on, what happened?"

Griffiths told them about the retreat from Malaya, the futile struggle to defend Singapore, the fruitless courage, the cowardice and desertions, followed by three and a half years of constant horror and brutality inflicted on the Allied prisoners of war by their Japanese captors.

Tucker ground the stub of his cigarette into the metal ashtray. "Japs! Vomit-coloured bastards." he said, disgust and venom in every syllable.

"I drew the book from the WRVS library at Kuala Lumpur. It's for GBH. His uncle was in Singapore." Griffiths slid the book onto his locker.

"I'm going to the O Group," he called to Rhys. Both men left the cool of the thatched basha and emerged into the sunshine outside. The platoon, briefed by GBH, left in two three-ton trucks, an hour later, the dust from the road rising like a fine grey cloud as the platoon passed from sight.

★ ★ ★

On a hand signal from Griffiths, the patrol stopped. Gethin Hughes moved forward, his left hand holding the compass. He gave the Owens gun to Griffiths, and took the map from the leather case that had been his father's. Carefully, he scanned the map, took a compass bearing, and, with a pencil, marked in a cross at the map reference he believed was accurate. He nodded to Griffiths, winked, replaced the map into its case and retrieved his weapon. He slipped the strap of the case over his shoulder, the fawn leather contrasting with the olive green of his cotton jacket.

Griffiths turned to lead the patrol, and then he paused. To his right, an unfamiliar shape was apparent in the greenness. He gestured to the officer, mouthing the word 'look'. The man came forward and followed Griffiths' finger.

"What is it?"

"I don't know, but it's not part of the jungle; there's a definite shape to it."

Gethin Hughes moved forward. Griffiths turned to face Parry as Tucker pushed his hand out and down. Both men knelt. Gethin Hughes moved up to the structure, which was a good twelve feet tall. He stepped on something that seemed yielding. There was a loud crack, and his left foot disappeared into a blackness that was the jungle floor. Griffiths stepped forward to help. Gethin Hughes held up a restraining hand, motioning them to 'stand still'. He indicated a fallen branch and, transferring his weapon to his left hand, he stabbed and hacked at the towering greenness. As he did so, he was showered with dark leaves, twigs and moss. The branch was biting into the green mass, then, a different sound was heard, as if the branch were hitting metal.

With a mounting sense of excitement, Hughes saw a patch of metal, and then some faded streaks of colour. He started to use the branch to attack the green mound directly in front of him. A raised bubble came into sight, then more metal and a raised arch. He pushed forward, hearing more cracking noises underneath his jungle boots. He stumbled on, his hand reaching out to steady himself. As the remainder of the greenery was falling away from the raised arch, he turned to Griffiths, exclaiming, "We've found ourselves a plane!"

There were more crunching sounds as he bent lower, to look into the blackness.

"It's the cockpit. I'm standing on what I think must be a

wing. That," he indicated the obelisk standing out up towards the sky, "must be the fuselage."

He leant forward again and slung the Owens gun behind his back. He put both arms into the cockpit. There were muffled sounds from inside. Then, Hughes rose up and turned to face Griffiths. "Well, I'll be damned! Bloody Hell!"

Griffiths stared at the astonished face of Hughes, and asked, "What is it?"

Three

Malaya

Negri Sembilan Gemas – 15 February 1957

SWEE POE WAS NOT HAPPY. It was his very first time in the jungle and he found it terrifying. He was lathered in sweat and his head throbbed, his stomach seemed full of knots, and a twisted pain passed through his abdomen with regularity. For three days they hacked and scrambled their way south from Seremban. They avoided roads, the rubber estates. The running dogs, the British Soldiers, regularly patrolled both, and there were paid informers amongst the rubber-tappers.

The overnight stops were the worst. The jungle seemed to invade their very minds; it was full of sinister sounds, noises that could not be explained. On the second night, something had slithered over his feet. Poe had lain paralysed with fear. He was a city man, born in Penang. He had worked in Ipoh, Kuala Lumpur, and, finally, in Malacca, where he had been recruited. He had seen the British soldiers in Malacca, all in civilian clothes, but every one of them armed. They swam at Tanjong Bidara, and then went to the bars and brothels in Malacca. They always seemed to be in a good mood, spending dollars on Tiger beer and women. The cell he had joined was a money and courier unit, taking money, collected by force sometimes, and information and orders to the independent platoons that operated in Northern Johore and Negri Sembilan. The English newspapers were full of 'Emergency' news, lists of the contacts and ambushes, names of the British units and casualties, and also of the dead and captured terrorists.

Poe was not a stupid man, he possessed a curious and enquiring mind, but he was also a thief. Twice he had been sacked for stealing from the printing houses he'd worked for, and had narrowly missed a jail sentence the last time. Only the intervention of a Chinese merchant, who had repaid the stolen seventy dollars, saved him from prison. It was the merchant, who had disclosed his Communist Party connections, who had recruited him. Poe was envious of the money that the British soldiers had to spend. He had learnt that the conscripts, National Service men they were called, were paid $25 a week. He was lucky if he earned that much in a month, and so he reasoned that, if the Communists gained control of the country, some of the spoils were his for the taking.

The three other men in Poe's party had come to a huddled halt. He eased his way down to squat alongside them, as much for their physical presence as anything – safety in numbers. All four men were armed, the leader with a Colt revolver, two others with, ironically, British Lee Enfield rifles. He had been given a .22 pistol, effective at very short range but not really a soldier's weapon. It had been explained to him that, as a new recruit to the cause, he had to take what was given to him. They also carried $250 each; it was deemed unsafe for one man to carry all the money, for if he was detained, killed or captured, all the money would be lost. What was not said was that $1,000 was a very considerable sum and even Communist terrorists could be tempted.

The leader was speaking. He was annoyed, his voice a hoarse hiss, the scolding tone very unsettling.

"Show me your leg," he ordered, and the slighter of the Chinese pulled up the loose-fitting trouser leg.

Poe grimaced. The man's calf bore a red, angry sore.

"What is it?" he whispered.

The leader was scathing. "It's a leech's head and it's become infected. I've told you before, burn them off with a cigarette end. You pulled that off, didn't you?" he accused. "Now we've got to go into the rubber and find a doctor, a doctor we can trust."

Poe hid his jubilation. The rubber estate offered creature comforts, basic, but anything was better than the jungle.

"We rest fifteen minutes, and then we head for Kuala Pila Estate."

"How far is that?" Poe asked, but the leader took the question as a query of his judgement and authority.

"We go straight on. The rubber is less than a quarter of a mile away, and don't question me again." The leader turned his back, discouraging any further conversation.

Poe made a decision; this would be his first and last foray into the jungle. Once into the rubber, he was going to desert. The $250 was a comforting bulge in his uniform pocket. If only he knew where he was, he would feel easier. All the jungle was the same, either up hill or down hill. He felt apprehensive, but the thought of leaving this place was the one ray of sunlight in this green hell. The four men ate a meal of cold rice and vegetables, being careful not to spill any rice. The leader stood up, scanned the home-made map, and turned at right angles to the previous path. He motioned to the others to space themselves out, four paces apart, as they set off. By the leader's watch it was 9.38am, and by 10.00am they would reach the rubber. A reconnaissance was made, to ensure that there were no security forces around, and then they moved on through the rubber plantation, avoiding any contact with the tappers, most of whom were Tamils and no particular friends of the mainly Chinese Malayan Liberation Army. The men disappeared into the undergrowth.

★ ★ ★

Griffiths watched as Gethin Hughes stepped back from the plane.

"What is it sir?"

The officer's voice was level.

"Interesting, corporal, interesting." He fumbled for the clasp of the map case, and put something inside. "It's 9.38. We go back." He indicated the direction with his left hand, and the tiny patrol moved off in a new direction. The golden rule of jungle warfare says: never go back the same way you came out. Griffiths adjusted the sling of the Bren gun. It weighed thirty-one pounds and the sling could cut deep into the shoulder. Without a word, he moved to the leading scout position, and the patrol moved silently into the greenness.

★ ★ ★

Poe's stomach was hurting again. The leader was still in a foul mood, slashing at the undergrowth that impeded progress, the parang, razor sharp, slicing into the dense foliage. The sudden stop and absence of the parang's whistling action caused Poe to stumble, and then bump into the static figure of the Chinese in front of him. The leader wheeled round, a finger to his lips. The jungle seemed to still; nobody moved. Then, as if a curtain had risen, Poe took in the scene immediately in front of him. He could see lines of regimented rubber trees, somewhere a bicycle bell rang, and there were other noises, a shout, and then, several people talking.

Poe's eyes drank in the view before him, but all he could think of was how he could desert. The Malayan All Races Liberation Army had a fearful reputation regarding their treatment of deserters and traitors. They were hunted down, a 'trial' held, and then the prisoners were hacked to death with a parang.

He decided to wait his chance. The leader put his hand palm downwards and lowered his arm; the four men knelt. Poe listened intently; the noises were getting fainter, a car or lorry engine sounded in the distance. The jungle closed over the four men.

* * *

Griffiths paused, unsure of himself. He raised his hand in the halt sign and leant his body forward, in order to hear more clearly. Then, he was sure; there were voices, relaxed voices, and sounds of laughter. He called forward Gethin Hughes with a silent wave of the hand.

"What is it?"

Griffiths motioned to his front. "Listen." The single word was whispered. Both men stood motionless. The voices were coming closer.

"Tappers," mouthed Griffiths, and Gethin Hughes nodded agreement. "We must have come further east than I'd planned to," he said.

Getting lost in the jungle was not unknown but it rarely led to any danger. If a patrol got really lost, it would find its way to a stream; follow it downstream till it came to a river, where there were always settlements. The voices were trailing off, and soon there was only silence.

"Wait," the officer whispered as he turned towards Griffiths. He lifted his leg off the ground and tapped his jungle boot. Griffiths understood. In the rubber estate, jungle boots were exchanged for hockey shoes, the same as those worn by the tappers. Sharp-eyed tappers could spot the shoe prints, and if they were Communist sympathisers, they would warn security forces in the vicinity.

"We'll take a look and try to get an accurate fix with this compass," suggested Gethin Hughes. A compass held close to the steel of a gun could give a wildly inaccurate reading.

"I'll lead." The officer motioned to Parry and Tucker. The soldiers moved forward unimpeded, for there was no fence around the rubber trees. Gethin Hughes slid out of the jungle, followed by Griffiths. It was like walking onto a brightly lit stage from the gloom of a curtained backdrop. Parry and Tucker were still several paces behind. Gethin swung his right hand, holding the Owens gun away from him, his left hand holding the compass. He saw the needle quiver and then stop.

At that precise moment, three Chinese terrorists walked straight out of the undergrowth, less than ten yards away. Poe was seven or eight paces behind the third man. The Chinese leader and Gethin Hughes saw each other at the same time. The terrorist's eyes took in the soldier's arm, holding his weapon away from his body. The second soldier was already swivelling to bring the Bren gun to bear. The terrorist fired his revolver: once − twice − three times. Gethin Hughes had only time to scream, "Jesus!"

The second of the revolver's rounds slammed into his head. He fell at Griffith's feet, the crimson blood spurting over the corporal's boots. Griffiths saw the agonised faces before him; the squeezing of the trigger was purely automatic; the Bren jerked in his hands; the heavy 303 rounds ripped into the leader's chest, the second and third men momentarily frozen. The second man started to bring the long rifle up to his chest, and Griffiths swung the Bren. The noise was indescribable. The Chinese seemed to jump backwards, the force of the bullets punching him hard in the chest. Griffiths was conscious of Tucker and Parry bursting up behind him, both firing. The third man dropped into a crouching run and veered to his right, trying to hide between the rubber trees. He only managed to gain a dozen yards, and then he was thrown face down by the bullets ripping into his back.

Poe had been engulfed in a violent explosion of noise. He neither knew what was happening, nor what he should do. In a spontaneous act, he crouched and ran as he'd never run before. He didn't know where to go but he had to get away from that awful noise. Thoroughly winded, his chest heaving, his legs jerking in a nervous spasm, he collapsed onto the jungle floor.

Unaware of how long he'd lain there, he sat up, put his fingers in his ears, but found no blood. He examined his chest and stomach; there were scratches and grazes, but again no blood. He drank heavily from his water bottle, and then, without knowing why, he began to cry. He cried and sobbed for several minutes; his lungs seemed to be like bellows, pumping out the tears that rolled down his cheeks.

The crying stopped and he started to collect his thoughts. Go back to where the ambush had been? How would he find his way? No. What had the leader told him before they'd started out? "Don't get lost. If you do, find a stream; that'll bring you to a river, and there'll be people there." He rose unsteadily to his feet, but which way was he to go? He turned around in a full circle. He must get out of here; he would not be able to survive a night on his own. His eyes caught something to his right. It looked like a hole punched in the green all around him. Nervously grasping his pistol, he moved towards it.

* * *

Griffith's whole body was numbed into a shocked stiffness; spent cartridge cases lay spewed around his feet. Tucker's face was chalk-white. "Is he dead?"

The slumped form of Gethin Hughes lay at Griffiths' feet.

"I don't know. I think so."

Parry was kneeling beside the body. "He's not! There's a pulse. Give me your wound dressing." Gently but inexpertly, he applied the field dressing. "He's losing a lot of blood,"

Griffiths felt some normality returning. "He needs to be air-lifted by chopper. Tucker, get their weapons and search them. Leave the bodies where they are. Parry, find a track or road, bring back some transport, and here, take this." He handed the Owens gun over. "Leave your carbine here and keep the safety catch off."

Tucker came back, carrying two rifles, with a revolver stuck in his belt. "I'll search them now."

"Help me move him into the shade, first," said Griffiths. He removed the map case put it over his shoulder, and took the spare magazines out of Gethin Hughes' pouches. Gently, they lifted him and laid him on the warm grass.

"That didn't take long," he said. A Dodge truck with three turbaned Sikh security guards in the back was approaching. The driver was the rubber estate's manager. He paled visibly at the blood and crumpled bodies.

"He's badly wounded. He needs to get out of here, quickly," Griffiths urged.

"There's a direct line from here to Tampin Army Camp," the manager replied.

They lifted the deeply unconscious Hughes into the back of the very dusty truck. The Chinese were laid on the ground.

"We'll come back for them," the ashen-faced manager added. "Their murdering days are over."

The lorry did a laborious three-point turn and moved sedately down the track. Thirty-seven minutes later, a Royal Navy Whirlwind helicopter landed the injured Gethin Hughes at the army camp, where he was whisked away to the medical centre. The remaining helicopter was loaded with the three dead men and Griffiths, Tucker and Parry.

Poe approached the spot cautiously. The object hidden there revealed its shape as he approached it. It was like the cockpit of a plane, he thought. What was it doing here, in the jungle? Tentatively, he went closer; the metallic cracking sound underneath his feet made him even more nervous. He carried a drawstring bag that held a torch. With its batteries removed, it was an emergency rice holder. He pushed the switch and a light came on. With his pistol in his right hand, torch in his left, he peered in very, very slowly. The beam picked up something gleaming on the floor of the fuselage. Curiosity getting the better of him, he leant further into the void. In the darkness, the torchlight seemed to be stronger. What he saw then was to fill his dreams for the rest of his life. He played the beam of the torch along the darkness of the interior, looking for a way to get closer to what he had seen.

The snake was a King Cobra, nearly seven feet long, poised, the hood fully puffed up, not a foot from his face, with gleaming eyes that seemed like the devil incarnate. Poe's scream never made it past his throat, but some sort of primeval self-preservation instinct made the pistol fire. He hit the open hood of the snake, and he fired again. The snake lashed out in its death throes. Poe staggered out, dropped his torch, the light still on; ruled by self-preservation again, he grabbed it and, for the second time in his life, ran as fast as his legs would carry him.

★ ★ ★

The intelligence officer was coldly persistent in his interrogation. What was the exact time of the contact? Were they certain there were only three terrorist? The dead men's fingerprints were taken and photographed. A huge follow-up operation had taken place, hampered by the absence of the Ibans, sea Dyaks from

Borneo, who were employed as trackers. The only two in camp had reported sick on the previous day. The Medical Officer suspected that they were, in fact, homesick. Two other trackers were on home leave. Parry mentioned that he thought he had heard a further two shots, but the helicopters were coming in and he wasn't sure.

* * *

Two days later, a bedraggled Poe, covered in mosquito bites and very, very hungry, walked up the road to the army camp in Gemas. The previous forty-eight hours had been a living nightmare as he stumbled his way through the jungle, haunted by fear of snakes, soldiers and just about everything all around him. He'd found a stream, and then a river, a wooden bridge, a track, and then, mercifully, a road and then, incredibly, a bus. He'd boarded it, paid for his ticket, ignored the other passengers, and got off at the terminus at Gemas, two hundred yards from the army camp. He'd hidden the pistol; armed terrorists the soldiers shot, unarmed ones they took prisoner.

The sentry called out the guard, and Poe soon found himself answering a lot of questions. He held back nothing; supplying the name of the Chinese merchant, the route they had travelled to the meeting point for the jungle trek, house names, locations, everything he knew. The Malay Special Branch raided houses, and took away maps, documents and money. Poe pored over the photographs he was shown; he was taken up in a helicopter and used a greatly amplified loud-speaker to call for the surrender of his erstwhile, albeit briefly, comrades-in-arms. He grew a goatee beard, wore spectacles and, with a bounty of five thousand Malay dollars, a 'resettlement grant' as it was termed, and a priceless UK passport, he was given nine weeks of lessons in basic English. After this, he left by ship from Singapore and sailed to Adelaide, in Australia. His business cards read, "Raymond (Elvis) Lee."

Poe left the world he knew, but he took with him in his head all that had happened and what he had seen.

* * *

Griffiths, Tucker and Parry returned to normal duty. Griffiths made enquiries about Gethin Hughes, and was told that he had survived and been flown back to the UK, where he was in a neurosurgical ward in a Hampshire hospital. Griffiths asked his company commander how he could contact Hughes, for he still had the map case with the bloodstains on it, but the major said he didn't know the hospital's location.

"Keep it. It was his father's, you say? Give it to him when you get back home. If the army takes it back I'll have paperwork from now to kingdom come."

Griffith put the map case in his kit bag.

Parry left in May, on demob leave. In June, Tucker was made up to lance corporal, again. In late June, the battalion went back to the UK. Griffiths was standing on the boat deck as the Johore Baru and Malacca Straits came into view.

"That's the last time I see this place – and bloody good job!" He turned and entered the busy corporals' mess, revelling in its warmth and companionship.

Four

The Magistrate's Court

Aberystwyth, Wales – August 1981

The courtroom had once been the ballroom of a grand, seafront hotel. The walls and ceilings were painted a soft shade of blue, but the high ceilings gave the room a desolate, cold air. The acoustics were not good and sometimes the words of magistrates, court clerks, solicitors, police prosecutors, witnesses and defendants were almost inaudible.

★ ★ ★

The car journey was a bonus. Griffiths had finished work early and picked up his wife from the university department where she was senior secretary. Bethan loved seafood and there was a seafood festival in New Quay, twenty-three miles down the coast; scallops, cockles, prawns, oysters. It promised to be a very enjoyable afternoon. It was holiday weather, bright warm sunshine, blue skies, and Cardigan Bay was dotted with white sails; the Aberaeron regatta was well underway.

Griffiths and Bethan had married in May 1963. They had met two years earlier, at a trade and business exhibition in Cardiff. She had been manning one of the trade stands and there had been an instant attraction between them. Bethan was blonde, self-assured, with a lovely smile. He'd asked whether she would have lunch with him. After a lunch hour that sped past on wings, they had arranged to meet the following evening. Their stories unfolded as their friendship deepened. Bethan was from Aberystwyth but had moved to Bridgend, to work for an electrical supplier. She liked the job, but not Bridgend, and was homesick. Every weekend, she'd drive back to Aber, as she called it. Griffiths told her of his engagement to the schoolteacher, how they had broken it off; he spoke of his branching out on his own, working for builders and contractors.

It was all so gentle, the looks across a room, holding the car door for her, the unspoken agreement, put in an old fashioned way, that they were meant for each other. They made love three weeks after the first meeting, each surprised at the other's boldness. Griffiths moved back with her to Aberystwyth, where they married, rented a local and rather poky flat for nearly three years, and then, with enough money saved for a deposit, they moved into a bungalow three miles from the town. They were very contented, but hospital checks confirmed that Bethan could never have children. They had explored the legal minefield that was adoption but some of the questions asked they considered intrusive, some even seemed ridiculous. Upset and exasperated, they eventually resigned themselves to a childless marriage. They walked in the superb countryside and on the mountains; they made friends and they lived for each other. Life was good. Griffiths was never without work, and they both enjoyed the social life of a university town.

Griffiths never spoke to Bethan about his time in the army, nor did he admit to liking the Malay people and the Malayan country. Whether her woman's intuition was responsible he couldn't say, but she guessed his nostalgia for the old days, and encouraged him to attend the yearly reunions in Cardiff. Griffiths was surprised at the warmth of his welcome, when he attended his first. Tucker, Parry and a hundred and eighty former fusiliers were there. Noisy, exuberant, beer-fuelled evenings always followed. It was later, in the early 1970s, when

Gethin Barrington Hughes reappeared for the first time. A bright scar was still in evidence at his left temple, and his words were sometimes, but not always, slightly slurred. Griffiths, in the time honoured manner, shook his hand, made small talk, and then moved back into the other ranks' table. After the speeches, the four old comrades settled at a corner table. Griffiths told them of his life since leaving the fusiliers, remembered the homecoming, he spoke of the ignorance and indifference of the civilian world, and he bemoaned the increasing greediness of a South Wales society that had been nurtured on the chapel, shared troubles and a spontaneous generosity, all of which seemed to be rapidly disappearing.

Gethin Hughes told them of the eleven months he had spent in various hospitals, the complete lack of recall of the action, the depression that seemed like a fog in his mind, lifting to allow periods of lucidity and a tenuous happiness, and then coming down again, to cloak his mind in self-pity. Later, he'd met Ruby; the personality, warmth and compassion of the woman had lifted him up to a level of life that approached normality. He was grateful to a degree that impressed his former comrades.

"She's a Ruby – a real diamond."

Griffiths tried to explain that he no longer had the map case. "I've moved three times since coming back from Malaya. I can't find it. I'm very sorry."

Gethin said, "I can't remember a map case."

"It was your father's." Griffiths told him, hoping that this would jolt his memory.

"No, I don't know anything about a map case. There are some things that I can remember, but a lot I can't." He shook his head. "If it turns up, well and good, but I'm not keen on seeing or remembering anything regarding the incident that left me like I am today."

Parry changed the conversation by placing photographs on the table, careful not to encroach on the beer stains, and explaining, "This is the wife, and these little chaps are the Parry commandos." A woman in her thirties gazed back at them, and two boys, who looked very much alike. "They are nine and eleven. Tearaways, the both 'em."

"What does your wife do?" Gethin Hughes' stammer was controlled.

"She's a demonstrator for some of the biggest stores in South Wales; irons, ovens, hairdryers, and all types of electrical household goods. Her boss thinks the world of her, always giving her overtime. She's a beaut." He picked up the photo and kissed it.

The men talked of their home lives and work. Tucker alone contributed little to the conversation. When the others had gone to the gents, Griffiths probed Tucker.

"Everything alright, Tuck? You're very quiet. You okay for money?"

Tucker sipped his bitter. "I'm alright. Just a bit of woman trouble." He took a big swallow.

The other two slid back onto the chairs. They met very nearly every year thereafter.

★ ★ ★

Gethin Hughes had telephoned and invited Kevin and Bethan to his home in Welshpool. With some surprise, Griffiths learnt that, despite his handicap, Gethin Hughes was a solicitor and, judging by the size and contents of his house, a successful one. The visit led to return visits, and then to shared holidays, and the years were kind to them. A good, honest friendship developed, and it was a very sweet, warm world.

When he attended the reunions, Griffiths noted that the numbers were steadily decreasing as men moved away or died. Parry was in trouble and drinking very heavily. His wife had been having an affair with her boss for, apparently, several years; the overtime had not been not what Parry thought it was. The divorce had been bloody and messy, and he confided that only being allowed access to his sons every other weekend was creasing him.

Tucker also had problems. He was working as a bouncer at a Swansea night-club, and could easily hold his own with the drunks and thugs, but his wife was running rings around him; always making demands for more money, Spanish holidays, a better car, a new kitchen, better clothes. He regularly lost his temper with her. He had once, in a blind rage, hit her. It was the end of the marriage and she moved out. Initially despondent, Tucker, surprisingly, grew to appreciate the quietness, the lack of tension and rows, just emptiness. He became more and more reclusive, avoiding friendship. His job was his safety valve – the ejecting of troublemakers taking some of the suppressed violence out of his body and mind. Bouncers were bouncers. If you wanted trouble, they'd give it to you. The ferocity that Tucker was increasingly responsible for was beginning to attract the attention of the South Wales constabulary. The management was told to rein him in, or else the police would. A bare three weeks later, on a Saturday night, a visiting rugby team was in town. One of the flankers, who himself had a history of violent conduct, was badly beaten by Tucker. The blind-side forward made a complaint to the police, from his bed in casualty. The police, not in a position to apportion blame, cautioned both men and, more importantly, the night-club owner was warned that, in the event of any more such incidents, their licence would be withdrawn. Inevitably, Tucker was sacked.

★ ★ ★

The door at the end of the courtroom opened. A woman and two men filed in and took their seats at a raised table. The people standing nodded respectfully towards the bench.

"Please be seated."

The side door swung open and three young men entered. The chairman of the magistrates indicated his annoyance. "This court is in sitting from 10 o'clock. Why are you late?" None of the men answered. "I will ask you again."

The defendants' solicitor was quickly on his feet. "I'm told there is heavy traffic between Synod Inn and here, sir." The middle defendant openly smirked.

"Very well, continue."

The proceedings unfolded slowly. The case was this: a car driven by one of the defendants had collided with a vehicle driven by Griffiths. Mrs Bethan Griffiths, a passenger in Griffith's vehicle, had been killed. All three men, under oath, denied being in the crash vehicle when the collision had occurred. They claimed that their car had been stolen, fifty minutes earlier, after they had parked it in the car park of a public house.

Griffiths' version of events was read to the court. His car, a Marina, had been overtaken by a red Ford Escort that had approached at speed from behind him, lights flashing, the horn sounding. It had overtaken his Marina on a blind bend, and all three occupants had gestured obscenely. The driver was wearing a red Welsh rugby jersey. Five miles further on, the Escort had emerged at speed from a village side street onto the main road. The ensuing crash had killed Bethan Griffiths in a jumble of noise, screams, running figures and anxious voices. Ambulance, police, fire brigade, the undertaker's hearse and a crash recovery pick-up had all attended the scene. The police constable was an experienced witness for the prosecution. All three men were questioned.

"You were all in the Ford vehicle involved in this crash, but who was driving?"

All three defendants denied that they had been in the car. It had been stolen from a pub car park, they insisted, while they were window-shopping further up the village. The policeman then called as witness a Mr Gwilym Morgan, who farmed just outside the village. He had seen three men, white, in their early twenties, running from the road junction, close to the scene of the accident.

"Do you recognise those men?" he was asked.

There was a pause. "Those are them."

The defending solicitor was polite and even-voiced. "You are quite sure, without doubt, that those are the men you saw running?" He omitted to mention the word 'away'. "What were they wearing? Describe their clothing?"

Mr Morgan's finger was steady and accusing. "Him and him, shirts and jeans. Him, jeans and a replica Welsh jersey."

"Do you realise how many people, women as well as men, wear replica Welsh jerseys?"

Gwilym Morgan was emphatic. "He did," he indicated to the court, his finger stabbing out.

"Mr Morgan," the solicitor's voice seemed to have moved down a gear, the words only barely audible. The court was absolutely quiet and still, "did you do National Service?"

"No."

"Why?"

"I'm a farmer. I work the land. I was exempt."

"That is correct. Farm workers were exempt from National

Service until they reached the age of twenty-six, provided they were employed in agriculture." The solicitor carefully laid his papers and glasses on the desk in front of him. "But, when you were twenty-three, you left your employment with a Mr Samuel Roberts after a dispute. Am I correct?"

Gwilym Morgan's face was grim.

"Yes, I did briefly leave, but found employment with another farmer. I now own that farm." The last sentence was a challenge. He was a man of substance, well respected in the community.

"I'm sure you have worked hard, but in the time after you left Samuel Roberts and before you gained further employment in agriculture, did anything happen?" The words were seemingly mild. Gwilym Morgan shook his head, not understanding what lay behind the question.

"You received War Department orders to report for medical classification at Swansea, Castle Street. Correct?"

Again, there was no answer. The eyes of the packed courtroom were fixed on the now seemingly lonely figure of Gwilym Morgan.

"Mr Morgan, what is the colour of my tie?"

The solicitor was facing the witness, the tie a scarlet ribbon on the white of his shirt. "You are colour-blind, aren't you? You failed a War Office medical for exactly that reason, didn't you?"

The accusation seemed final, even brutal in its correctness. Gwilym Morgan nodded in acknowledgement and defeat. The solicitor glanced across to the policeman; no words were spoken, but the officer, magistrates, defendants and Kevin Griffiths accepted that the solicitor was master. He had won. The magistrates retired. Twenty-three minutes later they returned.

"Defendants found 'not guilty'. No order for costs."

Griffiths sat slumped. The court was gradually emptying. There were commiserating hands on his shoulder, but he felt as if he were the loneliest soul in the world. Bethan had been killed and the culprits would walk away, scot-free.

He left the courtroom. The outside air seemed cold for mid-summer. He went back to the bungalow, the emptiness an accusing companion to the stillness of every room. He made three phone calls: one to Bethan's invalid father, one to the general foreman of the contract he was working on, and the last to Gethin Hughes. He explained briefly the court's verdict, and then put the phone off the hook, and fetched a bottle of gin and some tonic from the fridge. He drank himself into unconsciousness, but still the faces came: Bethan's, the driver's, every mark, and every feature in sharp detail. He wished he were dead. He awoke to find that he wasn't.

Five

Aberystwyth, Wales

August 1982

The telephone and Bethan's wedding dress were the only items he took from the bungalow. The furniture, every piece, he left behind. A neighbour's wife gently packed all of Bethan's clothes and took them to a charity shop. Griffiths had decided to buy a house in Aberystwyth town centre; the village had, since the crash, been too small, too confined; everybody knew everybody else. Aberystwyth, with its trades-people, student population and visitors, was far more anonymous.

Outwardly, he seemed the same, he still worked hard, but he was aware that he was drinking too much; a sociable drink in the club, and several more in the quietness and solitariness of his house. It was still just a house, not yet a home, and all the time, he nursed a gnawing, nagging hurt. He missed her, her smile, her warmth, and yet he refused to wallow in self-pity, but in the dark stillness of the bedroom, he thirsted for a way to seek retribution on those who had robbed him of his wife.

The phone was ringing.

"Kevin?" Only one person spoke his name with the accent on 'in'.

"What is it, Auntie Dil?"

The voice was loud as always, positive, not afraid. "I'm sorry, Kevin, but Uncle Glyn's dead. We've been up to clear out the house, and there's some stuff of yours there. We did ring you yesterday." The voice was scolding. "You lodged there years ago, when you were working in Bristol. I expect that's when you left stuff behind. We'll bring it back with us after the funeral."

"Thank you, Auntie Dil. Do I need to come to the funeral?"

"No. There's a crowd coming from here. You won't be missed. Glyn left here forty years ago, but blood is thicker than water – at least, it is in our family."

Griffiths gave a silent wince. Auntie Dil had not been invited to his wedding, and he was positive that he was still not forgiven.

"When is the funeral?"

"Tuesday. We'll expect to see you soon."

"I'll be there Saturday. Thanks for ringing and thanks for bringing my stuff back. All the best." He replaced the receiver.

It had been something like twenty-four years since he had lodged briefly in Bristol, with a rarely seen uncle, whilst working on a major store development. The house had been clean and welcoming. He'd been recalled back to South Wales at very short notice.

He visited his aunt, collected the bag, ate a dutiful meal, thanked her for everything, and drove back to Aberystwyth. The 'stuff' was unquestionably his: a creased, unlocked, olive green kit-bag that still bore his regimental number, rank and name. He opened it and emptied out the contents: boot brushes with his army number stamped on the wooden backs, two pairs of army socks, an olive green jacket, a *Western Mail* newspaper dated January 1958, and a brown map case.

"Well I never!" he exclaimed. He touched the case, resolving to phone Gethin Hughes in the morning. He was beaten to it. The phone rang just as he was pulling on his shirt, ready to go out. He recognised the voice immediately.

"Hello, Ruby, how are you?"

Her voice was strained. "Kev, Gethin is in hospital – in London. He was admitted to Shrewsbury on Friday and then transferred to St Hughes. He was operated on today."

"How is he? What is the matter with him?" asked Kevin, dreading the reply.

"I've just left him in the recovery room. The op. took over five hours, and he's already been another seven in recovery. They say he will be alright. He wants to see you. I'm stopping here till he's discharged. There is something else. His father died last week, and the local paper reported it. His father's name was George – George Barrington Hughes – same initials as Geth. Also reported in the obituary was his father's service in the South Wales Fusiliers, but, strangely, his age was not printed. He was eighty-five. The thing is this: I had a caller on Friday. I didn't know him but he said he'd served with Lieutenant Hughes and was a long-standing friend. He asked if he could he obtain any item of equipment, something to keep as a reminder of their service and friendship together.

"Kev, the strange thing about him is this: he was Chinese. As far as I know, George served on the Western Front, in the First World War. This man was in his, I'd say, late forties. He was nothing like old enough to have been in World War I. I wonder... Do you think he could he have been mistaken, thinking George was Gethin? I haven't said anything to Geth. He's got enough on his plate. They said that, barring complications, he can come home in about ten days. I'll ring you when he gets here. He wants to see you, but you can't be expected to go to St. Hughes. I'd best get back to him. Goodbye."

Griffiths replaced the phone, finished dressing and went out, his mind struggling to accept what Ruby had told him. She hadn't said what was wrong with Gethin. She seemed far more concerned about the mysterious visitor.

The following morning, the phone rang again. It was Sunday, and Saturday evening's beer and gin were still weighing on him. The voice was Tucker's.

"Griff? It's me – Tuck. I've got bad news."

With a sense of near despair, Griffiths asked, "What is it?"

The voice the other end was flat. "It's Parry. He's dead. Car smash. I don't know for certain, but he was probably pissed. He has never been right since the divorce – drinking like a fool. I'll find out what I can, day of funeral, where, and I'll let you know."

After a muted conversation about Parry, Tucker rang off. Griffiths gave a deep sigh. He rose, went to the fridge and reached for the gin, his fingers finding the cold comfort of the bottle. He didn't know why, but he withdrew his hand and shut the fridge. Whatever he had to face, it would not be done in a state of drunkenness or confusion.

* * *

Swee Poe had worked on the Snowy River dams and hydro-scheme in Australia for four years. He found the Australians loudmouthed, foulmouthed, and with a propensity for calling everybody 'bastard', including members of their own families, which Swee Poe found particularly offensive. Armed with his British Passport, he left for America, where he immediately found work in Alaska, on the Distant Early Warning System. It was the early 1960s, the Cold War was in danger of becoming a very hot war, and there was the burgeoning conflict in South East Asia as well as the Cuban Crisis clouding the international horizon.

America poured billions of dollars into an early warning system, in case the Soviet Union started lobbing nuclear weapons over the Bering Straits and into the densely populated American cities. American arms corporations needed labourers and roughnecks to work in the frozen Alaskan tundra and they paid top dollars for these men.

Swee Poe gained employment as one of a gang of twenty. Toughened, but not filled out with labouring in the Australian sun, an incident occurred one day that altered the course of his life. Every gang of twenty or more men was allocated a cook. One cook left and his replacement was a barrel-chested man, who took to wearing Marine Corps denims. When asked his name, he growled, *Gyrene*, which was Americanese for marine. The evening meals were always the same: steak, onions and French fries. On the first night, the usual meals were thumped onto the tables, but there was a difference. Some men were still in the showers, some were on the telephone, ringing far off families. Gyrene picked up the untouched plates and threw the food out of the front door.

"When I cook, you eat," was the growled, or to be truthful, snarled explanation. The same thing happened on the following two nights. There were cursing and scuffles, when men who had spent eleven hours of physical, heavy work, found their food thrown outside, with total disregard for their wellbeing.

Things could not carry on in this way, and they didn't. On the Thursday, all twenty men ambushed Gyrene, and set about him in a wild, swinging, punching mêlée. He was bodily thrown out of the front door. In a welter of high fives, handshakes and shouted congratulations, the men set off for the kitchen area. In the next five seconds, there was the most blood curdling and fear-pierced scream anyone had ever heard. The men stopped in their tracks. With a crack and almighty crash, the front door flew open. Gyrene, his face a mask of pure terror, stumbled into

59

the hut, followed by a massive, fully-grown Polar Bear, roaring wildly. Pandemonium reigned. The man who saved them was a Mexican, a small, dark, quiet man, who wrote to his family every night. He had the foresight to grab a rolled up newspaper, thrust it into the pot-belly stove and, once it was flaming, he jabbed at the beast's face. It worked. The bear, roaring in rage, turned and hurtled out into the freezing night.

The general consensus was that the bear had been deprived of its supper. The steaks thrown out by Gyrene the previous nights had, by their smell, attracted the Polar Bear. Gyrene went to his cubicle; the only sound to come out of it was the gurgle, gurgle of Bourbon whiskey entering his throat, illegally, for all alcohol was strictly banned. There was a hit and miss breakfast next morning, but when work was finished and the men returned to the hut, Gyrene was gone.

The construction boss, who drove a utility truck with 'RAMROD' painted on the side, looked around the assembled group. There were nine different nationalities. He gazed at Swee Poe.

"Hey, Chink, you cook? All Chinkeys cook? Right?" Swee Poe nodded acceptance. It was a turning point, from being a labourer, albeit a well-paid one, he now had the chance to learn a new skill and learn it he did.

For the next four years, he was constantly employed as a cook. He noticed how wasteful some of the men were with their food. Huge steaks were sometimes barely half eaten, so he carefully noted which workers ate less than others, and gave smaller portions to them. Nobody complained. He introduced boiled, poached and scrambled eggs for breakfast whereas before it was always fried eggs. A two-egg scramble looked as big as a three-egg fry. Every Saturday evening, he went to the huddle of houses and shops that passed for a town in Alaska, and sold the surplus food to the shops and the inevitable lone hotel. He made sure hot fresh coffee was always available after the evening meal, for happy workers are good workers. The construction bosses recognised this and he received regular bonuses. When he went into town, he always paid a visit to a branch of the First National Bank of Alaska. The banks always stayed open on Saturday afternoons, to accept the D.E.W. men, as they were called, who came to deposit their cheques and make withdrawals. Swee Poe never made any withdrawals. On his periods of leave, he never visited cities in America with large Asian populations. He found Canadians easier to get on with than Americans. He didn't gamble, and never paid to have a woman. He found that women in North America were, to his conservative, if not puritan, Chinese mind, very promiscuous. Women seemed to want a 'good time, Honey' and he felt obliged to supply it.

When the D.E.W. work ended, he drifted south, always keeping his eyes open to the people around. The Malayan People's Liberation Army had boasted that *every* traitor would be tracked down, wherever in the world they were. He knew that the Emergency in Malaya was declared over in 1960, but snippets in the press reported that there was still a hardcore of terrorists fighting on, coming out of the jungle, beheading a policeman here; ambushing soldiers of the Malay and Federated regiments there. It was wise to keep his guard up, and every night he thought of, frequently dreamt of, what he had seen in that black cavern that was a plane's fuselage.

The money in his bank account was now very substantial. He was treated with the utmost respect whenever he visited the bank. He invested in stocks and shares, listening courteously to bank managers and trust fund advisers, but it was he who made the decisions. He was, above all, meticulous about renewing his British Passport.

He had just come out of a Vietnamese restaurant in Los Angeles, in which he had invested, when he was aware of being watched. A Chinese with a pock-marked face was pretending to read a newspaper. Swee Poe felt a sensation in the pit of his stomach – a feeling he had not known for nearly twenty-five years – that of fear. Apparently unconcerned, Swee Poe took the freeway south to the house he owned in San Diego, but he constantly checked his rear view mirror. Once home, he telephoned the three banks where he had accounts, his investment broker and San Diego International Air Terminal booking office.

Six

Aberystwyth and Welshpool

August 1982

The chapel had seen better days, the once superb light oak pews and stalls badly needed a good scrub. The lofty ceilings, which had echoed to glorious singing, were damp and stained, with flaking paint. The congregation was not large; this few looked and sang like irregular chapel-goers. Parry's coffin stood on a wheeled trestle in front of the pulpit. The brass handles gleamed defiantly in the surrounding drabness. His two sons stood, somewhat uncertainly, beside a grey-haired woman. Griffiths judged her to be their grandmother. The service was brief; the voices singing the two hymns were stumbling and hesitant.

Griffiths had picked up Tucker at the appointed time, and Tucker told him the story as they drove along. The inquest established that Parry had been well above the drink-driving limit, but he was not the driver of the vehicle. His death was recorded as accidental. As is the way of things, the driver who had given Parry a lift, his last lift, was a lifelong teetotaller and had, apparently, suffered an epileptic fit. The car, in excellently maintained order, had skidded on a valley bend and rammed into a large electric pylon. Parry had been thrown through the windscreen and had died instantly. The minister concluded his homily by offering words of comfort to Parry's mother and his sons. The sombre bearers wheeled the coffin past Griffiths and

Tucker. Both muttered, "Goodbye, Parry."

Griffiths drove Tucker back to Aberystwyth, Tucker was virtually silent all the way. Tomorrow, they were to drive to Gethin Hughes' house in Welshpool. He had phoned earlier in the week.

"Ask Tucker if he will come as well? Would you be willing fetch him?

Griffiths answered in the affirmative. The next sentences surprised him. Gethin said, "I'm phoning from a phone box in Newtown. I'll explain why tomorrow." The phone then went dead.

"Do you ever get a feeling, tingling, perhaps, that things are not what you think they are?" asked Griffiths.

Tucker was laconic. "All the time. Why?"

Griffiths changed down from fourth to third. "I don't know, but something's not right with Gethin. I can sense it"

"You some sort of gypsy with extra-sensory perception, perhaps?" said Tucker sarcastically.

"That's a big word for you."

"I know plenty of double-barrelled words: mushroom soup; corrugated iron." Tucker smiled, "You're not the only clever sod, Griff!" Both men laughed, their friendship was to be cherished.

They arrived back in Aberystwyth and went to a restaurant for food and a beer. The food was good, the pint of draught beer excellent. Tucker was appreciative.

"Parry and I went out for a meal, a couple of months ago, but his idea of a meal out was fourteen pints of bitter and a ham sandwich. God, he could drink!"

Both men fell silent. It seemed hard to realise that Parry was gone. His Christian name was Godfrey, but that had disappeared into the mist during his army service. Men were known by their surname, followed by the last two digits of their army number. In Welsh regiments, with multitudes of Jones, Williams, Evans and Griffiths, it was usually the last three.

They enjoyed the meal, both men relieved that the funeral was over and done with. "Another?" asked Tucker.

Griffiths refused. "You have one. I'm driving tomorrow."

★ ★ ★

"Hello! Look at this." The car, a red Citroën, was parked across the entrance to a drive. Ruby waved them down, her voice was concerned.

"Is he alright?" Griffiths asked. He could tell she was on edge.

"Geth's fine – he's waiting. Follow me, Griff."

She drove off ahead of them, and several hundred yards further on, she turned into a driveway and pulled up outside the front door of a large Victorian house. She killed the engine. "He's in here."

They entered a hallway, Ruby's heels clattering on the stone tiles. The room was large and comfortable, a lived-in room; bookshelves held scores and scores of hardback books, the settee and easy-chairs were covered in dark green leather, Chesterfield style, and a gas-fire glowed and flickered.

Gethin Hughes did not rise to greet them.

"Ruby, be an angel and fend off anybody who comes on the phone. I'd like not to be disturbed for a while. Oh, and a pot of tea would be good." He paused, waiting for approval from Griffiths and Tucker. They nodded. With a limp hand, he motioned them to sit down.

"I'm, still not fighting fit, and so I'll try to be as brief, and, I hope, as lucid as I can be. Firstly, I can now remember just about everything from that time, twenty-five years ago – the contact, the killing, and my time in God alone knows how many hospital wards, and the way I nearly got you all killed."

Both men sat silent, for the voice telling them this carried no trace of a stutter or stammer. It was as Griffiths remembered it.

"Right. I was operated on in St Hughes; it's in London. The surgeon was a specialist, apparently one of the very top neurosurgeons in Britain. He was also a territorial soldier, a Lieutenant Colonel in a Medical and Surgical field hospital. After the pounding he gave me, followed by a spell in recovery, he came to see me. He gave me theatre tickets, for his wife and Ruby to go to see a musical. I told her to take herself off to the flesh-pots and enjoy herself, assuring her I'd be alright.

That doctor and I talked for nearly four hours. I don't know, perhaps all my fears and doubts came out. If I hadn't been so bloody careless, holding a compass in one hand and the Owen's gun in the other..." His voice now seemed hoarse, his face, in the light of the wall lamps, looked strained. Griffiths put his hand out, as if to stop the narrative.

"No, I need to finish. I must say it. It was entirely my fault that they got the first rounds off. After we had been talking for some time, the doctor gave me an injection. He said it would ease any stress. Whatever it was, I trawled up all the things my mind had hidden for all those years. I told him about that murderous fight and about finding that plane. I must have dozed off after that because the next thing I remember was Ruby waking me up and giving me a cup of tea."

Both Griffiths and Tucker remained silent.

"You must be wondering why we're meeting here?" Gethin

shifted in his chair, as if he was uncomfortable, but he continued to speak. "This is my father's house, or was. The point is," he said, and his hands opened as if to release his emotions, "I think my house has been bugged – phone tapped, whatever. Whilst we were in St Hughes, and then while I was in the officers' convalescent home, somebody broke in to my house. Nothing was stolen. My, I should say 'our', safe behind the airing-cupboard had been opened and, again, nothing taken. But I *know* somebody had been in there." There was an element of pleading in his voice. "I thought I might die during the operation, so I had placed all my papers in that safe: my last will and testament, bank books, accounts, house deeds, in strict chronological order. When I opened the safe, they weren't as they had been. The safe and contents looked the same, but I *know* they were not as I'd left them. Someone has turned my house over and they were looking for something. But what? I haven't got a bloody clue."

He slumped back into the comfort of the armchair. Ruby appeared and silently placed a tray laden with tea and biscuits, down on the richly carved coffee table. Then, she left the room.

Gethin Hughes drank from the cup, his hand steady.

"The plane – you both remember the plane? I saw what was inside. There were the remains of a man; no flesh, just a skull and bones, and then I saw it."

Tucker spoke softly. "What else did you see?"

Gethin Hughes set down his cup, his hand still steady. "It was gold. There is no metal in the world like it. Gold can lie buried in the ground, or in the sea, and when it is retrieved, it's as bright and shining as the day it was smelted. It was gold, ingot after ingot, in some sort of casing. It *was* gold," he insisted, his voice losing its urgency.

Griffiths rose and switched on the main light.

"Firstly, and Tucker can speak for himself, but as far as I'm concerned, you don't have to apologise. What happened, happened. It wasn't your fault."

Gethin Hughes' eyes were fixed intently on Griffiths' face.

"Malaya was Malaya; nobody ever knew what was around the corner. We had a contact. Three Communist terrorists were killed, one member of the security forces wounded; end of story." Tucker nodded in agreement. "That's my opinion."

Tucker stretched out his left hand, "You've been through hell. Don't make it worse on yourself, Geth." The brief sentence seemed to have a calming, even comforting, ring. "What bothers me is this: what are they looking for?"

The implication that his story was believed was not lost on Gethin Hughes. "I don't know," he said.

"I think I do." Griffiths stood up. "I'll be just a minute."

When he returned, he lowered something gently into the lap of the former officer. "I believe this was your father's. I've only just got it back. It was in lodgings I had in Bristol."

Hughes' face was at first uncomprehending, then, as realisation sunk in, he opened the fawn map case, fingers struggling to unlock the catch. A creased, discoloured map came out, and something metallic fell onto the table. It was a corroded metal disc.

"Dog tags," Griffiths said, picked up the metal, spat on it and rubbed at the grime, spat again, accepted a paper tissue, and rubbed again. The stamped words slowly emerged. "LT. SPANO. J. U.S.M.C. 66897 R.C."

Tucker accepted the coin-like disc. "I wonder who the poor bastard was."

Gethin Hughes leant forward. "This is like something out of my nightmares." He looked hard at the identity disc.

"You said you saw gold?"

Gethin Hughes nodded. "I did, definitely."

"How much?"

"Several ingots. They gleamed like sunshine. The casing round them seemed to stretch back and upwards."

"What do you think this gold is worth?"

"I have no idea. It would depend on how much of it there is. Do you accept that I did see gold, and this is not some hallucination of a mind-crippled wreck?"

Griffiths' answer was slow in coming. "If you say you saw gold, then you saw it. The point is, what do we do now? Go to the police, the army, the Government?"

Gethin stood up slowly, but held himself erect. "None of those. We go back to Malaya, or Malaysia as it's now called."

Griffiths and Tucker were shocked.

"Are you serious? Could you find the plane again?" Their questions came simultaneously, urgently.

"I could now." Gethin tapped the map with fingers that trembled slightly. He opened out the map very gently. The pencil cross was easily visible.

Griffiths was persistent, "Are you sure, Geth?"

"I am!" he insisted. The room with its comfortable chairs, its familiar lived-in, loving, family feel about it suddenly seemed cold, even hostile; the men as if frozen in time and memory, the very air seemed different. The foetid, wringing damp of the Malayan jungle, the overpowering smell of the rotting vegetation seemed to be all around them.

Tucker was the first to speak. "Two things. One, I can't go back to Malaya. I cannot bloody afford it. I've no real job; and I owe money for the wife's maintenance." He refused to utter her name. "I just about survive. Secondly, this business of Geth's break-in. It couldn't be crooks; they'd have filleted the place. What sort of 'banana' breaks into a house, then steals nothing, Gethin?"

"Apart from us and that surgeon, who else have you told?"

"Only Ruby, and she hasn't told anyone. Whilst I was in dock, she did have a caller. Believe it or not, he was Chinese and he claimed to have served with Lieutenant GB Hughes. He asked whether he could donate money towards the cost of the funeral, and could he have something to remind him of the friendship and comradeship he shared with Lieutenant Hughes."

"What happened?"

"Nothing, Ruby fobbed him off. She didn't tell him that Lieutenant GB Hughes was my father."

"How old was this guy?"

"Ruby says late forties, our age."

"How old was your Dad?"

"Eighty-five. But, something like this has happened before. Dad had a sister, Gwendoline. She had two sons; one died in infancy and the other joined the Royal Air Force. He was a fighter pilot. From what I can gather from family gossip, he was something of a hero, a Battle of Britain pilot. Apparently, he had three confirmed kills, plus a couple of probables. Then he was posted to Singapore. He's still there, because he was declared, 'Killed in Action', while trying to defend his airfield. You took a book, Griff, out of the library for me, *Singapore, The Naked Island*. I finally read another copy, in my basket-case days, in a hospital in Southampton. Well," he paused, "I'd like a drink. Whiskies?"

He poured over-generous measures into three tumblers.

"Auntie Gwendoline received letters from him."

"What was his name?" Griffiths interjected.

"Samuel, Sam Morgan Price. He wrote home right up until Singapore fell. How the letters got past the censors I don't know. They were full of the incompetence, arrogance, indecision and cowardice some people showed in that debacle. Gwendoline had callers, two men, who said they were Special Branch; they asked if she would come to Cardiff, where a 'brass hat' from the RAF wanted to speak to her. They even hinted that he might have news of her son. Naturally, she went, but they kept her hanging about for hours in Cardiff, and when the RAF man finally saw her, he asked half a dozen innocuous questions. No mention of the fate of her son, except to say he had *probably* been killed. She arrived home very upset and distressed and then, exactly like me, she found that her house had been searched. Sam's letters had been read and put back in the opposite side of the drawer from where she always kept them. She contacted Dad. He drove from Salisbury Plain, where he was working as a civilian. He reported the break-in to the police, the police said they'd look into it, but Gwen heard nothing more, and she died in 1944. Dad thought she'd never got over losing her son."

Both Griffiths and Tucker sipped at their whiskey.

"You told us you think your phone has been tapped?"

"I do."

"Well then, let's test it. Phone me tomorrow evening, at eight o'clock, and ask if Tucker and I had a safe journey back to Aberystwyth, and then say that you'll meet me at Tan-y-Bwlch beach next Saturday, at two o'clock, and add that you've got something important to tell me — too important to discuss on the phone. Okay?"

Gethin scribbled notes ion the A4 pad he kept at his side.

Both men stood up, ready to depart. They felt uneasy. Tucker gave a sideways glance at his companion. "I'm getting one of your funny feelings, Griff. Let's go."

They shook hands with Gethin and called out their farewells to Ruby.

They drove the fifty-seven miles to Aberystwyth in silence, each with his mind on what had been said in Welshpool. Tucker finally broke the silence.

"This gold Gethin was on about; if it's there, what do we do with it?"

"Keep it, I suppose!"

"That's stealing, but if it is there, surely, there will be some sort of reward."

"Who from?"

"I dunno. The Malaysian Government? Our Government?"

"How many pints of best bitter will it buy?"

Griffiths laughed, "Bloody millions!" He struggled to wipe out the mental picture of Tucker and himself surrounded by thousands of pint glasses. "When we get to Aber, we'll have four or five on account."

Still chuckling, both men were unsure of the outcome of events that might or might not come, but secure in the knowledge that they would face it – the three of them together.

The sun was shining, the land and hedgerows green, the road quiet. Griffiths felt his unease slipping away. He pumped the horn.

"What was that for?" Tucker smiled.

"Just to let the world know that we're not dead yet."

Aberystwyth and best bitter were just down the road.

Seven

London

August 1982

The restaurant was on the north bank of the Thames; it had a run-of-the-mill foyer, but the further in you went, the more the décor and furniture said class, privilege, money and power. Its clientele on weekdays were city men, and, now, more and more city women, Members of Parliament, visiting dignitaries, the occasional Heads of State of smaller countries and, sometimes, members of the British Secret Service. The Company Records Office stated that the building was owned by a company registered in Liechtenstein, but the building was, in fact, owned by Her Britannic Majesty's Government, and was the direct responsibility of MI9. The Michelin chefs were paid exorbitant wages, as were the waiters – there were no waitresses. The manager was paid an excellent salary, which was provided by a little known bank buried deep in the area known as 'the City'; everybody else was paid by the Liechtenstein company.

The building itself, all its rooms, dining-room, toilets, foyer, staff bedrooms, kitchen, including wine cellar, were monitored, 'swept' in surveillance jargon, twenty-four hours a day. By the standards of 1980, the building was regarded as 'safe', much of the technology was American. By reverse engineering, the original American features were eliminated, changed and restructured. The photographic devices gave clear picture quality and pin-sharp images in close-up; the sound was meticulous, mumbled or fumbled words clearly audible. The rooms had, over the last eighteen years, been used for entrapment and exposure, and on three occasions, they were the prime reason why three suicides had occurred. Men with power all seemed to think they were bomb, fire and criticism proof; they very rarely were.

★ ★ ★

Both men knew each other well. Michael, the older of the two, had been an England Rugby International, and was now a career civil servant, originally in the quaintly named 'First Division Table'; he was suave, educated and very clever. He had been married twice, divorced once, and was currently separated from his opera-loving wife. His one child, a son in his last year at Cambridge, was expected to obtain a First in Law. His father was tolerant, but wearily resigned to the fact that his son was a homosexual.

Scott, the younger man, would, in the 1920s, have been regarded as a 'White Hunter' type – fit, tanned, handsome, the sort of man that well bred women with rich parents would have swooned and lusted after. He was the archetypal clean-cut male, who they imagined would hunt lions in Africa and tigers in India, and make love to them in the coolness of their expensive hotel rooms. Scott was, in fact, the classic family man, married happily for twenty-three years, with two teenage daughters and, incidentally, he was afraid of large dogs.

They nodded amicably.

"How is the spying game?" Michael asked.

Scott gave the well worn answer, "On the up. How's the lying game? Shall we order the fish?"

The waiter took their order and brought a bottle of dry white wine in a bucket of crushed ice. He deftly removed the cork, poured a little wine into a glass and left. The two men at the table had been 'twinned' four years earlier. Scott collected and sifted information on known terrorist suspects, and sought out the identities of those who were suspected of terrorist activities. His brief extended beyond mainland Britain, to Ireland, north and south, Europe and the Middle and Far East. He ran thirty-seven Grade I operatives and had many other sources of information. These were people who kept their eyes and ears open; some had police or military backgrounds, others simply reported suspicious activities and received a modest amount of money in exchange. Their 'something for you' was carefully processed, electronically and manually. His team considered themselves to be professional, and much more competent than regional crime squads and special Branch. Scott had never been reprimanded in his eleven years in MI9. He was regarded as the role model of a spymaster, a title he liked, but pretended not to.

Michael had left Cambridge with a First in Pure and Applied Mathematics. He had entered the Civil Service a month after coming down from university. A vigorous and not overly dainty wing forward, he had moved smoothly into an England jersey. The game of Rugby Union was an amateur one, mostly. Players in Wales and some of the rougher edges of Britain, the West Country and Cornwall, were reputed to be handsomely rewarded for their endeavours on the field, and, certainly, his rugby prowess did not hamper his progress up the promotion ladder. With his high achievement came the diplomatic skills that made him a particularly good, possibly brilliant, solver of problematical political 'hot potatoes'. He read and commented on all the briefs, memos and files that came over from Scott, telling his political masters what they had to know, sometimes what they wanted to know, and sometimes what he thought they should know. He was not well off, despite his, by some standards, obscenely high salary. His first wife had seen to that, and the second one was doing her best to catch up on her predecessor.

The fish was excellent; both men would have been offended if it had not been. The wine was cold and refreshing.

"Something has come up." Scott was holding his glass by the stem. The Thames, grey and sullen, was busy with small craft passing up and down between its banks. Michael remained silent.

"What do you know of the fall of Singapore?" Scott asked.

Michael seemed disinterested. "What can I tell you about that? It was probably the biggest defeat ever suffered by the British Army, worse than the Somme. In a nutshell, you could say it was the definitive 'cock-up'. 135,000 soldiers, ours, Australian, Ghurkha and Indian, were killed, wounded, posted missing and captured – the vast majority of the poor buggers were captured. That was when the real evil started, the casual bayoneting, beatings, beheadings. The Greater Co Asia, as the Japs called the Dutch East Indies, Malaya and Singapore, was never the same again. It still isn't. The white men were proved wanting. Asians could fight and beat them easily. Why do you ask about that old history?"

Scott unlocked his attaché case and extracted two sheets of paper.

"These are photocopies. The originals aren't brilliant. It's 1941 typing and 1941 paper."

He slid both sheets across the table. Michael read them with practised speed, and read them again, memorising names and dates. Scott slipped the sheets back into the case.

"It's a flight plan that was drawn up for an American dive bomber, a Vindicator; the pilot was a Lieutenant in the American Marine Corps. His name was Jake Spano, twenty-five years of age. He was loaded up with cargo at Seletar Airfield, Singapore, on December 20th 1941. He was ordered to fly to Sumatra. He was told his cargo would be unloaded there, and then he was to fly back, to rejoin his squadron."

"So!"

Scott leaned forward. "It's there, in the flight plan. Sumatra from Singapore is south-west, but his plan was to fly north. The Japanese were in total air superiority down as far as Singapore itself."

Michael slid the empty glass forward. "Fog of war, mistake on somebody's part?"

"No, definitely *not* a mistake. The cargo he was carrying, and incidentally he was never told about it, was very important. I repeat *very* important."

"What was it?"

"Part of the cargo was gold, every ounce from every bank in Singapore, its weight in excess of 1,960 lbs, nearly one ton, value then unknown. The finance section are still trying to work it out, and their calculators went off the scale. Today's value has to be something approaching thirty million pounds sterling. That was only part of the cargo."

"Part?" Michael reached for the Chardonnay bottle, which was reassuringly cold. His antennae picked up a sharp rise in tension.

Scott looked directly at him. "I can't say anything, not here, anyway. It has to be in the PM's office."

"How far up the line does this go?"

"Right to the very top!"

"She's a busy woman."

Scott nodded acknowledgement. "Agreed, but if I told you that the second part of the cargo has been top of the worry list of *every* Prime Minister since the Second World War, you can bet she will find the time to see us."

"How has this come to light? When and where did you find out about this?"

"One of our contacts, a surgeon, told us that an amnesiac patient revealed just about everything, after anaesthetic. We checked, and checked again. The papers and documents about that cargo have all been locked up, and are to remain so for one hundred years.

Michael was impressed. "A hundred years! I didn't think we could do that."

"We can do anything. D O R A, Defence of the Realm Act, remember. That's sacrosanct, not for nosy people, historians, revisionists, unfriendly politicians and the like, to pick the bones over. We need to see the PM."

Michael refilled both their glasses. "This might sound at best simplistic and at worst stupid, but how can an American plane, albeit full of gold, which crashed in 1941, warrant the personal intelligence briefing of the PM?"

"I assure you it can. The Japanese were supposed to have invented the 'Divine Wind Tactic', i.e. suicide bombing of Allied ships, but, I rather think the American and British War Cabinets pre-empted them. The plane piloted by Lieutenant Spano was sent north, two Brewster Buffaloes were scrambled to escort him. He was to proceed northwards and then bear west."

"He was bait?"

Scott looked down at his hands. They were well-cared for. "He was, yes. The Japanese Army was going through Malaya like a dose of salts. Any Allied plane shot down was to be searched. The gold was not thrown away. A cache that size warranted very senior Japanese officers being informed, and that is where the second part of the cargo comes into the frame."

"What was it?" Michael was intrigued.

"I can't tell you, Michael. I won't know myself, until I am sanctioned as fit to know, and that will have to be approved from above."

"How far above?"

"Both of us are in the intermediate pool; the really high diving pool is not for us. The political implications for this are immense, possibly – no probably – world-changing events could result if this is not handled ..." he mentally rejected the word 'properly', and substituted, "professionally."

Michael signalled to the wine waiter. "Another bottle, please." He turned to face his colleague. "This isn't like you, Scott. We have always enjoyed an open relationship. You tell me half a story, but refuse to reveal the second half – the end game."

Scott felt uncomfortable. "I do not know any more. I repeat, I do not know what else was loaded into that plane, but we've done some digging into every file, every published paper about Singapore, every newspaper cutting, surviving censored mail, which incidentally still exists, every memo from the British War Cabinet that we've been able to locate, and just about everything our American cousins have on file and tape. I can only hazard a guess, and until that file that is to be held for a further sixty years is opened, only then can I state specifically and with clarity what that American pilot was transporting." His voice was little more than a whisper. "You must arrange a briefing for us. Trust me, Michael, this is truly vital."

Michael gently twirled the wine glass. "The old adage, 'cry wolf' comes into mind, but you've never cried wolf before. I have enormous respect for you, Scott, but..." The pause lasted for several seconds, "what if this story of long forgotten gold, and the other so far unexplained cargo, is just a figment of somebody's imagination?" Michael leant back, his chair somehow not as comfortable as it previously was.

Scott took his time before answering.

"Take the first part, the gold. The CIA followed and phone-tapped a former United States Army Air Corps pilot for a dozen years, because a cargo of gold on its way from the Americans to the Nationalist Chinese, to fund their armies to fight the Japanese, crashed in the Himalayas, going over what was called 'the hump'. A British officer operating in the Balkans mislaid just twenty gold sovereigns. There was nearly a Court of Enquiry about that. Governments covet their gold; if it's lost, they want it back and usually no questions are asked. Thirty millions. Think about it – build a lot of schools or hospitals, that would, or, with things as they are, several infantry battalions could be raised. But, it pales into insignificance alongside this particular cargo. If the so far unknown part of the cargo reveals what I suspect, I repeat, suspect, it to be, it's time for a decision, Michael. We need *that* file opened and then we need to brief the PM. My reputation, my job is all on the line. What do you say? I can go over your head. I've several tame politicians in the closet, but I don't want to use them. I need your experience and expertise to back me."

Michael remained silent, his mind recalling the occasion of his first cap against France, when he found himself lying trapped on the wrong side of a ruck, with French boots thudding and stamping into his rib and thighs; then, just when he thought the shoeing was over, a kick landed directly on his face. He felt like that now. Scott was not some maniac French forward, but a good, valued and, up to a point, a trusted friend. After the match, they had all shaken hands. The Frenchman offered his and muttered "*Enchanté.*"

Michael pulled his mind back to the question in hand. "I will think things over. There are some people I must see, and some people I must speak to. You said your job was on the line but, with respect, Scott, so is mine. This may, or may not be, as the song says, bigger than both of us. Now, what about a dessert?"

Scott watched Michael's face. There was no discernible trace of emotion or any physical clue to what he was thinking. He leaned back. "I'll try the rice pudding. I'm told it was first invented in Malaya."

Michael grinned. "Right you are; it's rice pudding for one, and, for me, some mince pies. Not yet Christmas, I know."

Scott said, "Christmas starts earlier every year. Presents to be bought. Don't leave it too long, or we might find Santa Claus has been down the chimney, all our presents have been taken back up the flue, and all we are left with is an empty stocking."

"Give me three weeks. I'll be in touch."

Michael scribbled on the proffered meal chit. It had been a first-class meal, but the price was gold-class. "How are your daughters?" he asked, somewhat as an afterthought.

Scott nodded, "Fine, thank you."

They left together, and parted at the main door, but there was no handshake.

Eight

Aberystwyth

Late August 1982

Griffiths let the phone ring five times before he answered it. Gethin's voice was matter-of-fact.

"Kev? How are you? Ruby's fine. I'm not quite fighting fit but feel a hell of a lot better. The reason I'm ringing is that I've found something. Remember when we had our little 'difficulty' with the Communist Terrorists, well, the map I used to mark the spot - I've found it. It was in my father's house. He must have collected it with some of my other stuff, when I was doing my grand tour of hospitals. I'll bring it down with me next Saturday. Ruby and I are going up to Harrogate tomorrow. Ruby's mother lives there, so we'll be away for three days, home on Friday. I'll slip down on Saturday, if that's all right. Where shall we meet? Tan-y-Bwlch beach. Okay. What time? One o'clock. If it's raining we'll go to the pub. I need your help; I would like you to sort out this map for me. I keep wondering if I got the map position right. It's important to me. See you Saturday."

Griffiths felt strangely elated, for the first time since Bethan had been killed. It was a small sense of reality, knowing that he was doing something positive, not just drifting through time; the schoolboy pretence of the conversation he'd just had; the laying of a trap had stimulated him. If Hughes had said he'd seen gold, he probably had seen gold. If he thought his phone might be bugged, it might be. The two may, just, have some repercussions. In a surge of optimism, or bravado, he wasn't sure which; he wished there would be repercussions.

Hughes turned the ignition key. The engine of the Jaguar, bought brand new by his father in 1955, turned over sweetly. He pushed his foot down on the accelerator and, in the confines of the garage, the noise sounded like the snarl of a beast, alive and angry. On the previous Friday, before phoning Kevin, he'd driven to Hereford. The Army & Navy Store carried a comprehensive stock of surplus ex-army, navy and RAF clothing, boots, webbing and equipment. He purchased a jungle green water-bottle-holder and map case, paid in cash and drove back to Welshpool. Next, he did a strange thing. He put both items of webbing into the stream that ran alongside his father's house and left them there overnight. When he retrieved them, he rubbed them through the dust on the floor of the outside toilet and dried them with Ruby's hairdryer. By 11 o'clock, both objects looked creased, crumpled and somewhat battered.

Hughes drove to his office and photocopied the crinkled map, memorising the grid squares. He placed the copy in his wallet, then, he carefully rubbed out the pencilled cross marked on it, and with a dry cloth he wiped away all traces of pencil and rubber dust. Then, with a pencil from his bureau, he faintly marked in another cross, one and a quarter inches to the left of the original cross that had been pencilled in on that day twenty-five years ago. He wiped the photocopier and drove back to his home, placed the creased map into the green gloom of the map case, and left it on the coffee-table in the front room. He collected Ruby from the hairdresser's and left for Harrogate. If anybody had measured the two pieces of webbing they would have seen that the side of the map case was exactly four inches from the edge of the coffee-table, and a closer examination would have revealed a human hair, one of his own, placed precisely, just over the top of the map inside the case. Also, the water-bottle-holder was lying north to south, precisely seven and a quarter inches from the map case.

On the following Saturday, Hughes kissed Ruby goodbye and left for Aberystwyth. Nine miles south of Welshpool, he pretended not to notice the two bikers who had appeared in his rear mirror. As he gently eased the Jaguar up to just under seventy miles per hour, both riders stayed with him. They eventually passed him going through Talybont, seven miles from Aberystwyth.

Griffiths saw the gleaming, cherry red Jaguar parked in the tiny car park, and noticed the admiring glances of a group of holidaymakers.

"The Birmingham Navy." He nodded at the holidaymakers who were circling the vehicle. "Brummies – if anybody knows their cars, they do."

Hughes clasped him around his shoulders.

"Good to see you, Kev. Let's sit down on the shingle." The pebbles were hard and unyielding against their bodies. "Look at the paper's preview of Welsh rugby, page twenty-seven." He handed over the paper. Griffiths flicked quickly through the pages.

Page twenty-seven had five postcard-sized yellow stickers, marked 1 – 5 in descending order, stuck to it. The first note said simply, 'I was right; my phone is bugged, and we did have visitors again. I'll explain later.' The second note was very brief. 'Tucker, you and me must meet. Somewhere where no-one can overhear.' The third note simply said, 'Without any obvious look, clock the two fishermen.'

Hughes remarked, "I think Wales' glory years on the rugby field have gone. That's a very pessimistic preview." He folded the paper, handed it back to Griffiths, and glanced around. "What's that up there?" He pointed to a nearby hill.

They stood up and looked at the monument rearing starkly upwards on the top of Pen Dinas. Griffiths folded the newspaper, shielding the notes.

"Wellington's monument. It's supposed to be a cannon with the mouth pointed to the heavens – an end to all wars."

Hughes was smiling. "I'll drink to that."

They turned around casually and observed who else was nearby. The two fishermen were also bikers, sporting black leathers and impressive bikes. One was casting, the other appeared to be selecting a rod from the contents of a black box. The rod was telescopic and it had a large reel. He apparently rejected it and placed it upright in the shingle. Griffiths noted that the reel was pointing directly at them.

"What did you want to see me about?"

Hughes shook his head. "I had this idea, quite a mad notion, that perhaps not all of that bullet is out of my head. I had been wondering if you fancied a trip back to Malaya, but when I spoke to Ruby, she was dead against it. She asked if I really wanted to undo all the good work that the British National Health Service says it is doing for me. Ruby's a gem, and very nearly perfect in her advice. If she says no, then, no it is. Come on, I'll take you for a spin; we can leave your car here. We'll come back for it later. Let's go and have a pint of this draught bitter you're so besotted with." They both laughed.

The biker was still fiddling with the fishing rod, the reel now pointing left, towards the Jaguar. Hughes revved the engine; the holidaymakers looked on enviously as they made their exit quickly.

"Turn right."

The Jaguar cut across the main road, flew up a short steep hill.

"Left!" Griffiths commanded and, in a cloud of dust, they merged with the hundreds of cars, campers, vans, bikes and caravans that were dotted about the camping ground. Griffiths was apologetic.

"Sorry for the terseness, but those bikes can shift, electric ignition... we only had thirty, forty seconds to get away from them."

Both men were excited, united by the bond of friendship and a sense of victory.

"Open page twenty-seven again," instructed Hughes.

Griffiths smoothed out the crumpled newspaper. Sticker 4 said, 'The words about not going to Malays were poppycock.' Sticker 5 simply said, 'Are you with me?'

Griffiths looked at the finely polished mahogany dashboard, the myriad of dials and gauges, and he could smell the luxury of the upholstery. His right hand came out and grasped the hand of the man whose life he had once saved.

"Try and stop me."

They sat and talked. "First, we bring Tucker into the picture," Hughes said, "but where can we meet? It has to be somewhere absolutely secure. Who, or what, is tracking me, I don't know. It must be something to do with that Yankee plane we found in the jungle."

"How did you know your house had been infiltrated?"

Hughes explained about the trap he'd laid. How the map case had been moved to five and three-quarter inches from coffee table edge; using a magnifying glass, he found the human hair on the floor, and the water bottle holder had been left just two inches from the map case. It was all wrong.

"Ruby will phone you from a public callbox in Shrewsbury. Be sure and take down *all* the details because she'll only phone once."

"When will she call and where shall I be?"

"She'll call the number of the phone box by the pier, the one nearest the Chinese restaurant, at two o'clock, next Friday afternoon. I need till then to organise things."

"Remember, if we ask Tucker to join us, he hasn't got any money."

"Tucker doesn't need money. I've got some. Dad was careful with his coppers. There's plenty."

"Take the long way home; go over the old mountain road to Rhayader, turn left back to Llangurig and then, take the route via Llanidloes and Newtown to Welshpool. I'll walk back to my car. Will you be alright?"

When he smiled, Hughes's face was almost boyish.

"I will. I've got this." He reached into the side pocket in the car door and pulled out a heavy-duty spanner. "If I'm attacked, somebody's going to have a sore head. And, I don't see why not. I've had one for years."

★ ★ ★

Swee Poe decided that he disliked the United Kingdom. People were always hurrying and scurrying, and some were rude. In Manchester, he'd passed a group of youths and girls; they had wild haircuts, wore rouge, lipstick and earrings, and they were the boys, and they all smelt. He was later to recognise the smell as cannabis, and these stinking boys were called Punks. He recalled his time in America, and the derisive term Punks seemed a very apt description. He quickly integrated himself into the Chinese community, never disclosing his true identity, and paid scrupulously for his food and rent and the tribute to the local Triad, careful never to excite comment or speculation. He explained, in a very carefully compiled and rehearsed story, that he was a widower. His wife had died in California, and he had a death certificate to prove it. The grief was a burden, the insurance money was a buffer, he just wanted to get away to see the world. How far away were the Mountains of Wales? Swee Poe discovered the answer to that easily enough.

In a reasonably smart car, Swee Poe drove down to Wales and headed for Cardiff. The South Wales Fusiliers' Museum was housed in a large, cold building. Poe was polite and respectful. He explained to a uniformed attendant, whose mind was wandering to a grandmother from Barry, whom he was meeting for a drink and a 'chat', that he was a journalist seeking material about the Fusiliers' tour of duty in Malaya from 1954 to 1957.

"In there, pal," the former sergeant said, pointing to an alcove.

"Thanks very much."

"Sir, no smoking I'm afraid," said the sergeant, cheerfully accepting one of Swee Poe's expensive cigarettes. "I'll just go outside and check the weather." The sergeant enjoyed a good smoke.

Swee Poe had paid over $300 for the camera, bought in Ottawa. It took excellent photographs. He went down the files of names, the click of the shutter and light of the flash recording them all. Satisfied, he left, after waving to the returning sergeant.

The notice in the Obituary Columns had been a massive bonus, overshadowed by the rejection of his advances by the tall, blonde, Anglo Saxon lady. It was only in the pub afterwards that he discovered that George Barrington Hughes was eight-five when he died, and that his son, Gethin Barrington Hughes, was the officer who had served in Malaya and had, apparently, been badly wounded. Swee Poe noted the address, postcode, location of the police station, and left for his new-found friends in Manchester.

"When I said 'secure'," I did not envisage being under the Lord's protection."

Tucker was quietly indifferent. "This is my job; I'm a caretaker. I look after the buildings, sweep them, clean them and carry out maintenance, repairing broken windows, mostly."

The building in Tucker's care was a Salvation Army Church hall. Tucker occupied a tiny bed-sit, and his meals were paid for at a busy little café down the road. His wages were very small. He was content. The Salvationists were good, kind people, nearly all elderly; their few children and grandchildren were always courteous and full of fun. Tucker was aware of people's respect and friendship towards him. From his indifferent attitude to Christianity or, indeed, any religious teachings and sermons he had listened to, he was experiencing something valuable. In its heyday, the congregation at the Citadel had numbered well over two hundred. Today, it usually comprised twenty-five to thirty, but something of the old, hard, Evangelical spirit remained. Three times a year, the forty-strong Salvation Army Band from Llanelli came to lead the Salvationists in worship. Tucker prayed with them. He accepted the fact that he was changing. The black moods of yesterday were now fading and he slid quietly into an acceptance that his life was in the hands of the Lord.

There were still some worrying forays into the world outside; a gang of youths, fifteen, sixteen years of age, nine or ten in number, girls as well as boys, had taken to throwing bricks and stones at the building. Tucker had fashioned a catapult, and, wearing rubber gloves purchased from the DIY shop, he collected pebbles and stones from the quarry. On light nights, he practised his aim at beer cans, and quickly found his range with the catapult. The first teenager to receive a bullet-hard pebble in the teeth, as he prepared to lob a quarter brick at The Citadel, had let out a loud squeal. In the next three minutes, another youth and two girls earned broken noses. That the missiles came from a hilly mound beside The Citadel convinced the youngsters that they were under attack from a rival gang. The subsequent police and newspaper revelations, which dubbed the teenagers as 'The Bent Nose Gang', finished the stone-throwing epidemic. Tucker was modestly pleased that he had defended his property. But the real end to the stone-throwing came when the District Council Chairman, in this case Chairwoman, chose to publicise the trouble, by inviting a local TV current affairs unit to transmit a programme about how her council had, under her dynamic leadership, turned a rebellious teenage faction into an integral part of the law-abiding and voting community. Shortly afterwards, while undertaking an official engagement, she bent down to unveil a commemorative a plaque, and Tucker's pebble hit her on the backside with considerable force. The subsequent television footage of the incident ran for days and the lady lost her seat on the council at the next election.

Hughes and Griffiths accepted that Tucker was, somehow, a different man.

"We're going back to Malaya. You don't have to find a penny towards the cost; it's on me," explained Hughes. There was a slight pause, while Tucker thought about it.

"Always said officers had more money than sense."

"Good," said Hughes, reporting to Tucker everything that had happened recently.

"How far off course is the new cross?" Tucker asked, referring to the altered map.

"About six hundred yards, but in the jungle, that could seem like sixty. I've done some homework and obtained a large-scale map of the State of Negri Sembilan. In those days, the manager of the rubber estate was a Mr Watson. He retired to the Scilly

Isles, of all places, where he died four years ago. His widow confirmed the name of the estate, the date of our contact, and also confirmed that a Commie Terrorist had surrendered to security forces at Gemas. Her husband had mentioned that the estate and jungle had briefly swarmed with soldiers, and one of them had said they were hampered because they had no Sea Dyaks, Ibans, as trackers. As far as he was aware, nothing of significance was found. The follow-up operation lasted for a further three days. Apparently, the CT who surrendered was the last of a four-man section, and, as far as I can discover, he survived the action and melted away. This brings us to a problem. Was Ruby's visitor in anyway connected to our unknown CT Chinaman?"

"What about the bikers? Who are they working for? They weren't Chinese, were they"

"I don't know anything about them at all. What I do know is this, that somebody was in our house, and the map was examined and probably copied."

"This surgeon; could he be the mole who spread the word? Did he tell the army, the government?"

"If he told anyone, it would probably be Army Intelligence."

Griffiths shook his head. "We just don't know, so we play it as it comes. If there is someone out there, Chinaman, Spook, or whatever, it makes sense to get back to Malaya as soon as possible."

The others nodded in agreement.

"Tucker, have you got a passport?"

"As a matter of fact, I have. I got it when we had our honeymoon in Spain. There's still a couple of years to run on it."

Griffiths said, "Mine's still in date."

Hughes stroked his tie. He was obviously in deep thought. The others waited.

"Right," he said. "We do it this way. I'll book the three of us to Amsterdam; we'll spend two nights seeing the sights, and then we'll take a direct flight to Kuala Lumpur. Ten days in KL, find the plane, and then see what has to be done next."

"What if we do find the plane and there is gold, what do we do?" asked Tucker.

"The authorities, Malayan and British, have to be told. The plane will be designated a war grave because of the body still being there, so we can't remove anything. However, there might be a reward for locating it. From a legal viewpoint, I believe there will be treasure-trove status, similar to the law that governs metal detection rules. I'm not that much bothered. I simply want this business out of my head. It's like living in a glass bottle, and there's a bloody big fly in there with me, buzzing in and out of my mind. I have to go back. I have to find that plane."

The three men lapsed into silence. The sparseness of Tucker's bed-sit was obvious as the light faded; the tick of the cheap alarm clock made the only sound.

"I've stated my position. What do you say, Tucker?"

"I'm content here. I don't really want anything. I might as well be honest. I'm now a Christian. God alone knows why and how. All I want is to work and follow Christ. I'll go with you." He spread both hands out as if offering his views to them.

"Kev?"

Griffiths felt numb, like the numbness he felt when Bethan had died. His voice was very quiet. "What do I want? I want to *kill* the bastard that killed Bethan."

"I can understand that. Okay, we'll go to Malaya first, and after that, we'll see." Griffiths rose, it was time to leave.

"Griff, Ruby will phone you as agreed. Tuck, ask the Captain of the Salvation Army whether you can have two weeks' holiday. Kev will let you know when." Hughes offered his right hand, and Griffiths and Tucker placed their hands on his. "You know what to say."

The three men seemed to straighten up. Twenty-five years ago, they had been young soldiers. The words were spoken quietly and in unison: "Once a Fusilier, always a Fusilier."

There was briskness in their movement now. Hughes shook hands with them both as he said his goodbyes. Three men, with widely different motives, were about to embark on a huge journey; one was going to conquer the demons that had tormented him over the years, one out of loyalty and to ease the poison in his mind, and one because he felt the Lord approved of the journey. Tucker reflected to himself that you couldn't get more diverse reasons than that.

Nine

Soho, London, England

September 1982

With some care, Swee Poe had dressed in a dark, expensive suit, white shirt, a gentle, subdued tie, shoes vigorously polished. The story about the streets of London being paved with gold was patently untrue. London, on this September day, had a tired, world–weary air. The victory parade of those who had returned from the Falklands had been and gone, so too had what the newspapers called 'the Falklands factor'. Swee Poe had agonised for a long time about whether he was doing the right thing. The very idea of a meeting with the unquestioned leader of one the British Chinese communities had been unthinkable just a few weeks ago, but subsequent events had changed everything. Swee Poe realised that he needed help. He needed someone in Malaysia, who could steal a map and lead him to the exact location of the plane. Increasingly, he thought of it as *his* plane, and he needed to get possession of a weapon. The prospect of returning unarmed to the Malayan jungle was as unnerving as a parachute jump without a chute.

He arrived punctually at the appointed place and was ushered into a large, airy room. The handshake of the man he had come to see was firm but not intimidating. Swee Poe accepted a large dish of tea. They made small talk, Swee Poe always deferential to his much older host. Swee Poe proffered his business card, which all but shrieked quality, with its black edge and the lettering in gold. It gave Poe's name as ELVIS LEE and carried, too, his Manchester telephone number. He smiled as the old man took his card, and noted that ELVIS and LEE were in capital letters. Eight was the total number of letters; eight was the number revered by the Chinese; eight meant wealth and much good luck.

Swee Poe gave his revised version of his personal history: born in 1935, only son of a small but prosperous Chinese businessman. He spoke of the horror of the Japanese occupation of Malaya and Singapore, and of his father's death shortly after Liberation. 'The Emergency', the killings, had not started till 1948. His mother and he had left for Australia a month before the first unrest. He lied easily and skilfully. On his twenty-first birthday, he said, his mother, who was never very strong, had told him of his inheritance, a very substantial sum of money secreted away from those wolves, the Japanese. Shortly to come into his possession was a map showing the location of his rightful legacy. In answer to a question from the old man, Swee Poe said it was not buried, just hidden. What he wanted was a gun, and a guide who could find his way in the jungle and retrieve a map, by which Swee Poe which meant steal a map. The old man's eyes showed no emotion. Swee Poe felt that he should enlarge a little on his story. The gun was for his protection; he had relatives in Malaya, bad, greedy people, who would not hesitate to rob him of his rightful legacy. He might have to defend himself. The money was still in Malaya because the people who now had the map had been, like him, away from Malaya for many years and also, like himself, carving out a living in the western world. The weapon had to be made available in Malaya. Guns were not allowed on aircraft. If he were caught carrying one he would be in desperate trouble. He was sure the respected gentleman would appreciate his concern.

The old man, his face thin to the point of haggardness, nodded. What was the amount of money Mr Lee had in mind, he enquired, bearing in mind that guns in civilian use were rare and unlawful. Both men tried to look sincere. Outside, in the cool September air of a London autumn, leaves were beginning to drift and swirl down to the pavement. Swee Poe knew he would be asked to pay an exorbitant amount of money for what he needed. The old man knew Mr Lee would barter for a smaller sum.

"You ask for a very big favour," he said. "I have many contacts, but a gun and a thief who can recover *your* map! In this world, Mr. Lee, nothing is free, unlike the old times, when friendship alone could be counted on. The cost is two thousand British pounds. That is for an automatic hand-gun with a full magazine, and will include a person to retrieve your map and guide you to your inheritance." The last word was spoken slowly, almost in a whisper.

Swee Poe gave a tiny shrug. "I have money, but, with great respect, I cannot afford that amount. I regret that we cannot do business. It is most unfortunate, but I thank you most sincerely for your hospitality and your very valuable time. I'm afraid I must seek help elsewhere." Swee Poe bowed his head respectfully, and reached out to retrieve his card.

The old man's fingers were very thin. They moved in a defensive screen over Swee Poe's business card. "It would be wrong to lose friendship without an offer from you." He used the word 'friendship' but both knew that he meant 'face'.

"I can afford one thousand pounds." He paused, and then added, "Plus two hundred, when my father's money is mine."

The old man rose and turned to face the window, his voice was even.

"The British have a saying: 'A bird in the hand is worth two in the bush'."

Swee Poe allowed himself a moment's reflection. "One

thousand one hundred British pounds, shall we say, or the American dollar equivalent?"

Without turning, the old man replied, "It is acceptable."

Swee Poe lifted his expensive briefcase onto the table, the locks snapped open and he made a point of rustling the blue and brown banknotes.

"Eleven hundred pounds for a gun, a guide and someone versed in retrieving articles," he said, and slid the neat piles of notes towards the old man.

The old man made no move to count the money. "It is agreed. When will you require this service?"

Swee Poe stood up; he felt like an athlete in the starting block. "Very soon. I will contact you shortly before my departure. You will give me the contact name and telephone number on the day I leave?" The old man nodded. Swee Poe picked up his briefcase.

"Thank you, sir. Please accept my card. I hope to speak to you very shortly."

The autumnal wind was keen. Swee Poe turned up the collar of his overcoat, the cold air whirling around his ears.

The seat was in the first-class compartment. He glanced at his watch. 1.58 pm. The train left five minutes later and on time. Swee Poe was jubilant that he had started on his quest, but also strangely uneasy. Something, annoyingly, didn't seem right. He had hesitated about contacting the old man whose name was whispered as *the* man to speak to. Swee Poe had avoided contact with Chinese communities for many years, but he needed help and local expertise. He had finally made up his mind. The old man was just as the whispers said he was, but try as he would to be rational, Swee Poe felt twinges of unease. It was a little like heartburn, a sharp stab of fear, followed by a lingering, bitter taste in his throat. He ordered a large whisky and the alcohol started to soothe him, dispelling the apprehension. The train entered a tunnel; his reflection in the window stared back at him. He raised his glass in a toast to himself. The buffet attendant, eyes and ears tuned to near perfection by years of service, caught the gesture and inquired, "Another, sir?"

Swee Poe was expansive. "Why not!" The sourness was disappearing from his throat. As the train thundered on its way to Manchester, Swee Poe's mood changed. The great adventure was starting. He had only a few things to do in Manchester, and then he would be on his way Malaya, and the dreams of twenty-five years would be realised.

* * *

As Swee Poe was leaving Euston Station, a black Rover saloon, with a driver and two passengers, left Vauxhall and, in moderate traffic, headed north out of London, and, one hour and forty minutes later, arrived at Chicksands, in Bedfordshire. The car pulled up at a mediaeval priory, parts of which were listed in the 11th Century Doomsday Book; some of the trees in the locality were believed to be amongst the oldest in Britain. This was the headquarters of the Defence, Intelligence and Security Centre – DISC. Its covert activities dated back to the early years of World War II, when they were operated by various sections of the War Department. Post–war, in the early 1950s, it was home to elements of the recently-formed United States Air Force, which had succeeded the wartime United States Army Air Corps. As the Cold War wrapped its icy tentacles around the world, the centre was developed into a highly sophisticated and very expensive Radio Interception Centre – RIC. Concentric circles of ultra–powerful radio aerials were erected around the building, and easy-going American airmen guarded it. Local people sometimes grumbled about interference on their radios and the increasingly popular television sets, but it was infrequent, and well-paid jobs were available for cleaners, gardeners, cooks and drivers. Chicksands had by then reverted to the British, and it was now in Ministry of Defence use. Occasionally, uniformed sailors, soldiers and air force personnel were glimpsed in the grounds, but the buildings appeared to be in civilian occupation and were usually very quiet. Vehicles came and went and there was a benign, studious, bookish atmosphere about the place.

Some of the rooms were used to debrief agents: British and foreign, and moles within the Irish Republican Army. The building was pleasantly scented with pine polish and air-freshener, and everywhere looked impeccably clean, desks gleamed, panelled rooms were warm. All-in-all, it was an impressively maintained building. The quadruple-locked library and reference rooms archived many thousands of files, dossiers, tape recordings, micro-dots and 16mm and 35mm film, the files ranging from a barely-remembered past right up to current times. The vast majority of files were classified 'Most Secret', and the rooms also housed a mainframe computer that matched anything the Americans, Russian and Israelis had.

Michael and Scott alighted from the Rover. It was now considered elderly, but if anyone had been allowed to raise the bonnet, their eyebrows would have been raised, as well. Instead of the standard work's engine, it now boasted a squat 4-litre with an accelerator ratio that went off the clock. Similarly, the lovingly polished bodywork and windows were classed as bullet-proof up to the old 303 Lee Enfield rounds, bigger and heavier than the standard NATO ammunition. Both men produced their identification passes to the civilian-clothed men of the Royal Military Police, and they were ushered in front of a metal detector, X-Ray and Positive Proof Indicator apparatus. Their facial images were sent in nanoseconds to the receiver.

The RMP, as unsmiling as ever, returned their passes and they set off down the 150-yard-long gravel driveway, neither man speaking, the stones crunching under foot in an old-fashioned, positively English way, epitomising grand Victorian mansions, huge stately homes – a world long gone by.

They were met at the door that the RMP guard told them was their destination. A man was waiting for them, with a welcoming, outstretched hand.

"Good afternoon, gentlemen. This way, if you please," he said, knocking at the door and leading the way inside the room, where a man was seated behind a large rosewood desk. He made no effort to stand up.

"Good journey?"

"Yes, thank you."

Greeting and response were perfunctory, without warmth.

Scott and Michael removed their topcoats and sat down. The man who had shown them to the room was standing by the door, awaiting further orders.

"No interruptions. Tea with biscuits, sixteen-thirty. That's all. You may leave us now."

Scott and Michael studied the man facing them; he was known to them both. He was neither a government minister, nor Permanent Under-Secretary, but, on the face of it, a little-known Member of Parliament, someone who was rarely interviewed on television or in current affairs and politics radio programmes. Both men were aware that he possessed one of the most ruthless, shrewdest analytical mind in British politics. He had no time for small talk and came straight to the point.

"You have requested a meeting to tell me something you believe might have a direct political bearing on the security of the United Kingdom?"

"We do... I do," Scott corrected himself, nervous about what was to come.

"Please carry on, the floor is yours."

Scott spoke without interruption. From memory, he told of the information given to him by the surgeon, the surveillance of Gethin Hughes' house, the map found in the map case and copied, the microphone recording of Gethin Hughes and Kevin Griffiths talking together on the beach at Aberystwyth.

"I believe that the plane piloted by the American contained something other than the gold, something that, if brought to light, would pose the most serious threat to us since World War II. I further believe that a copy of a certain document might be in the National Archives at Kew. If there is a copy of that document in existence, it should be released to us in my section at MI9. I must add, that I do not know if there is a document that could incriminate this country, but if there is, then every effort, whatever the cost, should be made to retrieve it." In a noticeably quieter tone he added, "And examine it." He sat back into his chair.

The man turned to Michael and asked, "What are your views?"

Michael thought carefully about how to respond. He'd tackled big men before, in what was referred to as 'an exchange of opinion', 'a cuddle', 'a shoeing', 'getting your retaliation in first'.

"I'm a government official; you are the politician. I collate and restructure the information Scott gives me. I do it quickly and accurately. The briefs I give to Government are scrupulous. I leave no stone unturned. What you do with the briefings I give to you is your concern, not mine. The facts presented to you by me and Scott have been honest. Three former members of a British Army patrol, operating during the Malayan

Emergency, apparently discovered the wreckage of a wartime plane. According to the information given by the surgeon who attended one of those men, there was a large quantity of gold bullion in that plane. The facts are that *no* gold was recovered after the fall of Singapore. If there was any other cargo, then we, as the professionals, have no knowledge of it. But if there is a copy of whatever was in that plane, then that copy is in the National Archives. We do not have access to it – you do."

The man worked his left hand over his top lip. People who knew him would have recognised a danger signal. Although he was annoyed, his voice remained neutral.

"Three former soldiers were contemplating returning to Malaysia, to try to find the plane, according to information given to you by Scott. That is not now their intention, you tell me. However, a perusal of army records shows that three Communist terrorists were killed, but a fourth, apparently, surrendered two days later. As Surrendered Enemy Personnel, he was put through the standard resettlement programme and given a resettlement grant. He was provided with a new, British identity, and he left for Australia. Where is he now?"

"He is known as Raymond Lee," Scott said. "He went to Australia, then America. He is now in England – Manchester. Immigration people say he has never travelled back to what was Malaya, now Malaysia. Do you want him picked up? If so, on what charge?"

The man in front of them seemed to relax.

"For the time being, do nothing. Over one hundred and eighty planes were shot down, or crashed, in Malaya during the defeat, the vast majority ours. We know the approximate location of this plane. Hughes' map gave you that, you say. We cannot simply blunder about, looking for it in somebody else's country. A press release will be put out in ten day's time – it will be kept quite low level – saying that a frigate of the Royal Navy, with undersea search capability, will be sent to Singapore. The news statement will indicate the mission as a search for a wartime merchant vessel, and it will hint at possible retrieval of undisclosed articles of considerable value. The real search, in the jungle, will be very methodical, starting at the map reference we have. The cover story for that will be a geological survey, to establish whether the area is suitable for a palm oil estate and, eventually, the clearance of primary and secondary jungle. If and when this plane is located, the second phase will take place. If bullion is to be extracted no more than six service personnel will be drafted in. They will be the mules. All six will be senior NCOs, bound, of course, by the Official Secrets Act. The bullion will be transported by locally hired private cars, and will be taken to the port of Malacca, where it will be held at a totally secure point until the frigate, its search apparently fruitless, calls at Malacca, to enable the crew to run ashore. The onboard Lynx helicopter will transport the gold onto the frigate."

The man paused. "If anything other than bullion is found, whatever it is, documents, artefacts etc., it will be destroyed utterly and completely. That is a task for your section."

The pen was pointed at Scott. "Who's your head of station in Singapore?" The pen had dipped, poised to write the name.

"Wilkins, but it won't be him."

"Why not?"

"He's in the UK, in hospital."

"What for?"

"Piles. Why he's here and not in one of several first-class hospitals in Singapore, I don't know!"

"In that case, we'll involve the Americans. I'll get clearance from above." His head jerked upwards, the movement a clear indication that the Prime Minister would be contacted. He continued to face both men. "Your comments?"

Neither man replied.

"Good, we meet a week today. It's a straight forward operation; nothing should go wrong; nothing will go wrong. By the way, what's the name of the CIA head of section?" His pen was poised again.

Scott did not need to consult his dossier.

"I don't know, that's down to the CIA."

The pen moved quickly. "Good. I see no problems. Thank you, gentlemen. That will be all."

"Do you fancy a drink?" Michael asked Scott, when they were back in the car.

Scott nodded. It was a private code they used. 'Need to talk, but not in the car'. Once back in London, both men made their way into a pub frequented by City people.

Ten

Soho, London, England

Later that same day

The old man pushed the intercom and said, "Come in, please." Immediately, a slightly built young man approached. There was a noticeable likeness between them.

"Yes, grandfather." He bowed his head respectfully.

The old man gestured at some bundles of currency on his desk. "Please put this into number three safe, and then I would like you to check out this man." He passed over Swee Poe's business card. "Find out who he really is – his real name – what passport he is using and when it was issued, but first, connect me to this number in Kuala Lumpur. I'll make the call in here. Thank you."

The young man took the scribbled telephone number and left. A minute later, the white telephone on the old man's desk rang. Although there was a seven-hour time difference between London and Kuala Lumpur – it was midnight there - the phone had been answered promptly. The conversation, brief and careful in its choice of words, lasted only two minutes.

The old man rose and walked into the adjoining bedroom. His chest felt tight and his back ached, but he walked upright, his head held high, a soldier's bearing. He slowly undressed and selected a grey, expensively tailored and immaculately pressed suit from his wardrobe. He put on a shirt and tie, the grey suit and a pair of black shoes. He solemnly studied his reflection in the long wall mirror. The function tonight was important, business would be discussed, decisions made, contacts would be cemented, money would find its way into his accounts. Yet the face of Elvis Lee, and their conversation, seemed to linger in his mind. He crossed the bedroom, the luxurious deep pile of the carpet deadening any sound, and opened another built-in wardrobe. He switched on the overhead light and opened a concealed door within.

The uniform was impeccably pressed, the jungle green jacket, the slacks with knife-edge creases, and his cap, olive green and with a bright red star centre front. The full dress-uniform of a Comrade Colonel of the Malayan All Races Liberation Army hung impressively before him. The old man raised his right hand in a regulation, British Army salute. Ironically, the British had taught him that, after the bitter and shameful defeats in Malaya and Singapore. The British had learnt quickly and well. They had schooled him in discipline, taught him how to place booby-traps, given him fighting skills, weapons training and perhaps, more importantly, taught him the art of jungle warfare. He and his comrades, everyone a card- carrying Communist Party Member, had harried and disrupted the Imperial Japanese Army, with hit and run – hit and run tactics. The Japanese generals had complained that, when they sent fifty of their soldiers into the jungle, they found nothing, no trace of their tormentors whatsoever, but when they sent five, no one returned. When the Japanese surrendered in August 1945, the old man had even taken part in the victory parade in Singapore, in the October, when sullen, demoralised Japanese soldiers, armed with nothing more than sweeping brushes, had been forced to watch the stirring march past of British, Indian and Ghurkha soldiers.

Three years later, as a battle-hardened fighter (and decorated with a British medal), he had led his unit as it erupted into the street of cities and towns of Malaya. The time of the Communist insurrection had come. At first, as the killings, atrocities and intimidation swept over the country, they were winning. Then the British employed new tactics: money was ladled out to informers, people defected, 'new' villages were built; the predominantly Chinese were re-housed and surrounded by barbed-wire fences. British and Ghurkha soldiers stood guard; food, and information began to dry up. British and Commonwealth forces sought them out in the jungle, the troops, nicknamed 'Running Dogs' because of their relentless hounding of the terrorists, had long noses and quick movements, for they were fighting a hard, skilful war. In 1960, after twelve blood-soaked years, as a fifty-year old, he slipped, with what was left of his command, over the Thailand border. One year later, he moved to London, with a new identity and a large sum of money, 'collected' during the previous years.

He closed the wardrobe door and flicked off the light. The information he had requested from his grandson would soon be in his possession, and all the jigsaw pieces of the man who called himself 'Elvis Lee' would slot into place. In the office down the hall, telephone calls were being exchanged. The myriad contacts available to the old man were being tapped. The grandson was completely confident that, in the next twenty-four hours, the identity of Elvis Lee would be laid bare, complete and accurate. He allowed himself a small smile. Some of the people whose stories he had unravelled were no longer of this world; for them, their real identity had been *deadly* accurate.

★ ★ ★

The pub was busy; young, early evening drinkers, with an air of 'another day another dollar', seemed to pervade every nook and cranny. Men were drinking bitter or lager, and gin seemed the most preferred spirit. Women, and there were many of them, were into wine. Many smoked. Scott and Michael took their pints of bitter to one of the few empty tables and carefully put their briefcases between their feet.

Michael sipped his bitter. "Well, what do you think of 'laughing boy'?"

Scott spoke quietly. "Not a man I'd like to share a meal with, but he has the ear of the Memsahib and he could, if he wished, cause you and me a lot of grief. So, we'll just have to live with it." Scott took an appreciative swallow and continued. "That plane has been in the jungle for forty years. There was, apparently, no fire on impact. If there were any documents, plans, or codes, they would have been encased in three layers of Bakelite."

Michael interrupted him. "What's Bakelite?"

"It was an early form of plastic-like material, named after Leo Baekeland. It was used, amongst other things, as a protective cover on orders to various overseas' commands. The Bakelite would also have been encased in asbestos sacks, to protect it from fire and heat. I think there would be a fair chance that, if there are documents in the plane, they would have survived the crash and the jungle."

"How fair a chance?" Michael asked.

"After forty years, about fifty: fifty.

Michael leant back against the upholstered bench seat, the chatter of the bar all around them, and he asked, "Why are you so anxious about this? Is there something you haven't told me?"

Scott took his time about answering. "When the surgeon's information came in, I looked into it myself, from a purely military point of view. It seemed to me to be just another hard luck story, albeit a very lucrative one – millions in gold bullion rediscovered, an American pilot dead. Then, when I started the pick and shovel work, the real digging, that is when things started to come to light. A copy of the pilot's flight plan showed that he was heading north, straight into the advancing Japanese, not south and safety; temporary safety, but safety, nevertheless. That struck me as odd. Then, there was a meeting of a British War Cabinet on the 15th of December, eight days after Pearl Harbour and five after the sinking of the *Prince of Wales* and the *Repulse*. There was a minute taken of that meeting, which is possibly now in the Public Record Office at Kew, or, more probably, where we've just come from – Chicksands. Actually, I happen to know that there *was* a *copy* of that minute, a totally unofficial one. All the people in that cabinet were in their early fifties and sixties. Winston was sixty-six, but they are all dead. There was one person present who was only in her twenties, a temporary secretary. She was there because both regular secretaries were absent. She only had the job, at very short notice, because her father was a retired Brigadier General, who served with some distinction in the First World War, but was sacked by General Haig after a failed attack. Whether that had any bearing on her future conduct is something about which I can only speculate."

Scott took another long swallow. "She was apprehended, purely by chance, when she met an official of the Electrical Trades Union who was a known Communist. He was suspected of attempting to obtain information regarding Britain's military capabilities. Special Branch men arrested him and his girlfriend in a saloon bar in Bethnal Green."

Michael nodded. "Another pint?"

Scott swung his right calf over Michael's briefcase while the drinks were fetched. Michael was a while at the crowded bar before he was served. He returned and eased Scott's glass towards him. "This secretary... do we know where she is now?"

Scott raised his glass, sipped and answered. "We do, and her Trade Union friend. They're in Stratford cemetery, killed in an air-raid on that same night."

Michael's voice was very quiet. "Convenient, very convenient."

"Wasn't it just!"

Michael leant forward, "What happened to the unofficial copy of the minute?"

"The Special Branch men handed it to a Detective Chief Superintendent. He read it, went white at the gills, apparently, drove to Downing Street, was admitted to No. 10 and there, somebody – I don't know who –burnt it."

Michael allowed himself a mild expletive. "Bloody Hell!"

Scott leant back. "That's what I know. What exactly is in the original minute is something about which I can only speculate."

Michael lifted his briefcase from the floor. "Are you going to tell me your own thoughts?" His voice had a hard edge.

"No, we'll play it as 'laughing boy' says. That way if, as our American cousins say, the crap hits the fan, we should be out of range."

Michael nodded, but it was a neutral nod. He started to speak his own thoughts. "He used the words *you* on two occasions, not *us*. Would you think that he has seen the minutes?"

Scott picked up his briefcase. "Whatever those minutes were, their existence caused a great deal of panic. Clement Attlee, the first peacetime Prime Minister, was so shaken, he wanted them destroyed, but our laws would not allow that. So, there they are, apparently locked up for the next sixty years, or is it something that will be discovered in the wreckage of a forty-year-old, crashed plane?"

Michael drank the last mouthfuls of his bitter. "You are worried?"

Scott nodded. "I shouldn't be, but I am. We need to find out what exactly is, or was, in that plane. We'll await our political master's call."

They returned their empty glasses to the bar and stepped out into the chilly night.

★ ★ ★

Swee Poe arrived back in Manchester, went to a public phone box and dialled 192, for directory enquiries. He asked for two telephone numbers and noted them in his diary. Tomorrow, he would phone. Tonight was a night for some celebration. He hailed a taxi that took him to a Chinese restaurant in the city centre, where he was welcomed as an honoured guest. He was served an authentic Cantonese meal, not the food offered to Westerners, and drank the finest whisky, followed by a long night of mah-jong. He lost quite heavily, but was still in a buoyant mood when he left in the early hours. He failed to notice the Chinese occupant of a Ford Fiesta that pulled away from the kerbside as his taxi set off to take him home.

Eleven

Aberystwyth, Wales

September 1982

Griffiths woke up and had no idea where he was. It wasn't his own bed and it certainly wasn't his own bedroom, but as he gradually became conscious, he was aware that there was somebody else lying beside him. He remained still, realising he was hung over. His head hurt! He tried breathing deeply, willing himself to surface out of a fog that gripped his mind. The room was dark, but not cold, with a glimmer of light to his right, which he thought might be daylight. There was a sound, a low murmur that came from his left. He reached out his hand, which came into contact with a body that was warm and soft.

"Morning." The voice came drowsily from beneath the eiderdown, and Griffiths, curious, surprised himself by replying, "Morning."

The darkness was melting, the bed was large, and there seemed to be a dressing-table on his left. Just then, a warm, soft arm emerged from the bedclothes and caressed his shoulder. He slid out of the bed and immediately realised that he was naked. A sliver of daylight touched his hand as he reached up to open the curtains. He pulled harder than he meant to and daylight hit his eyes. He took in the greyness of an Aberystwyth Sunday morning. Griffiths was embarrassed at his nakedness, when the eiderdown moved and someone struggled to sit upright. A female voice asked, "Who's a pretty boy, then?"

There were clothes strewn over the carpeted floor: trousers, shirt, tie, knickers, stockings, suspender belt, a lady's shoe, but his footwear was nowhere to be seen. He searched for his underpants, and a hand emerged from the bedclothes, holding them out to him.

"Yours, I presume?"

Griffiths all but snatched them from her, then, facing the bed, he hurriedly pulled them up, unwilling to turn his back and compound his embarrassment.

"Come back to bed."

He eased his body underneath the warm sheets. A face rose up to meet him. The kiss was long; their lips moving against each other, a full body moving close him. The voice was firm, the lips only inches from his face.

"That's what I call a wedding night."

Slowly, he began to recall where he was – the wedding, yesterday: suited men, shirts, ties, carnations, but, as always, it was really the women's day; silk dresses, designer hats, gloves, tiny handbags, high heels.

He still wasn't sure who he was in bed with.

"How do you feel?" he asked.

"Like the cat that's got the cream."

She was cradling her head against his shoulder, but Griffiths desperately wanted to see her face. As if in answer to his prayers, the woman lifted herself up. In a moment of wild madness, he was reminded of old war films, the scene where a U–Boat surfaces, white water thrashing around as the sleek hull breaks the surface. The whiteness of the crumpled sheets seemed to froth as the woman sat up. Griff took in the tousled hair, the face still bearing traces of make-up, and her huge breasts.

"Coffee or tea?" she asked.

"Coffee, please."

The woman swung out of the bed and walked naked to the door, where a black and orange dressing-gown hung on a hook. She slipped it on and tied the belt.

"Ready in five minutes," she said, and left the bedroom, and smiled wickedly. Griffiths was reminded of a tiger.

He struggled to dress. One of his shoes was missing, and so, muttering crossly, he went into the bathroom, splashed his face with cold water, combed his hair and limped downstairs, with only the one shoe on. He found the woman pouring coffee into two mugs.

"Sugar, Kev?"

The use of his name was a surprise and he avoided her eyes as he answered. Taking the mug, he sat at the pine table. It was with genuine surprise that he at last recognised her. She was a divorcée who worked in a solicitor's office. That she was a divorcée was a stroke of luck. At his age, Griffiths didn't relish being cited in divorce proceedings. He watched her and judged her to be four, perhaps five, years older than himself. That would make her fifty-one, fifty-two. Oh, God! Was she still of childbearing age? He panicked.

As if she had read his mind, she brushed her hand over his.

"I'm on the pill, so you needn't worry."

Despite himself, Griff smiled, for there had been no-one since Bethan. He accepted at that moment that this was inevitable, there were bound to be women in his life. She was looking directly at him; he was conscious of her femininity.

"I've had my eyes on you for months. You're quite a catch. There are women in Aberystwyth would give their right arm to be where I am now."

He merely nodded, embarrassed, and tried to change the subject.

114

"Wedding went well. That's the most I've had to drink for years."

He was beginning to recollect the highlights of the previous day: the reception, the evening disco, the dancing to Glen Miller's music, "String of Pearls", "Little Brown Jug", "Chattanooga Choo Choo", everything, from wild rock-'n'-roll to waltzes; holding women in his arms – 'proper dancing', as one woman had called it. Then, this one, he was desperate to remember her name, had danced close, her body warm beneath her dress, pressing into him. Hell! What was her name?

"Help yourself to more coffee. I'm going to the loo."

While she was gone, the domesticity of the scene filled his mind, the lovemaking of the previous night, the lust, the fierce exultancy of their coupling; it was all coming back to him. It was wrong, all wrong. It should have been with Bethan, not a woman he hardly knew. The phone rang, rudely interrupting his guilty thoughts.

"Answer it, Kev,"

He picked up the receiver.

"Is Judith there?"

"Judith is upstairs. I'll call her. Hold on a moment."

"Who is this?"

Without replying to the caller, he shouted, "Judith, it's for you."

She padded downstairs and picked up the receiver. He moved away but could hear one side of the conversation.

"Oh, it's you. Well now, that would be telling. Actually, it's Kevin – yes, Kevin Griffiths. You know, the one you daydream about, the one you say looks like a film star. No, not Donald Duck, more Robert Redford. Well, he didn't deliver the milk. Of course he spent the night! Ten out of ten!"

There was a prolonged giggle at the other end.

"See you tomorrow. No, not this evening; we're going for a rematch." There was another fit of laughing. "'Bye, Steph. See you tomorrow."

Judith replaced the receiver and came up to snuggle against Griffiths.

"Come back to bed. I'll make breakfast later."

She smelt of perfume, the womanly smell of her body seemed to be smothering his senses and blunting his mind. He fended her off, his arms outstretched.

"I can't. It's wrong. Beth might be dead, but I still love her. Always will, I'm sorry. You are a very attractive woman, Judith, but I still can't. I must leave."

Judith's eyes seemed as round as saucers.

"After last night!" Her mouth tightened, the soft, smiling, seductive lines had gone. She stepped back. "All right, then, get out!"

Griffiths picked up his jacket from the arm of a chair and limped to the door, the missing shoe all too evident. He stepped onto the threshold, turned, as if to offer a further explanation, but with the door still partly open, he checked himself, and then shut it, the click of the lock sounding like the finality of the condemned cell door closing on a prisoner. He was on the pavement, when there was a loud noise as a first-floor window was flung open; the head and top half of Judith and her stupendous cleavage were all too evident. "Go, and take your bloody shoe with you!"

The leather missile bounced off Griffiths' shoulder. She leant further out of the window, the rage clear on her face and in her voice. "Fuck off!"

Gwilym Daniels and his wife were on their way to chapel.

She gasped in surprise.

"What was that?"

Gwilym, who had been a qualified surveyor for over thirty years and had an eye for quantity, took his pipe out of his mouth. "About a 42D cup, I think," he remarked.

Griffiths hopped awkwardly, stumbling as he put on the shoe, and made straight for home. He let himself in, spurned the gin in the fridge, and opted for a cup of coffee instead. The phone rang and, dreading the anticipated tirade, he lifted the receiver. However, it was not Judith, but Gethin Hughes.

"I'll be with you in five minutes," he said.

"You in a jet?"

"No, I'm in a public phone box in Bow Street. See you."

Griffiths replaced the receiver, but, reflecting on Judith's venom, which still smothered him, he took the phone off the hook. If she did call, his line would be permanently engaged, but he felt a coward, nevertheless.

Gethin had on his cross-examination face. "You look rough."

"I feel rough."

"What's the matter?"

"Woman trouble, and I had too much to drink last night – far too much, hence the woman trouble."

"You surprise me," said Gethin, and sat down. "In that case, Griff, brace yourself. We go."

Kevin felt a surge of emotion, part fear, and part exhilaration. "When?"

"Tuesday. We meet at Euston Station, at three o'clock, by platform No. 11. Ring Tuck, and use the phone box by the pier. This is your Malayan currency, and this is your Dutch money. One day in Amsterdam, twelve in Kuala Lumpur, including flights. Euston to Heathrow, Heathrow to Schipol, Schipol to KL. Ten nights at the four-star Pan Asia hotel. We are, incidentally, the advance party for a reunion of veterans, scheduled for next year. We'll hire a car in KL. Clear?"

Griffiths nodded, his hangover receding somewhat. "How will Tucker get to London?"

"You must drive to south Wales, pick him up and catch a train to Paddington. There's one that leaves Bridgend at 8.55am; that'll leave you plenty of time to meet me at Euston. Got it? Okay." He pushed a further two bundles of notes over. "This is for Tucker. If he demurs, tell him, 'The Lord will provide'. Now, what about a cup of tea?"

★ ★ ★

Swee Poe had made his two phone calls on the day after he arrived back in Manchester. The first was to Gethin Hughes' office in Welshpool. It was, as he had expected, answered by a female secretary. Over many years, Swee Poe had worked with, and lived amongst, people of many nationalities. His mimicked accents were uncommonly accurate. The one he used now was a slow Canadian drawl.

"Hi, honey, I'm looking for an attorney, I mean a solicitor. Your man, Mr Gethin Hughes comes highly recommended, and I could do with his advice concerning some business interests in your lovely country. When will Mr Hughes be available for a meet?"

The secretary, more used to terse enquiries and, sometimes, temper-laden invective, was charmed by Poe's approach.

"Mr Hughes will be away for fourteen days from next Tuesday. Any date you wish to choose after that, please let me know."

"Fourteen days? Sounds to me like a vacation. Am I right? Somewhere exotic?"

The secretary was forthcoming. "Amsterdam – Holland."

"Fourteen days in Amsterdam; sounds like fun. Is there an airport near you? Will he fly from there?"

She gave a dismissive snort. "No! He'll catch the 11.05 from Welshpool and take the train down to Euston, London, and then go onto Heathrow. He'll meet his friends there."

"Well honey, I'll be in touch after your boss returns. Thanks a million." He had omitted to tell the girl his name and she had not asked.

Swee Poe next called a travel agency and made an appointment to see the manager. He was immediately slotted in for twelve noon that day but this time, he adopted a basic Manchester accent, slightly loud, with the habit of repeating certain sentences.

"What I need is a ticket to Amsterdam, to Amsterdam I say, a return ticket for Tuesday, leaving Heathrow at either seven o'clock or the next flight. How much?"

They agreed on a price and Swee Poe paid in cash.

"Never trusted banks or bank cards. License to print money. They print it and I have to pay for it!" Swee Poe said, pocketing the tickets.

He called Malaysian Air Lines office at Schipol Airport next, again stating he wished to fly but was uncertain when exactly. "Is it possible," he asked, "to book at very short notice a return flight from Amsterdam to Kuala Lumpur?"

"Midweek, sir, there are usually plenty of spare seats. Would you be so kind as to let us know details of your desired departure time, as soon as you can? You may pay now, if that is convenient. "

"Yes, of course."

He gave his name and the number of his widely accepted American credit card. The detail done, he drove back to his house and parked the car in the shared garage. He collected a small, plastic suitcase, and took a taxi to Manchester Piccadilly Station, where he bought a single ticket to Shrewsbury.

The train was reasonably clean and had a buffet trolley. As he sank into his seat, he expelled a long, slow breath. Things were developing nicely.

* * *

"I have the information you require, grandfather," said the young man, and placed two sheets of buff coloured of paper on the desk. It was a code used between them. White sheets of typed paper were used when the information on the person, persons or business mentioned thereon were considered 'clean', i.e. there was no known criminal activity, no false names, addresses used, no financial irregularities. The use of buff paper signified that extreme caution was the byword.

Elvis Lee, aka Raymond Elvis Lee – real name Swee Poe, was born in Ipo in 1935. Background: worked as a newspaper and printing operative; petty thief; two convictions for stealing; obtained a British passport, number 23166897, in May 1957, first stamped in Sydney, Australia; next, in Seattle, America, in June 1962. Two days later, he entered Canada at Vancouver. Six years later, he was back in America. He worked as a labourer on a hydro–electric scheme in Australia, then, he worked on the Distant Early Warning Line in Alaska. As a reasonably wealthy man, he returned to the US, and spent time in New York, New Jersey, New Orleans and, lastly, San Diego. Businesses owned by him now include restaurants, property development and management. He is estimated to be worth over four million US dollars. In sterling, that is over two million pounds. We have a photograph taken circa 1957."

The old man peered intently at the yellowing black and white photograph.

"You are certain, grandson, that this information is accurate?"

"We, you, Grandfather, run a well-oiled machine. Oil ensures that parts move smoothly and in perfect sequence. Oil is very important."

His slim fingers made a deft movement of counting money.

The old man's face was still impassive. He pointed at the photograph.

"He is wearing a uniform, grandson; do you know what it is?"

The young man returned his grandfather's gaze.

"It is the uniform of a volunteer in the Malayan All Races Liberation Army." His voice had a slight tremor, when he asked, "Grandfather, will you tell me when my father was killed?"

The old man rose and put both arms on his grandson's shoulders.

"Your father was leading a courier unit in Negri Sembilan, when they bumped into a patrol of British Running Dogs. Your father and two comrades were killed. One volunteer apparently escaped; two days later, a volunteer walked into a British Army camp and surrendered."

He took his left hand from his grandson's shoulder and tapped the photograph. "That is the volunteer. He subsequently betrayed our army, took what the Christians call Judas money, and left for a new life. And now," his voice became stronger, "he has to repay."

The grandson was very quiet, emotions and thoughts in a stampede through his mind. "What will you do, grandfather?"

The man dropped his other arm from the young man's shoulder. "Honour must be recognised and praised. Dishonour has one outcome: death. Phone this number; it is in San Diego. Tell the man who answers your call to fly to Kuala Lumpur, where he will be contacted. Do it now. After that, phone this number in Kuala Lumpur. We must be patient and very certain and precise if we are to be completely successful. Then, what can go wrong?"

He pushed the photograph of Swee Poe back across the desk. "He will die. I promise it, for you father's sake, for our army's sake. He will die in the time-honoured way. Phone those numbers now, grandson."

The old man sat back into his chair. For the first and only time in his life he wished on his ancestors' lives that he were thirty years younger.

The calls were made; San Diego came through with a clarity that made conversation easy. The young man was explicit and brief. After he had finished the second call, his grandfather took the receiver from his hand and replaced it. He felt suddenly tired, drained.

"Grandson, I would like some tea, if you please."

Twelve

En Route to Kuala Lumpur

September 1982

None of them had flown in a Jumbo jet before. The Boeing 747 of Malaysian Airlines hurtled down the runway and swept into the sky. Gethin Hughes, who had a window seat, pointed down at the night-time lights of Amsterdam, which spread like a carpet of winking dots beneath them.

They had met at the gate of Platform 11 at Euston Station, and immediately taken a taxi to Heathrow. In the mid-afternoon traffic, it had taken them an hour and ten minutes to reach the airport. In a bar, they had whiled away the time until take-off, and boarded the Jumbo at 6.30pm for the hour-long flight to Schipol . A taxi took them to central Amsterdam, where they booked in to their hotel, freshened up and then went out, to take in the sights, which had to include the Red Light district.

Tucker was matter of fact. "I shouldn't really be seeing this." His eyes took in the purple neon around large windows, where women and girls, in various states of undress, were seated on comfortable-looking sofas, legs swinging seductively over the arms. Griffiths, with Judith's temper outburst still fresh in his thoughts, tried to think about the rugby season; not altogether successfully, for some of the women were startlingly attractive.

Gethin Hughes was jovial. "Take a good look. You're not going to see anything like that in the jungle."

The friends ambled around, found a bar and went in.

The barman was apologetic but firm. "No bitter, only lager and spirits." Reluctantly, they settled for lager.

"Gnat's pee!" Griffiths' face showed his disgust. He held up three fingers to the barman, "Three gins, please."

The gin was drunk neat. "That's better," Griffiths remarked. Turning to Tucker, who was not drinking much, he asked, "How are things in Holy Orders, Tuck?"

Tucker was not be taunted, and his reply was totally sincere. "I can try to change some things for the better, and there are some things that are doomed to failure. I just have to trust the Lord." He sipped his gin, adding, "You're right, it is better than the gnat's piss."

Hughes looked on with affection. They were, in their own ways, the best and most honest, loyal men he had ever met.

"What causes you the most trouble with your new life, Tuck?"

Tucker swivelled on his stool to face him. "Families that have splintered – divorce – separation – drunkenness – squabbling – children at a loss to know where their father and mother have gone. We have one family, the Hopkins. The father was killed. He had a very good job with the Coal Board. He was killed underground. Safety procedures had not been implemented. His widow sued and was awarded a very large compensation package. She had never handled large sums before, and so she immediately bought a Mercedes Benz. She had three crashes in as many months, and finally wrote it off. Next, came an Audi, but the same again – four crashes, this time entailing a spell in casualty. Next was the Rover. She's still got that, but only because she's had two six-month driving bans for dangerous driving. Along comes a man from Carmarthen, a widower, with a son with eleven convictions for being drunk and disorderly, violent affray and a permanent hot-line to Alcoholics Anonymous. There's a sister, who turns up twice a year in a fur coat, covering a mini skirt that's the shortest thing I've ever seen, and sporting an ankle chain. They are known as 'The Lot Family', Lancelot. Crash a lot, Drink a lot and Shag a lot. I tell you, it's beyond a joke."

Hughes and Griffiths burst out laughing, each trying to visualise what 'The Lot' family actually looked like. Tucker fell silent, remembering the children of that inadequate family.

They talked and drank until well into the night. Amsterdam seemed very tolerant. Only two policemen passed their table, no screaming sirens, and no flashing lights. Hughes and Griffiths seemed impressed, but Tucker said simply, "Fools' Paradise. It'll catch up with them."

"What will, Tuck?"

"Drugs, probably. We've already got a problem in the Valleys, and I think it will get worse, much worse. Come to think of it, the jungle is a lot cleaner and safer than some of our towns in Wales!"

Both men shrugged; in their hearts, they agreed with their friend. "One last drink, boys. Tomorrow, we fly to KL."

★ ★ ★

Eighty feet forward of the friends, Swee Poe was seated in considerable comfort. He had opted to travel Business Class. The accommodation was luxurious and practical as it meant he would disembark first. He could watch the trio exit the aircraft, and follow their taxi. He had done it in London and again in Amsterdam, always in the background. He changed clothes twice a day, donned dark glasses and a snap down Fedora hat in the morning: the image of an American. In the afternoon, a lightweight suit, and a camera with all the photographic accoutrements, and he could be taken for the ubiquitous Japanese tourist. When he'd left Manchester for Shrewsbury, he had phoned the old man in Soho and been given a telephone number in Kuala Lumpur.

"You will be met at Kuala Lumpur airport," the old man said.

"How will I recognise my friend?"

"Don't worry, he will identify himself. I wish you a safe journey and that, what you seek, you will find. I'm quite certain that you will receive what you deserve. Goodbye."

Swee Poe had boarded the Euston train at Shrewsbury. He had walked the two carriages, apparently looking at seat numbers. Gethin Hughes was at a table seat, the *Daily Telegraph* and an empty teacup in front of him. Swee Poe had settled into a seat four rows behind. Passengers had had to change at Wolverhampton to board the Euston-bound train. He found it ridiculously easy, yet exciting. He did the same in Amsterdam, keeping never more than 50-60 yards away from them. The direct flight from Schipol to Kuala Lumpur was exactly twelve hours and fifteen minutes in duration. Swee Poe indicated to one of the cabin crew that he would like a Chivas Regal. The liqueur, so carefully blended in Scotland, was immediately forthcoming and very much to his taste. The service really was first-class and he revelled in it. As the 747 winged its way over the roof of the world, Swee Poe snuggled further into the luxury of his seat. Life was good.

★ ★ ★

The call was unexpected. "Michael, Scott here. I've just received a request from our friend, 'laughing boy'. He's called a meet at Chicksands for three this afternoon. Be at the chauffeur station, one o'clock. I've no idea what he wants. Bring the same folder that you took last time. I'll bring mine. There have been no additions to it since we were there last. Okay?"

The same man as before met them with the same greeting and asked them to follow him. The hall smelt of wood polish and air freshener. They were shown into the same room as on their previous visit.

"There has been a development."

Both men sat down and waited to be told more.

"The Royal Navy is unable to send either frigate or destroyer to Singapore for at least twenty-one days. Apparently, battle damage in the Falklands was greater than generally realised. Our masters want this sorted out, nevertheless. If bullion is found, a Hercules will be despatched to KL, and sufficient personnel will be made available to deal with it. If anything else is found, documents, etc., any written orders, they must be destroyed completely." Michael was writing on his notepad. He was chancing his luck and knew it, but he said it anyway.

"These documents, papers, orders, drafts, or whatever, I want to be quite clear about this – they are to be destroyed, you say. Why? There are quite clear guidelines on sensitive documents, and under no circumstances are such documents to be destroyed."

"You are a paid official of H M Government. I am an elected Member of the British Parliament. I have received specific orders, that any documents found in that crashed aircraft will be *destroyed*. Do you have a problem with that? If you do, put your resignation on the desk of the Permanent Secretary to the Cabinet by 10.15 tomorrow morning." His pen was now pointing at Scott. "Your head of station, Wilkins, is he still hospitalised?"

Scott was still mentally catching his breath at the brutal treatment handed out to Michael, however, his voice was composed, when he replied, "He is, with piles."

The man's hand was now rubbing furiously over his lower face. "The Americans, the CIA, they have been asked to provide an agent, a senior agent?"

"They have. Langley were informed after our last meeting, when *you* told us to bide our time, to allow for the cover story of the frigate and an underwater search."

"Well, all that's changed. Between you, organise a Hercules flight to KL. I want it there by Sunday. *Tell* Langley, I *want...*" he corrected himself. "Tell Langley, we would like the agent there as soon as possible. Scott, you are to delegate all your immediate responsibility to your deputy. You are also to be in KL by Sunday. We'll meet again this Friday, same time. Any questions? No?" He stood up, the interview concluded, all in a scant four minutes. Both men picked up their attaché cases and left.

In the car, Scott read his folder. Looking out of the window, Michael was the first to speak.

"That's the 47th lorry carrying coal that we've seen. Something in the wind? Stockpiling coal? Miners getting strike-happy, possibly?"

Scott was thoughtful. "I do believe you're right."

The car dropped them at Vauxhall, and they entered Scott's office, where they sat down to discuss the events.

"Well, Michael, what would you say has rattled 'laughing boy's' cage?"

"He's seen the minutes, I'm sure of it."

"Whatever he's seen, it's made him pull his finger out, and pretty bloody quickly. What are you going to do regarding his ultimatum? Not resign, surely!"

Michael shook his head. "I've been doing this job a long, long time. I've got friends in high places, so high I get dizzy thinking about them. If 'laughing boy' thinks he can bully or intimidate me, I must persuade him otherwise. I played rugby against Wales three times, and those boys were the same. Huge, fisticuffs up front, stamping, a lot of verbal intimidation, but I came through it. I'll just have to give as good as I get, possibly with a little help from my friends."

"You played three times against Wales? Did you win any of the matches?"

Michael swung an affectionate clip at the smiling face. "No, I didn't, but I'm due a change of luck. Come on. Let's have a pint of very best bitter, to wash away all the nastiness."

★ ★ ★

The Malaysian Jumbo jet made a precise, almost delicate landing; there was no jolt, just an ear-jarring noise as the engines went into reverse thrust. Swee Poe followed the first-class passengers out. The warmth of the night air, after the chilly dampness of Manchester, felt like champagne in his lungs, and he allowed himself to dawdle as he waited for the economy class to disgorge. He kept a close eye on them, waited until they had walked past, and then followed. He had no further need for disguises; he was just another Chinese man in a land full of Chinese.

He followed the three men to the luggage carousel, which was already circulating. Suitcases, rucksacks and parcels were spewing out onto the conveyor belt, disappearing and then re-emerging. He picked up his own suitcase, and waited until the trio had retrieved their luggage and moved on. There was a clatter of wheels on the floor of the long corridor that led to the Arrivals hall. Swee Poe cast around for some sign of the person who was to meet him. He saw a large, hand-painted card that said simply, BLUE SUEDE SHOES. The man who held it aloft was Chinese, stocky and with a pock-marked face.

"Hi! I'm Sammy. Good to see you." They shook hands. "I've got a car. What do you want to do?" He had a slight American accent.

Swee Poe wiped the sweat away from his eyes. "Follow those three men, wherever they go, whatever their hotel. Then, I think I need an ice-cold drink. I'll explain everything to you when I get a chance."

Sammy's car was almost new and spotlessly clean.

"You want something taken from those men?"

Swee Poe nodded. "I do. I rely on you for that. You've received a briefing from London?"

"Sure have. We'll see what hotel they're stopping at. After that, leave it to me. I know what I have to steal."

"When will they leave on their little journey, Sammy? Did you find that out?"

"It won't be tomorrow; they'll be jet-lagged and so will you. I'll get the item and then we can start our own journey right away. They can follow, as I am told they will."

Swee Poe and Sammy pulled in behind the taxi used by the three friends, and tailed it until it stopped outside the Pan Asia Hotel. Uniformed porters loaded their cases onto a trolley and they followed it up the ramp and into the gleaming, air-conditioned foyer.

Sammy parked his car outside a modern block of flats, each with its own veranda. He killed the engine and went round to lift Swee Poe's case from the boot.

"You're travelling light?"

"There's a change of clothing. If I need anything else, I'll buy it here."

Sammy opened the door to one of the flats.

"This is number three, Noordin Street. It's rented for two weeks. It is yours." He opened a drawer, revealing a gun. "This takes twelve rounds, .275, effective at twenty-five yards, fatal at five." He held out the gun and Swee Poe took it from him. It felt heavy. Swee Poe felt powerful, exhilarated, like the first time he had sex.

"This is the safety catch," informed Sammy; his thick fingers pushed the little lever. "Always keep it on. To fire, swing it to the left and then squeeze the trigger. Squeeze, don't jerk it, and *never* point the weapon at anybody." Sammy's voice sounded like a schoolteacher. "Okay? Look after it, and respect it, okay? I'll leave you. You get your head down. The fridge is full of food and liquor."

Swee Poe had noticed the Americanism of Sammy's speech.

"How long were you in the States?"

Sammy grunted, his head moving in a dismissive gesture. "Several years."

"Where?" Swee Poe was mildly interested.

"Newark, Atlantic City, Philadelphia; east-coast mainly. Went to Las Vegas once, lost every cent I had." He shrugged as if the thought of it was painful. "You?"

Swee Poe trotted out his bogus CV. He went to the fridge and took out two cans of Tiger beer. Sammy shook his head, "Not for me."

"Do you think you can get the item?"

Sammy seemed to have an aversion to smiling. "It won't be me, but the man who will take it is very professional. He has, to my knowledge, never failed. I believe it is a map. Don't worry; he'll get it – he'll even take the watches off their wrists if you say so. Enjoy your beer. I'll see you tomorrow, sometime about 7-7.30."

Sammy turned and was gone.

Swee Poe went to his suitcase, snapped the catches, and took out a pack of playing cards. Pulling the ring on the Tiger can, he took a long swallow. He felt slightly uneasy about Sammy. It had to be sorted.

He sat at the cane table, took the first card and laid it face upwards. Three of hearts – Newark. Jack of Clubs – Atlantic City. Nine of diamonds – Philadelphia. Queen of Spades – Las Vegas. Swee Poe had played this game before. He had used it to make financial decisions. He placed a card on the left-hand side, representing the cities he had lived in when he was in America, large cities, but he'd been careful to avoid any China Town areas. He found that being Chinese, in Canada or the States, proved no big deal. Once, in a bank in Cleveland, he had accidentally overheard himself being described as: 'A banana, yellow on the outside, white on the inside'. He'd felt vaguely flattered. The card was a seven of diamonds – Cleveland. Next, ten of clubs – New Jersey, then, two of hearts – New Orleans. The Ace of Spades - San Diego.

Swee Poe allowed himself a long, heavy sigh. "San Diego," he said aloud. "Now I have it: the Chinaman who was pretending to read a newspaper outside the Vietnamese restaurant was stocky and had heavily pock-marked face. What is this about, and how can I be sure of him?"

Swee Poe sat for a long time, the opened can of beer quietly losing its coldness. Why – how – would a Chinese man in San Diego now appear in Kuala Lumpur? Who knew Swee Poe was in Kuala Lumpur? Only the old man. The questions raced around his mind, but no answers were forthcoming. He scooped up the cards, went to the drawer and took out the automatic. In the tiny kitchen, he found a tea-cloth and carefully wrapped it around the gun. He took a small holdall from his case, removed his toilet things and put them in the bathroom, replacing them with the gun. He switched off all the lights and lay down on the double bed. He waited for nearly two hours, and then, in darkness, carrying the small bag, he slipped out into the hot, humid night.

The three friends had a family room, furnished with four single beds, a large television set, a mini-bar, writing desk, two wardrobes and two easy-chairs, and there was a massive bathroom with shower, toilet, bath, wash-hand basin and a shelf full of complimentary toiletries. They would not go unwashed. They were all in high spirits. The lights, the sheer volume of noise, and the surge of people in Kuala Lumpur were intoxicating.

Gethin Hughes was a platoon leader again. "Wash and brush-up, a fresh set of clothes, a drink in the bar, and then out to explore KL's finest!" he suggested. Griffiths and Tucker agreed.

The bar was lush, the armchairs deep. An Indian lady was playing popular classical music on a gleaming grand piano. They ordered three Tiger beers, touched glasses, murmured their old toast: 'Once a Fusilier, always a Fusilier', and settled down to enjoy themselves. They returned to their room a little after midnight, all suddenly and embarrassingly tired. They had planned to stay out on the town, but jet-lag had caught up with them.

Gethin Hughes' voice was matter of fact. "We've had a visitor."

Griffiths and Tucker, in the middle of undressing, paused.

"The map's gone. The map case is still there." Griffiths' pointed to the faded leather case.

Gethin Hughes lifted up the case, turned it upside down and shook it. "No map."

"Did we drop it on the way up in the lift?" Tucker was trying to inject some hope, some reason for the empty case. "It doesn't matter; it's got the wrong location marked, anyway."

Grifffiths was looking at Gethin as he spoke. "Right."

For what seemed a long time, Hughes returned the gaze, then quickly, urgently brought out his wallet. The map was protected inside a clear polythene wallet.

"This is the *real* one. I keep it on me at all times. Now then, a map goes missing, the same map that was searched for in my house and then copied. Anybody got any ideas what's going on here?"

Tucker and Griffiths, although half undressed, were fully awake.

"Is it our Chinese man, the man who called at your house, Geth? If it is, how did he know we were here; or is it just some local opportunist thief? Tuck, check the safe!"

Tucker played with the combination. "Passports - okay, money – okay, plane tickets – okay. Nothing's missing."

Gethin Hughes shook his head. "Lock the door, Tuck. We'll try and make sense of this in the morning."

In a subdued mood, and muttering a brief good night to each other, the three settled into their beds, but, despite jet lag and exhaustion, none had a good night's sleep.

Thirteen

London – Kuala Lupur

Thursday 30 September 1982

Vauxhall, the old and now obsolete, tube station, was in very close proximity to the buildings that housed several departments of Government Security Agencies. Unlike its American counterpart at Langley, Virginia, which had public phone line access to the Central Intelligence Agency, Vauxhall was still shrouded in anonymity. There were no brass name-plates or department signs to be seen, and several intimidating young men would often be seen in doorways, or entering and leaving the buildings. It was rumoured that they were Royal Marines or Parachute Regiment personnel.

Scott entered the building, showing his security pass at both check-points. It was common knowledge that several people had been refused admission and escorted firmly off the premises; those who had forgotten or mislaid their passes. In the case of those who had forgotten their passes, they would return home, retrieve them and would then be admitted, but in the case of mislaid, they were immediately suspended and barred from entry and telephone access, until the elusive pass had been found and a thorough security sweep had been undertaken. One unfortunate member of MI5 had his pass returned from a brothel in Hackney. The resultant investigations led to several highly-embarrassing disclosures. The operative was subsequently given '*gardening leave*' and sent home to an extremely sceptical wife. The joke lasted for several years, and said that 'gardening leave' was granted so that the condemned man had time to plant ten thousand trees in the Sahara. The man in question subsequently asked for, and was granted, early retirement, with a very much-reduced pension.

"Morning," Scott greeted his secretary and slipped behind his desk.

Mrs Mann nodded and placed some letters, in order of priority, on his desk.

"This has just arrived," she said, and handed him a faxed sheet. Mrs Mann, five feet ten inches tall and weighing in excess of fifteen stones, still had the figure and posture of a woman several years younger than her fifty years. Scott knew that they called her 'He Man', in the department, but he had never had a more conscientious or astute secretary. Her private life, had it been generally known, might have caused a raised eyebrow, but she was the epitome of discretion.

"Important?"

He smoothed the fax sheet. "I think so. It could be very important." The message was dated, signed by the MP, and simply stated:

Imperative I speak with you and Michael today. Your office, ten o'clock. Please arrange.

"I wonder what 'laughing boy' wants."

Mrs Mann said, "I've faxed Michael's office, told him the time of the meeting and asked him to phone you, to confirm. Would you care for tea?"

Scott nodded.

Michael arrived at a quarter to ten. They prepared their strategy for the meeting.

"We'll give this bastard a run for his money; we're playing at home now, at Twickenham. You game, Scott?"

"You lead, I'll follow." Scott nodded and smiled despite himself.

"Something's spooked him; either the memsahib has given him a kick up the jacksie, or something else has gone wrong; either way, we'll very shortly find out. I must say, to have a couple of weeks in Kuala Lumpur is a bonus. I've been there once before. Lovely country, very good people. We'll see what happens, if anything. If it's wrapped up quickly, I'll get Linda to join me. The girls can go to her mother's for a week." He was cut short when there was a discreet knock, and Mrs Mann's face appeared round the door.

"Your visitor is here, sir."

It was an old tradition, that visitors were never named when visiting Her Majesty's Secret Intelligence Service. Both men nodded to the visitor, but did not get up. Scott indicated a once expensive, but now somewhat weary armchair. "The floor's yours, sir."

The MP, as was his habit, went straight to the point.

"Your – our – agent from the CIA is in place?"

"From twelve o'clock, our time, tonight; seven o'clock Malaysian local time."

The MP said nothing, just gave a penetrating gaze at both men. Scott was reminded of a men's final at Wimbledon and, as the MP's eyes swivelled from him to Michael, he felt an insane urge to shout, 'Advantage the Spies,'

"Have you his folder?"

Both men opened orange cardboard folders.

"This came this morning," confirmed Scott. "I've had two copies made; one for you, one for Michael." He passed the folder across the desk. "Our man is a former United States Marine Corps Aviator, retired in..." he paused to ensure that he had the date right, "...1975. He joined the CIA, after screening and security checks, in July 1976. Retired with the rank of full Colonel, something of a 'good ole American boy'. Served in Vietnam, in what were the 'Wild Weasel' squadrons, in Thunderchiefs. Most of the pilots were American Air Force, but there were some Navy and Marine guys seconded to the 'Weasels'."

"What were 'Wild Weasel' squadrons?"

Michael asked, aware that he was out of his depth, a bit like fumbling a ball with the line at his mercy. Scott moved to support him.

"The Americans had to develop some sort of strategy to eliminate what the American military called 'Triple A', i.e. Anti-Aircraft Artillery in Vietnam. These were conventional anti-aircraft weapons, 85mm, 57mm, 37mm, and deadly surface-to- air missiles, SAMs, as they're known. The 'Weasel' pilots and their back-seat weapons and electronics officers were generally regarded as the finest of the fine. They were tasked with eliminating SAMs and conventional launch sites, to allow the American bombers to get through to their designated targets. The 'Weasels' flew what were sometimes literally suicide missions. They were all trained in jungle survival, at Nellis Airforce Base in Nevada, and at Clark Air Base in the Philippines. The attrition rate of 'Weasel' personnel was amongst the highest of all the American military. They were, as I say, particularly brave men."

The MP sighed and gently shook his head. "Anything more?"

Scott was ready. "Our man was almost inevitably shot down over a place called Dong Hoi. He spent almost four years in captivity in North Vietnam, in not very good conditions, and he was repatriated in 1972. After a lengthy 'restabilising and normalisation course', as our American friends call it, he returned to duty, first in the Philippines, and then he was posted back to San Diego as a flight co-ordinator and weapons' instructor. All in all, as I've said, he's a 'good ole American boy'- a first-class man."

Michael shook his head, the pen flying over his note-pad. "What's his name?"

"Spano, David Spano, USMC (Retired)."

The MP leant forward in the chair. Michael sensed that his and Scott's counter-attack was due to come under retaliatory fire. The MP's cold, expressionless eyes studied them.

"I took the trouble to check on the three former soldiers, Hughes, Griffiths and Tucker, as well as Raymond Elvis Lee." His voice had a steely edge. "Where are they now?"

Scott was aware of the sting of the man's words. Uneasily he replied, "They should be in Wales and Manchester, respectively. Why? Do you know something about them that we don't?"

"Apparently, I do, because none of them, I repeat *none* can be found. They have all disappeared. I wonder where?" the MP enquired sarcastically.

"When did you learn this?" Michael retaliated, feeling his anger kicking-in.

The MP gave a look that bordered on contempt. "I make it my *business* to find out; a course of action not, apparently, at a premium in this department!"

Mentally, Scott and Michael moved closer together.

"You knew this and you did not inform us? Did you inform anybody? Immigration – Special Branch – Interpol?" The vehemence of Michael's words made a tiny dent in the man's façade. Scott's intervention seemed dramatic in its abruptness. He pressed the intercom.

"Mrs Mann, come in, please. I want you to witness a

statement. Bring the tape recorder."

The MP made a move to stand up and leave, but Scott raised his hand.

"You will wait here, or I'll summon Security. Sit down!"

He had only once used that tone of voice, to a boyfriend of his daughter's, who had turned up hopelessly drunk, at the age of fifteen, to his daughter's birthday party.

"*You* told us to wait. *You* gave us to believe that any haste would be counter-productive, and now, for whatever reason, *you* are screaming blue murder that people who should have been brought in, have disappeared. What exactly is going on?"

The MP placed both hands on the table.

"*Your* operatives, may I remind you, stated that *these* men had no intention of going back to Malaya."

"We were apparently wrong, but it was *you* who told us to wait. Mrs Mann, switch on the recorder, please."

Michael spoke first, his voice impersonal: "This is the office of Scott xxxxx, in Vauxhall. It is ten past ten on the morning of 30th September 1982. A surveillance and covert operation has been ongoing for several weeks. I am now going to ask Mr xxxxx, MP, for his comment. It is my opinion and that of Scott xxxxx, that this operation has been compromised by Mr xxxxx, who insisted on delaying the action necessary for a satisfactory conclusion to the aforementioned operation. Mr xxxxx, would you care to comment?"

The eyes of the MP were hard, his face barely moved, the shake of the head almost imperceptible.

"For the benefit of the tape, Mr xxxxx has shaken his head, indicating a 'no'. Copies to…" Michael gave four names. The MP's eyes registered surprise, then, as the last name was declared, he gave an intake of breath that seemed to be painful.

"Do you still want me to go to Kuala Lumpur by Sunday?" Scott was looking directly at the MP. There was a long pause.

"No, leave it to the Americans."

Scott told Mrs Mann to switch off immediately and prepare copies of the transcription.

The MP rose out of his chair. If deflated, he was not prepared to show it. "You will regret this, and that is a promise."

Michael eased himself back into his armchair.

"There's an election soon. You might not be an MP for much longer. You might do well to consider that."

The MP turned and left.

Scott pushed the intercom. "Mrs Mann, call Immigration, Special Branch and Interpol. Immediate flash alert." He spelt out the full names of Hughes, Griffiths, Tucker and Swee Poe. "Check all flights, from Sunday, 26th September, out of Heathrow and Gatwick, and arrivals at Kuala Lumpur and Singapore. Get Regional Crime Squad – Inspector level – onto this. Get them to go to their home addresses and places of work and make enquiries of neighbours, and as soon as anything comes in, let me know. Thank you."

Michael clasped his hands behind his head. If the confrontation had shaken him, he did not show it.

"Why would he leave it to the Americans? It's our gold, or it was."

"He's afraid of political repercussions. It's an American plane. If there is anything else in there, presumably the same order is to destroy it. That leaves Her Majesty's Government in the clear – smelling of roses, actually – and possibly thirty million quid richer! Look at what we've got. Three geriatric ex-soldiers, a former Communist Terrorist, and now a clued-up American Central Intelligence Agent, all converging on a plane that crashed in 1941, that might or might not hold gold bullion and something else, that could cause merry hell, if it's still there."

"What are you going to do?" Michael asked.

"Wait. It's all we can do. If our three friends and the Chinaman are in Malaysia, then we round them up pretty damn quick, and let the Americans have a clear run at anything else that might still be there. We should have some information back quite soon."

"How soon?"

"Late afternoon is my guess. Want some tea?" asked Scott.

As an afterthought Michael asked, "What time is it in Malaysia now?"

"Seven hours in front of us – that's half five their time."

"What time does it go dark out there?"

"Seven-fifteen, seven-thirty. Why do you ask?"

"It is, in my humble opinion, a lot easier to find people in daylight than it is in the dark."

Scott nodded. "It can't be helped. We wait."

The tea and biscuits were laid on the desk.

"Cheers!" both men raised their cups, wishing that they contained something a lot stronger than tea.

★ ★ ★

They had slept late; the room was orderly enough. As ex-service men, they were of a tidy disposition. They rang room-service for coffee and toast and then conducted a thorough, painstaking and frustrating search for the map.

"It's gone," Gethin Hughes concluded. "We might as well accept it; we've been done over. Who by? Will we ever find out? I doubt it. It seems to have been a professional job, no sign of entry, nothing else stolen."

"We going to report it?" asked Griffiths, sitting on his bed.

"No, it will simply draw attention to us. Let's get our shopping done and tomorrow we'll start on our search. First thing we have to do is hire a car. As for the rest of the stuff, I've started a list. Bottled water, food and Parangs - one each. Can you think of anything else? I also thought of sleeping bags, torches and mosquito cream; what do you think?"

Griffiths was still sitting on his bed. "Try for a Bren gun."

Tucker laughed, "You'd have forgotten how to use it, Griff."

"No! Cock gun – mag on – battle sight up – switch to repetition – first pressure on the trigger, then - fire!"

"You're a bloodthirsty bastard," said Hughes, smiling.

In a solemn voice, Griffiths admitted, "I enjoyed shooting people; it was better than soccer." He'd once said the same thing to a woman he'd worked for, a lady employed as a senior social worker. She had several qualifications but not a sense of humour, so, by mutual consent, he never worked for her again.

"Come on then, let's go and get our act together!" They placed the crockery neatly on the breakfast trolley and left for the morning's shopping. They locked the door carefully.

★ ★ ★

David Spano received the call in Austin, Texas. It was short but explicit.

"Fly to Atlanta; you'll be met at the airport terminal; board a United Airliner; there is a refuelling stop at Dubai, then fly onto Kuala Lumpur; report straight to the American Embassy; the First Secretary will brief you."

First Secretary? Huh! It must be important, regardless of the time. That clinched it, it must be very important.

He dressed quickly and forgot nothing: passport, CIA ID, shaving-kit, a streamlined Colt, and ten rounds, which he placed in his ankle holster. He was forty-three, pushing forty-four, but he still had his own teeth and hair and was, for a middle-aged man, in very good shape. He was careful about his diet, and he jogged and exercised, which kept his stomach flat. Women found him outwardly attractive but inwardly cold. He was conscientious, but would get furious with himself if he made a mistake. As a marine pilot, he'd learnt to kill with clinical precision. The bombs, napalm, and heavy-duty cannon shells he had discharged had killed many people. He did not deceive himself that the dead were all Vietnamese Regulars, or Vietcong and Vietminh. There must have been women and children as well, but they were the enemy, and he felt no animosity towards them and, on the other side of the coin, no remorse for his actions.

As a field agent, it was different. There had been the sleeping sentry in a Russian Tank Brigade Headquarters in Afghanistan, an armed Iranian security guard, who had disturbed him carrying out a burglary at a Chinese diplomat's flat in Tehran, and a member of the Egyptian Security Service, who had shadowed and spied on his movements for a week and two days, whilst he had used his cover as a journalist to photograph likely crossing points of the Suez Canal for a possible invasion of Israel. The man had gurgled when the eight-inch blade whipped into his heart. Spano had rolled the body down a steep bank into the Nile. The spot was a well-known location for crocodiles to sun themselves, and he doubted if the body would be seen again, let alone any of it recovered.

He was met in Atlanta; a special kerbside check-in had been arranged for him. He boarded the United Airways flight ten minutes before take-off. He had been provided with a complete itinerary for this mission, and best-guess prediction of possible action. He was to work alone but, surprisingly, the bullion, if there was any, was to be the second objective. The first, it was stressed, would be the recovery of any documents or papers. They were to be read for time and date and then they were to be totally destroyed. No traces of documents and/or their casings were to be left. Spano's written instructions indicated that a phosphorous grenade should be used for the purpose. The exact location and grid reference of the site of the downed aircraft were shown on the map that came with his orders. Privately, he pondered on the contents of the supposed papers. He had trained exhaustively in jungle survival, and trained in the Philippines, prior to Vietnam, a conflict that had been the defining and changing moment in his life. The Philippine jungle was not as thick or hostile as the Malayan, but he was absolutely certain he could find spot marked on the grid map reference.

The journey, with the refuelling stop, would be a long one. He took out his wallet, which held a photo, old and now rather faded, but well-protected and preserved by a stout polythene case in good condition. A young, handsome face stared back at him. The man in the picture had dark hair and a dimpled chin. He took a long moment to look at it, kissed his right forefinger and pressed the tip to the face, whispering, "'Night, Dad, God Bless."

His mother had remarried in 1944. His stepfather was a fine man, the son of a Presbyterian minister, who had reluctantly and against his father's wishes, left the Protestant faith and become a Catholic, to marry David's mother. David grew up in a contented, middle-class home; his education was smooth: high school; university, and then a commission in the United States Marine Corps. His mother, always fearful but loyal, had told him that his father had always kissed a photograph of them both, before he flew. David faithfully did the same. His mother had died of cancer in 1965. It was just a few weeks between diagnosis and the end, and she was only forty-six. The loss affected David profoundly. He grieved privately, throwing himself into the flying that he did so well, and he rose steadily up the promotion ladder. By 1968, he was an Acting Major, jumping the ranks from Second Lieutenant to Major in just eight years. Then, he was shot down, and the three years and seven months he spent in captivity were not good. Twice he was taken from the camp at Son Tay and put in solitary confinement. He returned, wafer thin, dishevelled but not broken. The other POWs looked up to and respected him.

He tucked the precious wallet into his jacket and put out his cabin light. Tomorrow would be a fresh day, and he would do his duty.

Fourteen

Kuala Lumpur, Negri Sembilan

Friday 1 October 1982

Swee Poe was nothing if not fastidious. He breakfasted on eggs and noodles, washed up the pans and crockery, made his bed, and dressed with some care in the short-sleeved shirt, grey shorts, and the flip-flop sandals everybody, men, women and children, seemed to wear. In his holdall were a pair of trousers, socks, a long-sleeved shirt, first-aid kit, torch and the automatic pistol Sammy had given him. He drank from the refrigerated bottle, the taste of water bringing back memories. It was Malayan water, not like the tepid tap water in Britain. He refilled the large, plastic bottle and sat on his bed and waited. Sammy arrived at exactly seven.

"We go now. We'll miss the early morning traffic."

Clutching the holdall and water bottle, Swee Poe followed Sammy out into the humid air, the coolness of the night already giving way to the heat of the day.

"This what you want?" Sammy was holding out a map. Swee Poe gave it a cursory glance, folded it and tucked it into his shirt pocket.

As if reading Sammy's mind, Swee Poe said, "It's an approximate location. We might have to root around a bit." He couldn't help wondering if Sammy had copied or memorised the map, and whether he harboured any thoughts of double-crossing and disposing of him. Then, the plane might never be found.

"What are we looking for, Elvis? If it's paper money, it's no good. Malayan dollars were changed for Malaysian Ringgits, some time ago; the old dollars are valueless."

Swee Poe swung himself into the passenger seat of Sammy's car.

"It's not notes."

"What then?" Sammy's voice was demanding, truculence not far from the surface.

"You'll just have to wait, Sammy." He spat expertly through the open window. "It all comes to those who wait. It's a British saying."

Sammy turned the ignition key, the engine purred and they drove out of Noordin Street into a jumble of cyclists, scooters and a few cars. Driving south on the Seremban Road, Sammy continued through Petaling Jaya, Seremban, and continued on towards Kuala Pila Pass. Swee Poe had heard of Kuala Pila and the infamous pass. There had been dozens of ambushes along its narrow, menacing sides. The 'Running Dogs' had always been on high alert, moving along it with their little convoys of fully armoured 'coffins', carrying supplies, money and soldiers, preceded by 'Dingos' or 'Ferret' armoured cars, the drivers and crews sighing with relief once they were through the pass, followed by a dry throat at the prospect of the return journey.

The sun was high and it was now very warm, but Swee Poe felt coldness on his chest and head. He realised he was very frightened. They turned off the dusty road and drove along a bumpy track. The rubber trees looked as if they were no longer being worked, there was no sign of tappers, it was a still, quiet place, and the trees immobile, like gravestones in a vast cemetery.

Sammy's voice was jarring. "Elvis, this is as far as we go. The rest is on the hoof. Malayan saying, OK."

They got out of the car and changed into the spare clothes they had carried with them. Sammy reached back into the car to retrieve the parang, which was in a wooden sheath decorated with Chinese symbols. Pulling it free, he waved his right hand and the blade of the parang seemed to hiss through the air. He made cutting movements again, the steel gleaming through its oily film.

"Why do you call it a parang?" Swee Poe looked and sounded like a city man, who had been dropped unceremoniously into the fringes of a jungle setting. "I thought they were called machetes?"

"Oh, they are, in some parts of the world, but here they're called parangs – a Malayan word. I'll lead the way. What are you doing?" Sammy had come to an abrupt halt, when he saw Swee Poe carefully easing his automatic into the waistband of his trousers. "Have you got the safety catch on?"

Swee Poe gave a nod, "I have, Sammy."

"You'd better have. A jolt or a fall with it off, and you might shoot your bollocks off! How are you going to spend your fortune then?" Sammy commented with a smirk, and walked on through the deathly quiet of the rubber estate. In a moment, he vanished into the jungle. Swee Poe hesitated, then, feverishly gulping air into his parched throat, he followed.

* * *

Hughes, Tucker and Griffiths had done a day's hard shopping, ignoring the temptations of ice-cold Tiger beer until their list was complete, when they steered themselves towards a bar, drank sparingly, and then ate cheaply at one of the many hawkers' stalls. An early night meant they were awake early.

"Well, today's the day," Hughes said in a subdued mood. "Come on, let's get on with it."

They dressed in their jungle green jackets and slacks, all of twenty-five years old, which they'd brought back with them from Malaya. Griffiths had had the waistbands let out and the jackets were given extra chest width, with a V-gusset inserted at the back. The seamstress in Aberystwyth had been curious.

"Where are you going, then?"

"A reunion at Cardiff. Everyone comes dressed as they were twenty-five years ago."

The woman was unimpressed. "Bloody army, shooting all those poor Argentineans. All they wanted was their own country back. I've got a son; he's never going into the army, I'll see to that."

Griffiths put the five pound notes onto the counter. "They probably wouldn't take him, at least, not in our army. Tell him to try the Swiss Navy; they're desperate for men."

The woman laid the garments on the counter. "What, no tip?"

"Yes," Griffiths offered, as he swept up the clothes. "Keep your mouth shut! My nephew was killed in the Falklands!"

The woman was shocked, her face revealing her surprise. Griffiths briefly regretted his lie. He had no nephew, but the woman was symptomatic of what was wrong with the British people: no real knowledge of the world or world events; rubbish newspapers; rubbish women's magazines; everything slap-dash. The social workers and Britain's legal system ruled; political correctness and money ruled; common sense and decency were nowhere in contention. He'd taken, surprisingly for him, a perverse delight in snubbing the same woman, on another occasion, by not replying to a birthday party invitation, and, subsequently, he pretended not to see her when they met in the street.

The hire car was loaded. Hughes was in the driving seat, Tucker next to him in the front passenger seat, and Griffiths in the back.

"Know how to get there, Geth?"

Hughes nodded, started the car and then switched off the engine. "Before we go, how do you two feel? Any reservations?"

Tucker yawned, stretching his arms. "Bit late for that, Geth. Come on, let's get this gold. If we do find it, the nice British Government might give us a little reward. What do you say, Griff?"

Griffiths eased himself forward off the back seat; he was already sweating.

"To be honest, I don't really care."

The first couple of days back in Malaysia had been exhilarating and exciting; sights, sounds and smells that he'd thought he'd never experience again brought back memories, but last night was full of memories of Bethan. She should have been here with him. He realised that the man who had killed her and then lied with contemptuous arrogance, was more and more filling his mind. He had tried to fight against it but he knew that it would have to be resolved. He did not fear jail, or the shame of a court case, but he knew that he must confront the man, or men, who had caused him so much pain.

His friends sensed the change in Griffiths' mood. Tucker turned and reached back to touch his old comrade's shoulder.

"I know what you feel; I felt like it myself. Like a big, black cloud over everything, but," he removed his hand, "don't worry. The Lord will help you. It might sound foolish, but He did for me. I don't know how or what is in front of me, how my life will turn out or end, but in Him I trust. Come on, Griff, it'll be alright. If you can't yet trust the Lord, then trust me."

Griffiths looked at Tucker's face, knowing the concern was genuine. He slumped back. "You should have been a preacher, Tuck."

"If it was up to me," said Hughes dryly, "he'd be the Archbishop of Canterbury!"

Griffiths found himself answering, "Does he go looking for gold with two other nutcases?"

The sombre atmosphere was broken and Hughes turned the ignition key again. "Let's go." They moved off to join the madness of the rush-hour traffic, the overpowering petrol and diesel fumes mingling with the warmth of the sun on the city's streets.

* * *

The American Embassy was lit by just a few security lights. The gate was manned by two US Marine Corps personnel. David Spano knew that another two marines were patrolling the neat wall that enclosed the Embassy grounds, and yet another two men were inside the building. He produced his CIA ID.

"Wait here, sir," the accent was a southern drawl. The corporal deftly tapped in a set of numbers on a large keyboard and spelt out his surname. "Somebody's coming to meet you, sir." the guard said respectfully.

A man in civilian dress strode quickly towards Spano and clasped his hand.

"I'm Clancy. I'm not the Second Secretary; he's away on business but, like you, I'm in the firm."

Spano shook the outstretched hand. "I was briefed that the Second Secretary would meet me. How long have you been CIA?"

Clancy, large and overweight, smiled and replied, "Longer than you, sunshine. I'm the man with the hammer, in Malaysia anyway. I'm the Section Head. I've heard about you, though. You had a rough time in 'Nam?"

Spano shook his head; the humidity of the air, even at night, was wearying. "You could say so."

"This way. I'll tell you everything you need to know and probably more. The Brits are going ballistic and I mean ba-llistic. Some wartime crash might, and I mean *might*, have some pretty sensitive documents stashed on board. Your job is to find the plane and destroy any papers, letters, confidential pouches, that you find. You don't read 'em, just give them the hereafter touch. Those are my orders." He pulled a cigarette from a soft paper packet and flicked a zippo lighter. "Those are yours." The smoke from the cigarette merged with the light from the guardroom.

"Why are the Limeys so wound up? What's in these documents?"

"Search me. All I know is that the plane, discovered apparently twenty-five years ago, has something on board, apart, possibly, from some gold, something the Brits – not Limeys – want blown out of orbit." Clancy noted Spano's raised eyebrows. "All you have to do is find the plane, search it, and dispose of any documents. If there is any bullion, we tell the Brits, they tell the Malaysians, and we keep out of it. Easy peasy."

Clancy was dragging furiously on the cigarette, the tip glowing bright orange in the darkness. "You might have company, though. There's a trio of British vets out here, and possibly a certain slippery Chinaman. The Brits have the idea of 'liberating' anything they find. You treat them as hostile and use extreme force if you deem it necessary."

The cigarette, its short life spent, was ground into the floor.

"You're on your own, Spano. No communication with the Embassy; none with us. Find this goddamned plane, if it's there, search it and destroy what you have to. Forty years is a long time. I have to say, you come highly rated, but, is there anything you want to ask me about this mission?"

"Why us? Haven't the..." he was going to say 'Limeys' but checked himself, "Brits any agents who can handle it, or are they too busy drinking tea and watching cricket?"

The reply was cold, aloof and professional.

"The Brits and we are partners. Special relationship; you heard of that? Just do your job." There was a pause, "Actually," he added, "I rather like tea. Everything you need is in a silver Toyota, on the right hand side of the motor transport compound. Leave as soon as you can tomorrow." Clancy turned and walked into the darkness.

Spano stood still, the night air full of the sounds of a far-east country. In Afghanistan, the nights were usually very cold; the days could be oven-hot, with a dry heat that seemed to suck every bit of energy and every drop of moisture out of a man. Vietnam was like Malaysia, a big yellow moon, a natural gentleness over sharp ridges and mountains, except, that is, when he flew. The Thunderchiefs were awesome, huge and massively expensive. A war correspondent had compared the American War in Vietnam to hitting a fence post with a gold watch. The fence post would eventually sink into place, but at what cost?

He began to recall that crash in North Vietnam. When he'd been brought down, it was not by some deadly surface-to-air missile fired from the sites that ringed Hanoi, but a burst of good, old-fashioned, automatic rifle fire. His mission had been in trouble almost from the moment it started. One of the F4 Phantoms in his flight had aborted at take off, with a flame-out; the plane had been lucky to avoid major damage, but the sortie was one kite short. They had homed in on the Vectors given by their backseat 'bears', as the electronic and weapons officers were known. The B52, although flying many thousands of feet above them, still had to take evasive action to avoid 'triple A'. Then, his wingman had sustained a burst of 57mm anti-aircraft shells in his port engine. The pilot's voice, matter of fact, had come in loud and clear.

"I'm exiting now."

Spano had watched the flash from the cockpit and seen the two ejector seats catapult into the night air, their parachutes billowing wide. He had pulled his own plane round in a tight turn, and then swept down and away from the descending 'chutes. The plane's nose came up, and he estimated he was four, perhaps five, kilometres from the parachutes.

He was now reliving everything that had happened afterwards.

It was then when he became conscious of the tracer rounds arcing up out of the darkness of the land. The rounds seemed leisurely, curving upwards towards the silk. Spano rolled the plane, dived, closed on the sites that the tracer was spitting from, flipped open the gun cover and pressed the hard, red plastic firing button. His plane shuddered as the air-to-ground missiles blasted into the distance. There was a three second pause, and then there were two explosions, a thousand feet away, to his port side. Almost immediately, his plane staggered; the noise filled his senses. He knew instantly, from the feel of the aircraft and the warning lights on the control panel display, that he had sustained battle damage. The head-up display was flashing one red light; there was another red light on his oil pressure gauge, and the inevitable smell of smoke was getting stronger. His backseat 'bear' shouted into the intercom, "Fire in starboard engine!"

"Okay, let's go, now!"

Two ejector seat handles were pulled, the cockpit, as if a giant hand had lifted it, disappeared, and Spano was aware of a huge thrust upward, followed by the sensation of falling. The jerk on his upper body and shoulders was hard and was followed by a floating sensation. It seemed only seconds since he was in his fighter plane, and now he was descending onto the dark landmass that was North Vietnam. He closed his legs and swung in his harness, but as he floated he could see no sign of his fellow pilot. Then, he landed – crashing, tearing at bushes; there was a splintering sound as a branch collapsed under his weight. Instantly, they were there, a jabbering horde of men dressed in shabby green uniforms and funny-shaped hats, but bearing Kalashnikov rifles. He was dragged, kicked and cuffed, and then there was quietness. A man holding a large flashlight stood over him. Spano noticed the stars on the epaulettes, and then he saw the pistol descending as if in slow motion, the butt hitting him on the forehead.

"You American Criminal, you die!" There was another burst of talking; the pain and blood had begun to restrict his vision. Spano saw another man move into view.

He said, "Well, American, welcome to North Vietnam." Spano had passed out.

Extensively interrogated, beaten and humiliated, Spano was put on a near starvation diet. The camp was known as Son Tay, and it was located just twenty-three miles from Hanoi. On two occasions, Spano and four other POWs were caged and paraded through Hanoi's streets, poked with sharp sticks and spat at. He frequently thought his life would end at the hands of an enraged mob or as a result of the beatings by the guards. Then, he was brought before Captain Choi.

Choi had the slight, small build of a typical Vietnamese. His face was serene, his manner composed, and he spoke English with a very slight French accent.

"You are well?" The question was ludicrous. Spano replied as he had a hundred times before: Number, Rank, Name.

"It is alright, David. You will not be harmed or hurt anymore."

Spano, on hearing his Christian name, had to struggle not to let any emotion show. 'David' meant a happy home, a loving mother and stepfather, barbecues, high-school dances, girls. The captain's hand came forward, and Spano winced. The cigarette case was small, neat, polished, much like the captain himself.

"Take one," he offered. Spano shook his head. "David," the captain's voice was mildly reproving. "You do smoke. I've read your file. They're not Lucky Strike, I'm afraid. They're English Senior Service, a very good cigarette." He tapped his cigarette several times on the desk. "I like them well packed." He held out the packet again. "Go on, I won't tell if you won't." The smile was spontaneous. Spano reached out to take a cigarette. The lighter sparked, and the smoke hit his throat and lungs. He felt light-headed, very nearly losing consciousness, wondering furiously if he had been drugged. The giddiness subsided.

"Is it good?" The captain leant back in his chair. "I'm afraid I smoke too much. Your western doctors warn that there are health risks, but I do enjoy a smoke in the morning."

Spano tried to pace his enjoyment of the cigarette, taking it out of his mouth, to delay the inevitable, but the effects felt wonderful. He wondered, fearfully, what was to happen next.

"There is a Swedish Red Cross delegation in town," continued Choi. "They have to stay at a place twenty kilometres away. The bombing, you understand. We are putting POW names forward for repatriation, which we hope will happen sometime soon, but we need those prisoners to reply properly to questions from our Swedish visitors, and sign a document, to confirm that they have been well-treated while they were our guests."

Spano ground out the cigarette butt. "I'll sign nothing." The words had a flat finality.

The captain moved his hands in a gesture of acceptance. "It is a small thing we shall talk about it later. Oh, here, have these." He withdrew five cigarettes from the packet. "I can't help you with matches, I'm afraid. For the time being, David, it is goodbye."

Choi's hand came forward, but Spano was unable to reciprocate, when the captain squeezed his hand. Choi stood up, called to one of his men and, as the door opened, a guard came in. There was an exchange in Vietnamese, and the guard took Spano's arm quite gently and led him away.

"There you are, David, your ordeal might soon be over. Think of it: pretzels, beer, American women." Choi's voice faded as Spano was taken down the corridor, not to his old cell, but a different, larger one, with a bed and a small battered writing-desk. The guard gestured towards the room, put his hand in his pocket, withdrew a box of matches, picked out five and handed them over, whilst making gestures of smoking, and he actually smiled. His mind in complete turmoil, Spano sat on the edge of his bed and, for only the second time in his life, he cried.

★ ★ ★

Swee Poe was stumbling along behind Sammy. It was just as it was in his vivid nightmares: the jungle all around him, the same unique, nauseating smell of rotting vegetation, and strange, sinister sounds. Sammy was slashing a path five paces in front of him, but every few minutes or so, he would stop to look again at Swee Poe's map. He did not look happy but, thought Swee

Poe, had Sammy *ever* looked happy?

"We're here, or at least your map says we're here. Recognise anything?"

Swee Poe shook his head. "Not a thing!"

"We'll split up. You go for three minutes that way." Sammy stretched out his right arm. "I'll go this way."

"No!" Swee Poe's voice was shrill. "We stay together."

"Why? Are you afraid that a tiger will have you? You've got your gun." Sammy's sarcasm was all too evident. "Okay, Tarzan, we go that way – together." Sammy turned right and moved on. Half an hour later, he stopped and declared that it was 'chow time'.

Swee Poe gingerly squatted down, facing Sammy. The rice and vegetables were sticky and moist. After decades of mostly western food, the meal was frugal in the extreme. Swee Poe drank greedily from his water carrier, such was his thirst. Sammy broke off a piece of bread and ate it; he was an uncouth eater.

"Look, Elvis, we go back the way we came, and then spend another thirty minutes, beginning from where we started. Then, you stop there, and I'll go north for ten minutes, come back to you, and then, go south for ten minutes." He held up a hand, brooking no disagreement, "It's the only way we'll cover the ground. If we find nothing, we'll move to the next square on the grid."

Swee Poe, extremely unhappy at the prospect of being left alone in the jungle, realised that there was merit in Sammy's suggestion.

"Okay," he agreed reluctantly. They came off their haunches and back-tracked until they arrived at the point from which they had started.

"How do you know this is it?" Swee Poe thought that all

the jungle looked pretty much alike.

Sammy nodded at an ancient tree; there was a fresh parang slash, three feet up its trunk.

"Wait here. If I find anything I'll come back." He noticed the fear in Swee Poe's eyes and grinned. "I promise." He moved off into the thick undergrowth.

For the first time in twenty-five years, doubts set in, and Swee Poe wondered whether the bullion he'd seen was really worth all this. He stood sweating, his throat was very dry. He checked his watch and waited.

★ ★ ★

Griffiths, Tucker and Hughes had been badly delayed on the Seremban Road, where a public works lorry had been involved in a collision with a scooter. The vehicles were now locked in an embrace mid-road. One-way traffic was controlled by two Malaysian policemen, who were allowing a slow and very hot procession of cars to pass. Clear of the accident, eventually, they sped on their way, trying to make up some time, for driving conditions in Malaysia were, on the whole, very good. British Colonial rule had given the country expensive, well-maintained roads, and they drove British style, on the left. With the windows almost down, the temperature inside the car was soon pleasantly cool again.

Hughes turned off the B road and onto what had been an estate road. Griffiths tapped his shoulder.

"Up ahead, three o'clock; see it?" They stopped alongside a Datsun. Tucker placed his hand on the bonnet.

"How long?" Griffiths wanted to know, as he walked around the car.

Tucker was non-committal. "Bonnet's warm, but it could

simply be the sun."

Hughes noted the registration. "This could be our visitor, or simply an estate worker – security or something."

"How does this correspond to the map, the one that's missing; the one with the duff information on it?" asked Griffiths, as he finished his inspection and was joined by Hughes at the driver's door. Tucker gave a tentative tug at the door handle, but the door was unyielding.

"This is roughly the area where I put the cross in the grid," said Hughes.

They fell silent for a moment, save for Griffiths, who kicked the offside tyre, and said, "This is very probably our Chinaman. What do we do about it?"

Tucker was looking at the ground. He tapped Griffith's arm and pointed. There was a very faint track leading from the car to the edge of the jungle, and where blades of long grass were disturbed and bent over on a dry bare patch of ground, a shoe print was just visible. They stood stock still, listening.

"Nothing," said Hughes, "Let's go to our grid. Don't slam the car doors. We'll go in first gear. I'll be as quiet as I can. I estimate about six hundred yards. Griff, take the map." Hughes fumbled in his shirt pocket and handed over the plastic case to Griffiths, slipped the car into first gear and gently crawled along the track.

"I said we should have had a Bren gun," remarked Griffiths.

Tucker turned, smiling. "What we need to worry about is has *he* got one?"

Just minutes later, Griffiths nudged his friend's shoulder and whispered, "By my reckoning, we're here."

Hughes reacted by turning at right angles and driving very

carefully into the deserted rubber estate. He pulled up, the track some eighty yards distant. "We're not invisible, but we're not obvious. It will have to do," Hughes concluded.

Already wearing their jungle greens, it only took moments to attach the sheathed parangs and water bottles to their belts. Lastly, they put on their hats. Finally, the precious map was placed in Gethin's pocket, and he gave the instruction, "Okay, let's go."

In single file, six paces apart, they headed into the menacing jungle, disappearing within seconds as the dense canopy swallowed them.

Fifteen

Kuala Lumpur

Late morning, Friday 1 October 1982

David Spano stretched his arm to take hold of the old-fashioned, wind-up alarm clock. The hands showed 11.07, so he had slept well. He rose, showered, shaved, and was dressing when the phone rang.

Clancy's voice was clear. "You okay? We've had a phone call from London and they want those former Brit soldiers picked up. Apparently, they flew out to Kuala Lumpur from Holland. The local cops are looking for them. They'll ring us when all three are in custody. The Brits want you to have a clear field, a home run. The real reason is they probably want to extract any British Nationals from the frame. Suits us; the plane was American. Anyway, stay put, see the sights. The Malaysian police shouldn't take long; three middle-aged Brits stumbling around KL should stand out like Father Christmas at Easter. I'll be in touch. There's something like eight hours of daylight left... two hours to get there... It doesn't leave a lot of time today, but tomorrow should be 'D Day'. 'Bye."

Spano went back to his bed. He ignored the can of Coca Cola in the fridge, instead choosing a bottle of pineapple juice. He lay on the crumpled sheets. Overhead, the large electric fan clattered, keeping the room pleasantly cool. Every time he lay down, his mind would go back to Vietnam, the blades of the fan reminding him of the distinct fluttering sound of Huey helicopters lifting soldiers and marines. It had been a bad war. Once, when on leave in Saigon, he'd met up with a Marine Corps Major, and they had got quietly drunk together. Spano had questioned the Major as to why the war was not being won. What was the *real* reason? The answers that the infantry officer gave were no big surprise: Politicians, political interference at every level, body counts – theirs, the VC – as many as possible, the Americans as few as possible. The politicians seemed terrified of public opinion. But the second reason was, in a practical sense, the more disturbing. The American forces were employing the wrong tactics, the Major had explained, slamming his right fist into a cupped left hand.

"We're the United States Marine Corps. Speed and fire power, hit them hard! The trouble is, the VC are rarely where we think they are. They seem able to slip away, disappear totally. We go in and there's nothing, then, two kilometres down the road, they mortar our positions! We *have* to fight them at their game, slow it down, use more intelligence and target all known tracks, paths and roads the VC use. It takes time, though. The Koreans have three battalions near Da Nang. They do just that and they've paralysed the VC in their area. But our army, our politicians, want quick victories. The Koreans and the Australian battalions go out in squads and platoons, and hunt down the VC. They copy what the Limeys did in Malaya, but again, it takes time – hundreds of man hours for a handful of kills, but," with the bourbon poised on his lips he paused, then swallowed, sweating profusely despite the air conditioning, "the real victory," he continued, "is that we will be hunting them and not the other way around. Morale, superiority; move by day or night, ambush and kill. *That's* the message we should be hammering home. I really wish to God the brass would take that on board."

The evening had lapsed into an alcoholic haze, but sometime later, Spano learnt that the Major had been killed, extricating his marine company from a fire base, after it was overrun.

Captain Choi had made an appearance some weeks after the first interrogation. Spano had laid the five cigarettes on the writing desk and spelt out 'NO' with the five matches, breaking two in half to form the letter O. They had lain there, ignored by the guards, until, one day, they were gone. Spano saw no one. He was given two subsistence meals a day, but had no contact with other POWs, although he gradually gained the impression that he was being watched. His hut had bamboo walls, the poles four inches apart; there was no place to hide, no privacy. Then, one day, in pouring rain, he was taken to the same room where he'd met Captain Choi before. He was told to sit down, and he waited and waited.

When Choi entered, the same smooth face, the immaculately pressed uniform, it was as though he were meeting an old friend.

"David, I'm glad to see you. How are you?" Spano replied with Number, Rank and Name. Choi gave a smile and chuckled. "It's alright, David; no pressure; you'll be going home soon." He was looking directly into Spano's eyes as he spoke. He took out his cigarettes, nodded at the packet in his outstretched hand. Spano shook his head and Choi placed a cigarette in his mouth and lit up. The cloud of smoke lingered between them. "You are a brave man, David, a good man, but what sort of America will you be going home to? People like these perhaps?" He reached into his briefcase and extracted a photograph. It was starkly pornographic. Three young couples, faces and genitals clearly showing, were lying on a grass knoll; there was a college building in the top of the picture, and a banner that screamed "SCREW – SCREW – SCREW THE WAR". The photograph had been syndicated across America, heavily censored, to avoid indecency laws. Choi produced another photograph, that of a high-profile Hollywood actress, posing at a North Vietnamese anti-aircraft gun station; and cuttings from daily newspapers across America. Returning servicemen from Vietnam had been photographed being refused service in bars; there was a report of a knifing in Idaho, during a family fight, and a photograph of a serviceman bleeding to death, another showed a sign that said simply MURDERERS; it was hanging from a state university where veterans queued to enrol.

"David, David, what is America turning into? Look, I know nothing I can say, nothing we can do, can make you betray the USMC, but America isn't the Marine Corps. College Professors are abusing their positions to urge all American troops out of Vietnam – peace at any price. I'll make a prediction. Vietnam will haunt your country and your people for generations."

Choi's smooth face was full of concern, the eyes sympathetic. Spano fought to stay in line. Number, Rank and Name. There was no snap in his voice, the words hung emptily in the room.

"Ah!" Choi stood up. "David, for you, your war is almost over. You will be repatriated next week, no trick, no lies; you're going home. I will not see you again. Goodbye." He offered no handshake, but turned abruptly and left, the flimsy wooden door swinging silently behind him.

Choi had been right. With a half hour's notice and no time to speak to other POWs, he was taking a shower, dressing in an immaculately pressed uniform and having a rattling, bumpy ride in a regular Vietnamese army truck. After this, he was sent on the two hundred metres walk across the bridge that spanned the de-militarised Zone. Flashlights, careful, helping hands, a whole barrage of salutes followed, but somehow it was not right. Spano saw the be-medalled uniforms and felt strangely remote, as if he were not physically present. He answered preliminary questions and was guided into the initial debriefing centre. He did not enjoy the first substantial American meal he had tasted in over three years, and his mind and body were tired.

Choi had travelled in a civilian car, immediately behind Spano's truck, observed the walk over the bridge and then returned to his office. He wrote neatly, in English, a three page summary of David Spano's behaviour and actions whilst a captive. The summary and conclusions were surprising:

Spano has shown a noticeable pattern of behaviour. He is a brave, outwardly confident American serviceman. There is no physical or mental means of us persuading him to betray or inform against the United States Marine Corps, but when he leaves his spiritual home, i.e. USMC, he might react differently. He came to Vietnam as a brash American Nationalist; he leaves as a deeply disillusioned man. He might (underlined in red ink) *be of use to us. Contact should be made, tenuously, but necessarily, in America.*

Choi had signed the document and passed it up to the Secretariat, where it was duly photocopied and filed.

Spano returned home, the massed journalists and photographers formed a solid wall on the airport tarmac. He gave a brief interview, understated, without a trace of self-pity, and was driven through the milling crowd of tearful wives and excited children who had surged forward to embrace their loved ones. He spotted a sign hanging from a large building; it said simply, WAS IT WORTH IT? BRING THE TROOPS HOME NOW. An enormous anger erupted in his mind and he swore obscenely. His driver, a senior NCO in the US army, had slowed the car.

"Want to go back? Shake your fist, let off steam? It'll probably do you good, sir."

The words were meant to be helpful, but Spano's rage had left him feeling physically sick.

"No. Drive on," he replied, and, in that moment, his life had changed forever.

He had undergone umpteen interviews, debriefings, answering coldly and with logic the questions posed. There had followed a posting to the Philippines, his promotion to Lieutenant Colonel, the meticulously calculated back pay, and then he was posted stateside, to San Diego. His immediate superior, a Brigadier General, was impressed with his skill as a weapons' instructor, but was concerned at the emptiness of the man himself. He had no family, and only irregular and purely sexual liaisons with women. He had asked Spano whether he wanted to take early retirement from the USMC. Spano took little time to think about it, before he decided to accept the offer. He folded his uniform, quit the unit, and was immediately enrolled into the Central Intelligence Agency. He passed all their tests, criteria, and aptitude challenges. He was, after seven months of rigorous training, accepted as a field agent. It was in 1978, two years after he had left the marines, that he received the first phone call. He was in Philadelphia, working as part of a surveillance team, taping and photographing a drug-running gang. The call had come to his hotel room.

"David? It's me, Captain Choi. You remember?"

Spano had been surprised, but gave no indication of it.

"Of course, Captain. What are you doing in America?"

"Well, I'm not a captain now; I'm de-mobbed, so to speak. I work for an American pharmaceutical firm." Choi named a well-known company. "I hoped we could meet over a drink. I'm afraid that I've fallen in love with your bourbon whiskey." His voice was the same: soothing, anxious to please. "David, I know practically no one here. I would be grateful for the company of someone I know and, incidentally, have a great respect for."

"There's a bar four blocks down from the hotel; the 'Ace of Diamonds'. I'll meet you there, let's say eight o'clock," suggested Spano. He toyed with the idea of phoning his section head, saw no reason to, and left for the bar.

The 'Ace of Diamonds' was typical of a South Philly bar, with its large TV and pool table, but it was half-empty. A morose barman placed a bottle of Wild Turkey bourbon, a jug of water and two glasses on the table, and went back to his newspaper.

"What do I call you these days?" asked Spano.

Choi smiled. "My Vietnamese name is unpronounceable. Choi is fine."

They talked freely, and Spano was surprised at the spontaneity of their conversation. Choi turned the bottle around. "Wild Turkey; not the same as Wild Weasel, is it, eh, David?"

Spano smiled for the first time in years. "You knew all along, didn't you?"

Choi nodded. "Your mother's death, your father lost in the Second World War, and your outstanding flying record. Yes, we knew it all. And did you know who really won the Vietnam War? It was you, the Americans. We are an impoverished race, suffering from trade restrictions, shunned by China. Everywhere, people are hungry, not really starving, but hungry, hungry for goods, for the better things in life. They see television from the west, the cars, the clothes, the food, the freedom of working people. There is no question, you won the war. I earn, believe it or not, twenty times my salary as a Regular Vietnamese Captain, which, in turn, was four times as much as a manual worker. All that blood, all that sacrifice, for what? So that our politicians can live fat cat lives! We have a saying in Vietnam, that the only way to frighten politicians is to mention free elections. You are looking at an embittered man, David. It doesn't make for good company, to grumble about this. Let's have another drop of this glorious whiskey." He poured two glasses, raised his and toasted, "To Honour, may it always rule us."

Spano touched his glass with Choi's. "I'll drink to that."

They drank a further couple of glasses, Choi insisting on paying the tab.

"I'll be in touch sometime in the future, David. It's done my heart good to have met you again."

They shook hands and Spano surprised himself by replying, "Don't make it too long, Choi."

Spano went back to his hotel, warmth not entirely due to the bourbon was in his chest, and he enjoyed a dreamless sleep.

Choi phoned three times over the next seventeen months. They met up in Cleveland, Gary, Indiana, and in a town in Texas, famous for its 72 ounce steaks. Choi had been amazed.

"I can't eat all this meat! There's enough on this plate to feed a Vietnamese family of eight and leave scraps for the dog!"

They had compromised, sharing a meal between them, and had wandered back to their motel, where Choi produced a bottle of Wild Turkey. He poured two glasses.

"To Honour," he suggested, and they drank, savouring the bourbon and their friendship. "David. I would like you to meet somebody. You have a lot in common. He is an aviator like you, and he was a POW."

Spano eased his legs forward, settling himself for a comfortable drink. "Marine, Air Force, Navy?"

"No, David, none of those."

"Air National Guard? Didn't know they had any POWs."

Choi had placed his drink on the table between them.

"His name is Dimitri. He is a Major in the Russian Air Force. He was shot down while piloting a Hind helicopter gun-ship, forty miles west of Kabul, in Afghanistan. He was held for eleven months, and then, an attack on the valley where he was held captive allowed him to escape. I believe he went three days without food or water. He climbed up to the snowline and survived by living off the snow. He wrote SOS in the snow, and was rescued, purely by chance, by a helicopter. He now serves in the German Democratic Republic, East Germany. David, he wants to come to America. In other words, he wants to live a different life. I don't think he wants to desert. Like you, he is loyal to his air force, but there is now a girl, a woman really, a librarian in Dresden. They want to build a new life together. As a favour to me, will you meet him?"

Spano placed his glass on the table and looked into Choi's eyes. "You know I'm in the CIA?"

"Yes, of course. Have I ever asked you any questions about the CIA? I respect you too much, David. Let me tell you about this man. I first met Dimitri in Hanoi. He was part of a visiting Russian Air Force training cadre. He seemed different from the rest, didn't go round staggering drunk on vodka. We talked about the war, and, clearly, he was interested in our country, our culture, the way we live our lives. I grew to respect him and we kept in touch. I had a letter from him only last week; it was posted in West Berlin. My firm has an office there, and it was in our mail. Here it is."

Choi handed over the short letter. "It's written by him, it's his handwriting."

It was written in grammatically correct English and expressed good wishes to Choi. The writer asked if they were going to meet again.

"It's our little code." Choi pointed to the capital A in 'Again'. "Dimitri is getting impatient. David. Will you meet him, give him any advice you can, to help him to extricate himself and his girl. What he'll give you in return I don't know, but the Hind has a very formidable weapons system; I believe it is as good as anything you have in the west. Whatever you do, don't compromise yourself or him. The East German Secret Police, the Starsi, are very powerful but Dimitri is not allowed into West Berlin; we can meet up with him in East Berlin. Anywhere else is out of the question. What do you say, David?"

Spano stared thoughtfully into Choi's face for a moment.

"I'll have to put it before my section head, who will have to take it up with Langley. I simply *cannot* take unilateral action. You must realise that, Choi."

"Of course I do, but please, David, be exceptionally careful. If the Starsi get any inkling of this, Dimitri is literally finished." Choi's hand moved across his throat. "When will you start, David?"

Spano downed his bourbon in a gulp, "Tomorrow, Choi, tomorrow."

Spano spoke to his section head, and was driven up to Langley, where he was painstakingly briefed on what to say, what not to say, and the emergency procedures to adopt if things went unexpectedly wrong.

He flew to West Berlin and met the man known as Dimitri. At their second meeting, Dimitri gave him the address of Olga Witchmann, in Portland, Oregon. Dimitri explained that she was a Starsi agent, a sleeper, and she owned a liquor shop. This information was passed onto the CIA in Oregon and, four weeks later, after an exhaustive observation, three men walked into Olga Witchmann's store and arrested her. She was a mine of information. Several people were rounded up and arrested on espionage charges. They turned out to be very low-level operatives, who were paid to pass on information about naval ships operating out of Seattle. Three were given prison sentences of up to two years, one was deported, and one, a licensed private detective, disappeared. The CIA was pleased with the outcome, but it would have been different had they known of the three unofficial visits paid to West Berlin by David Spano.

★ ★ ★

Hughes led Griffiths and Tucker through the foliage; they used their parangs sparingly, stopping every ten minutes, and kneeling on the jungle floor, straining to catch any sound that was alien to the jungle noises that surrounded them. After the third stop, Gethin Hughes beckoned them to his side.

"If I'm right, we're pretty close to site marked by the cross," he whispered. "Move out at right angles and if you see anything out of the ordinary come back."

His words were barely audible but the urgency in his voice was evident. They separated. It was Tucker who noticed what appeared to be a misshapen tree, without any discernible outline, just a mass of greenness. He moved closer, the parang in his right hand. His left foot stood on something, causing a metallic cracking sound. He moved his right foot tentatively and there was another metallic sound. He inched the parang down to his right boot as a huge, black and yellow spider scuttled furiously away. The parang probed along the jungle floor. A scratching noise came from the tip of the weapon. Tucker slowly straightened up. He slashed at the creepers in front of him, the blade quivering as it connected with something solid. He slashed again, attacking the foliage and mosses, and sending leaves and twigs flying off as the blade bit deeper. Then, just to the right of his face, a grey, rust-streaked, metal object appeared. Reversing the parang, Tucker banged the handle on the metal. A dull, hollow noise reverberated from the impact. He stepped back, his breathing heavy with his exertions.

Three minutes later, he caught up with Hughes and used a finger to indicate the direction from which he had come. Hughes indicated to him to stay where he was, and moved into the trees. Tucker heard them returning when they were almost on top of him. They followed him back to the object and entered the tiny clearing together. Tucker pointed his parang at the cut foliage.

"Be careful, there could be snakes."

Hughes walked cautiously towards the metal object. He scraped away the debris, the metal making a grinding noise as the blade worked its way over the surface. The three men began to strip away the dense undergrowth. They worked without stopping for thirty-five minutes. The plane had landed nose first, causing the propeller to be completely buried. They looked inside the black void of what had been the cockpit, parangs at the ready, in case there were any reptiles lurking. Hughes swept the bright beam of his torch over the interior, and when satisfied that there was no danger, he played the beam along the floor. His left hand found Griffiths' shoulder and he gripped it hard. The torch revealed what appeared to be several dozen bricks, lying haphazardly on the ribbed floor, bricks that gleamed like they had on the day they were smelted. Tucker followed, his eyes taking in every detail. He took the torch out of Hughes' hand and worked the beam through the blackness, revealing more bricks, and something else, which looked like a box. He waggled the torch for his comrades, drawing their attention to the object.

"There's definitely something else in there," Tucker said, his voice low.

They retreated a few paces and quietly gazed at the wreckage of what had once been a war plane. Griffiths looked at his watch.

"It's eighteen twenty hours. It'll be dark in less than an hour. It will take us thirty minutes to get out of here."

Hughes nodded, his chest still heaving at the physical work

of the past forty minutes. We won't go back to KL; we'll stay overnight at Seremban. We'll make an early start, get back here and we'll take one ingot back to the police station at Seremban. This crash is a war grave, remember. We can't mess with it."

"What about our Chinaman, if it is him?"

Tucker was already moving back from the clearing. Hughes shrugged.

"We can't stop here all night; we can't see in the dark, let alone in the jungle, and so neither can he. We'll get back as soon as it's light."

"Fair enough," Griffiths grunted. "There used to be a couple of brothels in Seremban."

"We're not stopping there!" Tucker's voice was sharp, final.

Griffiths looked at Gethin Hughes, winked and replied, "Spoil sport."

They moved easily out of the clearing. The night seemed to be closing in very quickly. After every thirty yards, Griffiths clipped a branch or tree just deep enough to leave a barely noticeable way-marker. They came back to the car, drove away in first gear and saw no sign of the vehicle they had seen earlier. Despite the fast-approaching gloom, Hughes did not switch on his sidelights until they came to the road junction. Within an hour, they were at Seremban, where they found a hotel. None of them slept well.

Sixteen

Kuala Lumpur

Friday evening, 1 October 1982

Sammy was driving far too fast, obviously in a foul temper.

"Elvis, we've spent eight hours thrashing about in the jungle, and all I've got to show for it are blisters and mosquito bites. For the last time, what are we supposed to be looking for?"

Swee Poe steeled himself. "You'll find out, when we find it."

Sammy's temper snapped and he brought the car to a sudden halt. His face was contorted with rage.

Swee Poe stared at him. "You've been paid to act as my guide. I paid good money for your services. You have a contract. Honour it!"

Sammy flung open the car door. "I have a contract, right enough, and I intend to honour that, but," Sammy hissed, "the contract is to kill you first, and then, whatever your stinking treasure is, steal it. Surprised?" He drew his parang clear of its scabbard and swung the blade. "You're a deserter from the Malayan All Races Liberation Army. You will not die slowly," he shrieked. He shifted to the front of the car. "Get out and move over to that drainage ditch!"

Swee Poe put his left foot out onto the roadway, simultaneously producing the automatic from his waistband.

"Ah!" Sammy was grinning, making his pock-marked features animal-like in the darkening sky. "You've got your gun. Okay, so shoot. See what happens. Fuck all! Blanks don't kill, not even at five feet," he said mockingly. "Go on, Elvis, shoot me!" The parang was pointing directly at Swee Poe's face.

"Okay Sammy, I will shoot you." He brought the weapon up and fired. The explosion seemed enormous; the impact of the high velocity round punched Sammy backwards, his eyes wide in disbelief.

"You've shot me!" The words were uttered in amazement.

"I have," agreed Swee Poe as he lifted the gun to Sammy's head. "I had the ammunition checked and changed in KL, the first night we met. You see, Sammy, we've met before, outside the Vietnamese restaurant in San Diego, when you were pretending to read a newspaper. Who do you work for? One of the Triads? Tell me."

Sammy was making croaking noises. "No, no, don't kill me."

Swee Poe shook his head. "Sorry, Sammy," he said, and squeezed the trigger again. Sammy's body gave a convulsive shudder, but his eyes stayed wide open. Swee Poe managed to drag his body to the side of the road and shoved it over the edge of the bank. It rolled down and disappeared into the undergrowth at the edge of the jungle. Swee Poe briefly toyed with the thought of covering the body with vines or leaves, but, instead, he climbed back into the car, sweating profusely. His hands were shaking. He switched on the engine and moved off. By the time he arrived at his flat in Noordin Street the panic had left him, to be replaced by a completely unexpected sense of exhilaration. He drank greedily from the refrigerated water bottle. He called the telephone number the old man had given him in London. The call was local and the voice that answered was business-like and sounded as if it belonged to a professional person.

"My name is Elvis Lee. I believe I have an agreement with you?" Swee Poe was conscious of aloofness in the voice at the other end.

"I'm sorry, Mr Lee, we do not have an agreement. What we do have is an arrangement; there is a difference in law. You have your inheritance?"

Swee Poe sensed a difficult conversation. "I expect to have it tomorrow, or Sunday – Monday at the latest."

The offhand voice cut in again. "I suggest that, when your inheritance is in your possession, you phone again. This is a premature discussion."

Swee Poe drew a long breath. "I phoned to find out your terms. In a nutshell, how much commission you will charge?" He forced some intensity into his voice. "I want *time* to examine my options."

"Mr Lee, you don't have any options. I am the only one you can deal with. The commission is the standard rate, 60:40."

Swee Poe gasped in astonishment. "You take forty per cent? That's exorbitant!"

"Wrong, Mr Lee. I take sixty per cent, *you*," the word sounded deliberately contemptuous, "have forty per cent. Take it or leave it!"

Swee Poe slammed down the phone, shaking with anger and frustration, his mind in turmoil. What was he to do? Gradually, his mind started to function. Everything led back to the old man in London. First things first. He had to find the bullion, *his* gold, and that meant going back into that accursed jungle, alone, but it had to be done. He reassuringly had his gun, but was still amazed that he had actually used it to kill a man. He tried to force the image of Sammy's face out of his mind, convinced that

Sammy would have shown no mercy towards him. The answer came to him suddenly. He'd follow the ex-soldiers, just as he had done in Amsterdam, and let them lead him to the plane. That meant he needed to get back to the rubber estate as soon as it was daylight, hide until they turned up, and then follow them into the jungle.

He immediately left his flat, went to a service station and filled up his car with petrol. On impulse, he bought two canvas shopping bags decorated with the legend, 'Penang the Golden Island'. He returned, ate ravenously, but slept badly. Images of Sammy, and the deafening noise of the gun being fired as the gleaming blade of the parang came towards his face, were ever present, and three times he woke up drenched in perspiration. The bed sheets became uncomfortably damp, and he moved to the sofa, put the light on and watched the clock, resolving to leave at five-thirty, which would get him to the estate at first light.

★ ★ ★

While Swee Poe was making his phone call, it was two in the afternoon Eastern Standard Time in Philadelphia. Magda Anna Crumpet was parking her Buick outside the recruiting offices of the United States Air Force. She walked up to the gleaming brass and glass reception desk, watched by a sergeant, resplendent in number one dress uniform.

"My name is Magda Anna Crumpet. I'm a retired police officer. I was a Gold Badge Lieutenant of Detectives in the Philadelphia Metropolitan Police Department. I want to see someone of a higher rank than yourself, if you please." She opened her handbag and placed on the desk a miniature of her gold badge, which she had been given on her retirement.

The sergeant looked at the replica badge, but did not touch it. "I'm on duty, ma'am, and these," he tapped the three dazzling white stripes on his sleeves, "give me the right to answer and ask pertinent questions." He nodded gravely.

The woman's hand again went into her handbag. She withdrew two large photographs from a cardboard folder. "Do you know what these are?"

The sergeant bent forwards to scrutinise the pictures, commenting with some sarcasm, "Photographs?"

Magda sighed, not a petite woman's sigh, more a notice of a call to arms. Within and outside the police department, she was very well known for two things. Firstly, she was completely teetotal. She had never tasted alcohol; the smell of it made her want to vomit. The second was her phenomenal, near perfect photographic memory. She often boasted that, if she'd seen something or someone, or read something, she'd remember it, usually with a time and date, and, in the case of text, she could repeat it word for word. Magda beckoned the sergeant. "In the course of my police career," she leant closer, "I've met many famous people: Congressmen, senators, and top military personnel. Sergeant, do you want me to pull rank? If you do, just come up with another dumb wisecrack. Your boss, and pretty damn quick! You understand?"

The sergeant seemed to smile, at least his lips moved. He turned, picked up the telephone and gave four quick jabs on the keyboard. "Captain Alvarez? Desk here. I've got a woman who insists on seeing somebody above my rank. She's brought in two photographs." There was a pause, and then, as he replaced the receiver, he said, "Take a seat, ma'am. The Captain is on his way down."

"I'll stand."

Captain Alvarez was twenty-seven. He had passed his Major's examination with some ease and was confident promotion would be a matter of course. His eyes took in the figure in front of him.

Something, an inkling of what used to be called self-preservation, flitted into his mind. "How can I help you, ma'am?" His smile was warm.

Magda indicated the sergeant. "As I was trying to explain to brains here, I am a retired police lieutenant. On my retirement, I did what everybody does, I travelled: Europe, London, York, Edinburgh, William Shakespeare's house, Stonehenge, Paris, West Berlin, Rome, Madrid and, finally, I went Stateside. These," she tapped the two greatly enlarged colour photographs, "I took when I was in West Berlin. These two men are in East Berlin."

"How did you manage to do that?" the Captain's smile had now gone.

"I took a tour bus along the Berlin Wall. The bus was ancient, with a plexiglas top, fitted with an old-fashioned trycicle gear that allowed the roof to be raised maybe eighteen inches. It was used as an air vent.

The Captain gave an affirmative nod but did not interrupt.

"Well, I stood on my seat, lifted my camera out through the vent and snapped. The Kraut driver went bananas, shouting, '*Nein, nein, Fotos verboten!*' He stopped the bus and went on ranting. I was told I could cost him his job."

"What did you do?" the Captain was looking into her eyes.

"Got off at the end of the tour and didn't give him a tip. When I came home, I had the films developed, and nearly two hundred, postcard-sized photographs printed. These two I had enlarged. Look." She pointed. "This guy I've seen before." Her painted fingernail tapped the civilian in the photo. "He's an ex-POW, name of Spano. He was a marine pilot. I saw his homecoming on TV and he spoke on camera afterwards. Also, eighteen months ago, I saw him again, here in Philly, coming out of a bar, the 'Ace of Diamonds'. I was on a stakeout across the block. What I'd like to know is this: what is one of our guys doing in East Berlin with one of their guys? See his uniform; that's no tram conductor; that's a Russian military man."

Alvarez looked hard at Magda Crumpet. He thought that if she had a cigar and a raincoat she'd pass for Colombo, the popular TV detective. "Sergeant, get me Base Security at Camp Jordan. Ask for the duty officer. Well, retired Lieutenant of Detectives, I'll try to find out what Spano was doing in East Berlin."

The sergeant passed the handset to the Captain as soon as he'd connected to Camp Jordan. Alvarez identified himself and explained the circumstances.

"I've a *lady* here, who took some photographs in West Berlin. No, she's not a service woman, but she's a retired police officer. I would say she's a very credible informant. Right, sir." He turned to Magda. "You've asked a question, ma'am. The Air Force is going to answer it. This way, if you please."

The airfield base security office contained four people: a major, a female telephone operator and two airmen clerks. The photographs were presented. Another three personnel entered, and then three more, causing a bit of a stir between the staff, until a one star Brigadier General entered. The prints were placed under a magnifying glass and photocopies were printed off. When the Brigadier General spoke there was total silence from the assorted uniforms. "This is odd. Send them up to Langley, by hand. You, Miss Crumpet, will go with them, if you please. Who brought them in?"

Alvarez stepped forward. "Captain Alvarez, Philadelphia Recruiting Office, sir."

The Brigadier had cold, very blue eyes. "Good, Captain. You've used your initiative. It won't go unnoticed." He turned to the Major. "Get in touch with Langley and tell them I've sent the prints up. From here on in, it's their ballgame." He snapped a salute, the uniforms stiffened and saluted back. Magda Crumpet was reminded of a scene from Peter Sellers' "Doctor Strangelove". She was excited and curious. It was just like one of her homicide investigations. She happily joined Captain Alvarez on the way to the airstrip.

The Brigadier returned to his office and lit up a cigarette, blowing a perfect smoke ring. He had already recognised the civilian, but had not revealed it.

"Well, I'll be damned," he muttered softly to himself. He picked up the phone. "Get me the incoming desk, Central Intelligence Agency, Langley, he requested curtly. There was a forty-second pause. "This may be urgent." He gave a lucid account of the base security meeting, told them his extension number and hung up.

The interviewing room at Langley was pleasant, with comfortable armchairs and large airy windows. Three modern prints hung on the walls. Two men sat opposite Magda Crumpet. They were large, faintly-tanned men, wearing button-down shirts, middle-of-the-road dark suits.

"When did you take these photographs, ma'am?"

Magda's reply was immediate. "18th July. I was in West Berlin on the 17th, 18th and 19th July this year.

Both men scribbled furiously, as they continued with their questioning. "You claim you saw this American civilian in Philadelphia?"

"No, I didn't *claim* that!" Both men looked up from their notes. "I didn't claim to see him; I *did* see him. He came out of the 'Ace of Diamonds' bar; it's in south Philly.

"How do you know it was the same man?" There was no

ma'am at the end of that question.

"Check my police file. I've been blessed with an exceptional memory. If I said I saw him, you can bet your pension I have seen him, and the other guy."

Both men in unison asked, "What other guy?"

The response sounded slightly comical, even to Magda. "He was an Asian, five feet six, slight, a hundred and thirty, maybe a hundred and thirty-five pounds." She drew her left hand along her face and lower jaw. "Judging by his jaw-line, I'd say he was Vietnamese."

"Would you recognise him again?"

"You still want to bet your pension?" teased Magda.

One of her interviewers leant back and pressed two buttons, and a screen slid down the wall. He operated a further button and facial images appeared.

"Say when you see him." The screen went blank and a further set of faces appeared.

On the forth set, Magda pointed, "Top left."

"Close-up," the interviewer suggested, and the image grew bigger. "Do you want further enlargement?"

"No need. That's him."

"You're sure, ma'am?"

She noted that the ma'am was back. Magda gave what could be described as a snort. "Of course I'm sure! Anything else I can do for you?"

The interviewers looked at each other and shook their heads. "We'll fly you back to Philly, but you are to tell no one of this interview, understood?" There was no menace in the words, just a caution.

"Of course," agreed Magda.

The journey back went smoothly, the Beechcraft aeroplane made excellent time; however, Captain Alvarez was disappointed and annoyed at being excluded from the proceedings. Magda revealed nothing, but as she alighted she patted his hand. "Nice flight Captain." He felt patronised.

The interviewers had gone directly to another office, where they were joined by a man who was smoking.

"We're starting to unravel things," he said. "On the 14th July, our man went on vacation to Flagstaff, Arizona, but he checked out of his hotel on the 16th. He checked back in on the 21st. The hotel clerk remembers him saying something about fishing at Jackson's Hole. He'd had had two other vacations in the previous twelve months: Miami, Florida, and a skiing holiday at Denver, Colorado. Check both out, including commuter airlines. He could have gone continental from one of the bigger airports."

The interviewers waited as the man stubbed his cigarette out.

"We must give this Diamond Priority."

The interviewers grimaced for, in twelve and fourteen years respectively, neither had been involved in a Diamond Priority; Silver, Ruby and once Gold, but never Diamond. They left their note-pads to be written up and filed.

The air-conditioning made the office suddenly seemed too cold. The man picked up the scrambler phone, 1950's technology, but still very efficient.

"I have to speak to you." There was a pause, and then he nodded. "I'll be there in twenty minutes. I'll bring what we've already got." He hung up, went to light another cigarette, gave a mental shake of his head, picked up the note-books, and headed for the filing and cipher room.

★ ★ ★

David Spano rose quickly from the bed and briskly filled a green, canvas holdall. He switched off the fluttering fan and left the room. He ignored the Toyota in the motor pool, nodded to the two marines at reception, and strode out into the seething streets of Kuala Lumpur.

Seventeen

Kuala Lumpur

Midnight, Friday 1 October 1982

David Spano had hired a scooter, one of the top of the range, 150cc models, together with a crash helmet. From a market stall he'd purchased a pair of dark blue jeans and a long-sleeved, dark blue, wool jersey. Although the night air was still warm, on a scooter it would be cooler. Dressed like this, he would be indistinguishable from the hundreds of Malay, Chinese and Indian riders buzzing around the city streets. He ate frugally and cheaply at a roadside food stall, calculating that in two hours time he would ride to the place on the map. He wanted to be there early; the night held no terrors for him.

★ ★ ★

Spano had used his vacations to travel to Europe, going once from Aspen, Colorado, via Toronto to London, then to Berlin; another time, from Florida through Paris and onto Berlin. He had travelled on his second passport; the one the CIA did not know existed. He had flown back to his holiday hotel and reported back on duty on the date and time he was expected. All told, he had been to Berlin on six occasions, meeting up with Choi in the offices of Choi's firm. Then, he had travelled in the back of one of Choi's vans through the famous Check-Point Charlie, into a courtyard a few hundred yards on, and then to the flat Dimitri 'borrowed' from a friend. Spano had never met Dimitri's friend, but had met his girl, tall, dark-haired, with a serious face, her lips sometimes twitching. Spano thought she was frightened but struggled not to show her fear. Spano and Dimitri had talked, Dimitri at pains to hide his eagerness to please. At the second meeting, he had produced details of the Hind M1-2.4 helicopter, range 450 kilometres and the still classified armaments. Spano, in return, gave an update on American movements to bring Dimitri 'over the wall', as he had put it.

"I've given you information, David," Dimitri persisted. "Can't you give me something? If I'm lifted I can tell them that you're thinking of defecting. I need something, anything, to explain my involvement with you, a Central Intelligence Agency operative."

"Okay, Dimitri, you have given me information, and I'll feed you some in return, next meeting. I promise."

Dimitri looked and sounded relieved. "David, do you really understand the risks I'm taking; Amelia, here, as well. If the merest inkling of this interchange got out, then, unless I can show some positive signs of a productive liaison ..."

Spano touched Dimitri's shoulder, as much to reassure him as for a sign of friendship. "Now, let's talk flying, Dimitri," he suggested. For the next half-hour they conversed in the jargon and camaraderie of pilots.

"What angle of attack did you operate in the Hind?"

Dimitri was unhesitating, "Thirty degrees."

"Really?" Spano's voice was mildly incredulous. "Bit steep! Are you sure? We used twenty-two degrees in 'Nam."

"Your Hueys are not our Hinds, and there are no steep valleys in 'Nam – nothing like as steep or deep as in Afghanistan."

Spano stood up. "I will go now," he said, and turned to Amelia. "Goodbye, we'll meet again, somewhere more conducive to open friendship."

Amelia nodded. Her dark eyes were troubled. "Goodbye, David."

Dimitri and Spano walked downstairs and out onto the pavement. It was raining gently as they shook hands. Choi's van pulled up, Spano climbed into the back and, with a wave, they moved off.

Amelia lit a cigarette. "Will he defect?"

Dimitri was undressing. He laid his uniform on the cheap settee. "Yes, he will, very soon, he is like a fish, not quite taking the fly, but he will."

Amelia dragged eagerly on her cigarette, "Should you have told him that stuff about the Hind? I thought that was all classified."

"The Mujahideen brought one down outside Kandahar, two weeks ago. Its vitals are now probably being photographed and reassembled at the American base at Frankfurt am Main, but it will make our man look good." He threw the huge decorated air force hat onto the bed. "I hate playing bloody soldiers. They are all so stupid." He drew out some civilian clothes from the wardrobe. Lieutenant Colonel Gerhard Elias GRU, Soviet Secret Service, stood in front of the mirror. "Let's eat," he suggested.

★ ★ ★

The Brits had found no difficulty in booking into a hotel in Seremban; no night-time sightseeing for them; a meal of Nasi Goreng, two bottles of Tiger beer each, then bed. Even Tucker, his thirst for alcohol greatly abated since his involvement in the Salvation Army, wanted to drink, and talk about what they had seen and the enormity of their find. Hughes was the quietest, his mind full of memories of the day his life had changed forever, twenty-five years ago. Now, he was back where that incident had occurred that had had such long-reaching mental and physical repercussions.

"What's the score, Geth?" asked Griffiths.

Hughes twisted in his bed, the bedside lamp throwing his face into relief. He shook his head as if to clear the thoughts from his mind. "We go back, park the car, walk into the jungle and pick up one ingot each. That box, or dispatch box, whatever it is, could be the pilot's. Did you see him?"

Griffiths and Tucker nodded, recalling the collection of whitened bones, the skull and fragments of what looked like a uniform. Tucker's whisper was just loud enough to be audible. "God rest his soul."

"We bring the ingots back here. There's a police station by that big municipal building. We go in there, hand over the gold and offer to take a police detachment back. Well just remind them that the plane is a war grave. Apart from the three ingots and that box, we have no right to remove anything. That's down to others."

Griffiths interjected, "What about the British authorities?"

"We don't know whose gold it is, or was. The pilot was American," answered Gethin.

"You've got his dog tags with you?" asked Griffiths, anxiously.

"I have," Gethin assured them, and he carefully withdrew the coin-like token from his wallet. "J. SPANO RC USMC. I can't read the number."

"Will we get into trouble for bringing the gold in?" asked Griffiths.

They had all speculated on this privately, ever since seeing the incredibly shiny, gleaming blocks.

Tucker spoke for them all. "No! We use the ingots to show

that we've found a crashed plane. We are handing them in, not doing a runner."

Griffiths whistled, "Some runner. I could buy Aberystwyth with that lot! What do you think it's worth, Geth?"

"No idea. Let's get some shut-eye. Up early – get there – get it out – back to the local coppers – back to KL – then sunny Wales. Goodnight!"

★ ★ ★

Swee Poe dressed and forced himself to eat something. He pulled his shirt down over the automatic in his waistband, picked up his holdall and two canvas tourist bags, and locked the flat door. Driving Sammy's car, he pulled out into the light, early morning Kuala Lumpur traffic. When he stopped at a red light, a large white car slid in behind him. With a shock that was nearly paralysing, Swee poe realised it was a police car. He raised his left hand in greeting. Two pairs of eyes saw the raised hand and ignored it. Red went to amber, then green and the white car accelerated and swung left. Swee Poe felt as if he urgently needed to urinate. The rear lights of the police vehicle disappeared into the distance. Swee Poe gunned the accelerator and went on his way. In an hour, maybe an hour and a half, he thought, he would be there, waiting for the Britishers. He knew their names; the Fusiliers Depot in Cardiff had revealed them. There had been four in the Running Dog's patrol: Hughes, Parry, Griffiths and Tucker. Now there were three. One of them, he guessed rightly, was no longer alive. Swee Poe kept within the speed limit. It was still dark, no lightening of the sky yet, as dawn was still some hours away. He felt frightened; the wheel in his hands seemed cold. Furiously, he told himself out loud, "Pull it together. You've come too far to lose now!" How would he get the bullion? Would he have to kill the Britishers? He had no idea.

Spano eased the scooter out onto the trunk road and went into the right-hand lane. A lorry, fully laden with timber, no doors on the cab, roared down on him, its horn blowing frantically. He swung back into the left-hand lane and opened up the scooter's two-stroke engine. The evening air was cool and, although late, there were still lights in the cafés and bars. He headed south to Seremban, confident he would do what he had to do.

★ ★ ★

It was a sight no one in living memory had seen before: a man *running* down a corridor in the offices of MI9, Vauxhall. The man stopped at the office of Mrs Mann and knocked boldly. He stepped inside.

"Mr xxxxx is wanted in the conference room. I couldn't get through on the telephone, or to you," he advised accusingly.

Mrs Mann spoke quietly into the phone. "Go back to bed. I'll be home at seven." She replaced the receiver. "He's on the phone now. I'll tell him," and she looked at the man's face, red and sweaty from his exertions, adding, "Who wants him?"

The answer produced an immediate effect. Scott terminated his telephone call abruptly and made his way to the conference room. A long-dead uncle, once a serving police officer in the Devonshire Constabulary, had once told him that the first thing drummed into probationers was *never* to run. Running was a sign of panic. Always use the measured tread; it reassured the members of the public. Even so, he quickened his pace, knocked and entered.

Michael was already seated, and facing a civil servant holding the position of Permanent Undersecretary, a Colonel with the red collar tabs of a Staff Officer, a female secretary, and their old fried the MP, 'laughing boy'. Michael and Scott sensed that there had been unwelcome developments.

"Sit down please." The Undersecretary snapped, and Scott pulled out a chair for himself. "There has been a series of communications between MI6 and the CIA. The CIA has a field agent in Malaysia, by the name of..." he glanced at the file for verification, "David Spano. They are now concerned that this agent has been compromised. They have told us at MI6 that he is to be redeployed; 'deflected' was the word they used, from any part of our recovery mission. They were most insistent. Spano is to play *no part* in this operation."

It was not yet the time for questions. They would be asked later.

"The CIA has asked for our help. Agent Spano has apparently left Kuala Lumpur, and not by the officially provided means of transport. You have precise details of the location of the site?" He looked at Scott for a reply.

"There is a map, the site marked with a cross. It was obtained by covert means but it gives the exact location of a wrecked plane, discovered during the Malayan emergency, in February 1957. We have two copies."

The MP cleared his throat and, when he spoke, he seemed to have a heavy cold.

"There is a map, and it was obtained, as you say, by covert means. Three former members of the British Army, the surviving members of a four-man patrol, are in Malaysia already, having used deception to travel there. What we do not know, of course, in view of their unorthodox travel arrangements, is whether the mark on the map indicates the correct location, or whether it is another deception." He coughed loudly and scowled at Scott. "If the cross is wrongly marked, wilfully or accidentally, it could take weeks to find the plane's location. The jungle is not neutral territory. Treat it in a disrespectful or cavalier manner and it will prove to be a formidable adversary."

The Undersecretary addressed Scott. "I believe you have a theory about what might possibly be found at the crash site? None of us here are interested in *why* you believe that something of a political or military nature could be found there, something that might cause Her Majesty's Government extreme anxiety. Simply tell us what you think, or surmise, could be found. In a nutshell, spell out *what*, apart from the alleged bullion, you believe could be brought to light."

Scott glanced at Michael. "Fair enough. This is what I suggest could be found." He spoke for twelve minutes."

The Undersecretary sat motionless throughout, with his pen poised above his folder, but he seemed to have paled somewhat. The Colonel had sat upright, rigid, his eyes clouded in disbelief and apprehension. The MP was tapping his desk with a finger, the irregular rhythm like a Morse code training exercise. The Undersecretary turned his head sharply and made a brief chopping movement towards his secretary, who took the shorthand minutes to the paper shredder, which made a metallic screech as it devoured them. She returned to her chair.

"What do we do now?" the Colonel asked.

The MP was explicit. "One: relegate the bullion, two: find and detain that agent. Does 'deflect' mean what I suspect it does?" No one answered. "What assets do we have in Malaysia?"

The Colonel was apparently preoccupied with Scott's summary.

"I am sure we have none in mainland Malaysia. I'll check Borneo and Hong Kong." Scott continued, "There's a Ghurkha battalion in Borneo; they always have a standby platoon."

The MP was ready to speak again. "Then, get them there; make all necessary arrangements with the Malaysian Government.

If necessary, hire, or commandeer, air transport and, critically, fully brief the officer leading the platoon. They travel with their personal weapons? Agreed?"

He stood up, reached for his attaché case and placed the folders inside. "I have to report."

Everybody knew to whom he was going to report. The MP turned around, with an afterthought, and stared at Scott and Michael. "If your theory is correct, and there are damaging, or incriminating, items recovered, the political due process will take place. If, on the other hand, this or these documents fall into, shall we say the 'wrong hands', then..." He did not complete the sentence. The threat was unspoken, yet explicit. He nodded vaguely at those present, and left the room.

Michael leant over, his voice a whisper. "Scott, what exactly is his game? He twists and turns like some demented rat caught in a trap."

Scott gathered up his papers, tapped them into a tidy block and slid them into his folder. "I don't know, but my guess is he's backed the wrong horse."

"Is it a loser?"

"Possibly, but, more to the point, have we backed the winner?"

They moved up to the Colonel. "We have some organising to do, sir. Shall we start?"

The Ministry of Defence in Westminster instigated several urgent phone and fax messages, as did the Foreign and Commonwealth Office. Computers were soon in action. Six thousand miles away, three former British soldiers, a deserter from the Malayan All Races Liberation Army, and a one-time American Marine Pilot were ready to converge on a point in the jungle of Negri Sembilan. Further east, a hastily roused platoon of the Ghurkha Rifles were drawing their self-loading weapons and preparing to leave barracks.

Meanwhile, on the east coast of America, a Brigadier General in the United States Air Force was desperately trying to contact a presidential aide in the White House.

Eighteen

Negri Sembilan

First light, Saturday 2 October 1982

Swee Poe made good time, once out of Kuala Lumpur. He turned left off the main road and carefully drove along the deserted track, turned right and edged up to what looked like an abandoned tappers' station, a place where the workers had gathered when the rains thundered down. It was dilapidated, dirty and obviously long out of use. He switched off the sidelights, got out, locked the doors and advanced some fifty yards, finally settling apprehensively behind a rubber tree, easing himself in as comfortably as possible. He was, without doubt, a frightened man, and he neither saw nor heard a figure rise up from a squatting position and effortlessly slip back into the darkness, a bare forty feet behind him and out to his right. Both men sat mute and waited.

The Brits had been delayed. The night clerk had asked to see their passports and had disappeared into the back office. Fifteen minutes later, no clerk, no passports and all three were on edge.

"I think we've got trouble," said Hughes curtly. "Let's leave the passports and go." They filed out of the hotel and started their vehicle, just in time to see the clerk waddling at some speed in the direction of the dimly-lit police station. The clerk had tried to phone the police but, receiving no reply, guessed, quite rightly, that the duty officer was asleep.

No one spoke as the car, driven by Hughes, flew down the tar macadam road. It wasn't his Jaguar, but he handled bends, corners and the straights as if it were. Tucker's hand signal was explicit.

"We're here. Turn left," he insisted. Hughes slowed the car. "We're nearly there. Look that tree," added Tucker. In the rapidly growing light, a slash mark showed through the bark.

"Go further on. Drive into the estate." Griffiths' voice was strained.

In silence, they drove on. Hughes did a neat three-point turn and reversed the car further back into the trees.

"We wait until its light. We'll stand-to outside." The use of army language seemed entirely appropriate.

"Bring back memories?" teased Hughes. Griff and Tucker nodded. "The worst by far about stand-to was putting on trousers and jacket soaking wet from the day before," admitted Hughes. "Dry, clean clothes to sleep in, back into jungle greens for the day ahead."

Tucker grimaced. "At home, my mother used to put any shirts of mine that she'd just washed and ironed against the mirror. If there was any condensation on the glass, she'd iron them again. Happy days."

Hughes was standing at the offside door. "Were either of you afraid of going into the jungle?"

Griffiths was tucking his trousers into his socks. "I was bloody terrified. What about you, Geth?"

"Yes, so was , in the beginning. Frightened physically, and more frightened that I'd make a cock-up," confessed Hughes.

Tucker laughed, "That's a new one, an officer frightened. I never heard of that one before. I thought the Officers' Mess was a branch office of Hollywood," and they all smiled.

"Saw no sign of our Chinaman, if it was him, or that car we saw parked yesterday," Griffiths said.

"I've thought about that." remarked Hughes, suddenly serious. "Tuck, you stop here – say, for fifteen, twenty minutes. If he, or anybody, follows us, come in after him. You never know, he might have Griff's Bren gun. That okay?"

Tucker nodded. "It makes sense. If he does have a gun, I'll wish I had Griff's Bren, not this oversized carving knife." He held his Parang in his hand.

"Give it ten more minutes, Griff," suggested Hughes. We go in, load up with an ingot each, and that box, whatever it is, then out, back to Seremban, the cop shop and probably a phone call to the British Embassy. We might need extricating from here."

Griffiths nodded. "Our passports, that bloody clerk, they're probably onto us by now. I'm expecting the Fraud Squad, the Flying Squad and the Serious Crimes Squad to arrive at any minute!"

Tucker was chuckling, "Well, at least it won't be the Vice Squad!"

They waited, the final traces of darkness making a swift retreat.

"Okay, let's go!"

Gethin Hughes and Griffiths moved off, seven paces apart, parangs at the ready; both felt and looked like soldiers. Tucker watched them go and glanced at his watch. Twenty minutes, that should get them to the plane. He stood, a lone figure amongst the silent rows of trees, but he was not afraid as he unsheathed his parang.

Swee Poe peered out from behind the tree. The movement of something a hundred yards to his right caught his eye. Men, two of them – even at that distance he recognised them – were moving straight ahead. No nervous, cautious, faltering steps: they moved as soldiers. In that instant, Swee Poe felt admiration for them and an overwhelming urge to run and join them, to blurt out, "Let me come with you; we can share the gold." The insanity of it came as a hard blow to his chest, when reality kicked in. He rose and, keeping his eyes firmly fixed on the moving figures, in a crouching run, he closed on the two men, curious about why there were only two? Where was the third man? He realised he didn't care. Soon, he would see again what he had first glimpsed twenty-five years ago, and what he had thought of constantly ever since. The two men were leaving the rubber and entering the jungle. Swee Poe's eyes took in the swaying, ever-moving foliage. He paused, withdrew his automatic and followed into the greenness.

Spano made no move or sound as the figure of Swee Poe passed him. His eyes, too, had seen the figures moving purposefully through the rubber. He stood up and silently followed, wondering about the man in front of him. He was obviously Asian. His briefing had mentioned a Chinaman. That he was not with the other two was obvious. The briefing had also said three ex-Brit soldiers, so where was the third? The first two had disappeared into the jungle. Spano saw the Chinese stop, withdraw a gun from his waistband and then, step forward, until he, too, was swallowed up by the mass of undergrowth. Spano heard a sound that stopped him dead, the unmistakable fluttering of rotor blades: helicopters, and more than one. He eased the Colt into his hand, aware of its coldness, and ran towards the jungle entry point. The helicopters were very close, and as he stepped under the green canopy, they passed overhead and went on their way, the noise diminishing by the second. To someone who had passed a jungle-training course, the trail ran straight and true: broken reeds, branches still quivering after human contact, the jungle floor heavy with footprints.

Tucker was just about to follow Hughes and Griffiths, when he saw a figure loping towards him. He froze behind a rubber tree as a man passed, no more than thirty feet in front, Gripping his Parang, Tucker made to move, but froze again. There was another figure, still and poised, watching the Chinese. Tucker saw the man's hand move to his ankle, and suddenly, he held a gun in his right hand. Tucker's thoughts at that moment were not religious, or righteous. Griff was right; they should have had a Bren. The man had moved, weaving between the regimented rows of rubber trees. Tucker immediately recognised someone who had had military training. This man was a professional; the first one was an amateur, and a frightened one at that. He waited until the second man had passed, before he stepped out. He did not know what was going to happen as he followed; he only knew that he needed the Lord's help with his task, and he needed it now. The man had walked unhesitatingly into the jungle's edge. Thirty-five seconds later, Tucker followed him.

The noise of the helicopters was loud and distracting. Not for the first time, Tucker had doubts about the outcome of the unfolding events. Hughes and Griff were in serious trouble, followed by two men, both armed. Instinctively, he ran, crouching, into the fetid mass in front of him.

Gethin Hughes was struggling with the swirl of emotion in his head; he was sweating furiously from the exertion and humidity, the beads of moisture running into his eyes. He blinked and moved the sweat-rag down over his forehead. He paused and turned to face Griff. His colleague's face was taut, his eyes wide, the left-hand moving to his lips.

"Someone's coming." The words were soundless but unmistakable. Hughes mouthed back, "Tuck?"

Griffiths shook his head, "Too soon. Move." The silent

conversation was terminated. He put both arms out and, swung them wide, in a swimming motion. Hughes immediately moved to his right, stepping back into the soft greenery as Griffiths went in the opposite direction. As if by telepathy, both men crouched down, each like a tiger, stalking and waiting to pounce on some unsuspecting prey.

Swee Poe was not certain, not certain at all, how it had happened. One second, he was following noises, the leaves and bushes still swaying, the sound of a parang as it cleared a pathway, and then nothing – no sounds, no movement, just a stillness – the only sounds coming from the jungle itself. He was close to panic, realising that the gun in his hand was of no earthly use in this cloying, choking wilderness. Both Hughes and Griffiths saw the figure pass them. They were close enough to smell his warm flesh, almost close enough to stretch out and touch him. Both noticed the gun in his right hand, they also registered the fear that was evident in his eyes. Griffiths stepped out in a bounding leap, his right-hand clamped on Swee Poe's wrist. Hughes saw the flash of movement and sprung from his hiding place. Swee Poe caught sight of the raised Parang and he screamed the scream of the desperate.

"No!" He shielded his face, "No! No!" The grip on his wrist was frightening in its brutality, the face in front of him contorted with rage.

"Who the fuck are you?" yelled Hughes.

"I came for the gold, only the gold; please don't kill me, please." He realised that he was crying, his chest heaving with the sobs.

Griffiths wrenched the weapon from Swee Poe's paralysed hand.

"I've got it!" He waved the weapon at Hughes for what seemed minutes, but in truth it was only seconds. The three men stood locked in a surreal posture.

When Hughes spoke, his words were calm; his face had lost its rage. "We're not going to kill you. Who are you and how do you know about the gold?"

The pounding in Swee Poe's chest was increasing, his voice still punctuated by sobs. "I found it... by accident... twenty-five years ago. Please, please don't kill me."

There was impatience in Hughes' voice. "I've told you, we're not going to kill you. How did you find it, twenty-five years ago?"

"I was in the Communist terrorist unit that engaged with your patrol. I was the fourth man. It all happened so quickly. I ran away. I found the plane by accident. I had no idea what to do, where to run. I just wanted to get away from the shooting and that's the truth." Swee Poe felt completely and utterly drained and was close to collapse.

Griffiths nudged Swee Poe forward.

"He's had it, Geth. He's no danger. Let's get on."

Hughes nodded in agreement. "Come with us. You'll see the gold, but that's all. It's not ours and it's certainly not yours. What's your name?"

Swee Poe found himself replying, "Elvis..."

"What?" both men stared in stark disbelief.

"It's true. I was given a passport after I surrendered. I could pick any name I wanted to, so I chose Raymond Elvis Lee." The absurdity of the situation made both men laugh outright. "What are your names?" asked Swee Poe apprehensively.

Griffiths grinning widely, and unable to check his laughter, and replied, "I'm Frank Sinatra, he's Dean Martin, and our mate who's following us is Perry Como. Bloody hell, I think I'm dreaming. Middle of the jungle and a Chinaman tells us he's Elvis!"

Swee Poe caught the humour in Griffith's face and voice and, as if a cloud of blackness had lifted over him, realised he was safe with these men in the jungle that terrified him, and he would come to no harm. He hurriedly asked, "You won't kill me, will you?"

Gethin Hughes shook his head. "We were soldiers, not butchers. Come on, Elvis, let's go to our plane. I want to get out of here. Griff, we'll pick up an ingot each and that box, wait for Tuck and hightail it back to the car." He turned to Swee Poe. "Follow me, Elvis, and don't make any noise."

With his heart rate now approaching a normal beat, Swee Poe followed.

The plane lay almost at an angle of forty-five degrees to the vertical; stripped undergrowth littered the trampled clearing. With parangs drawn, Hughes and Griffiths approached cautiously from separate directions. Any large stones or felled trees were the favourite haunts of snakes. At the wreck, Gethin's torch swept the darkness of the fuselage, revealing no reptiles. Carefully, both men lifted out an ingot, then, with a long, sturdy branch, poked and scuffed at a large oblong box. It gave a hollow sound as the stick gradually dragged the box closer to them. It snagged on several of the gleaming, smooth gold bricks. Griffiths leaned in, removed four of the ingots and laid them carefully on the ground, then, he grabbed the dispatch box, which, to his surprise had a plastic feel.

"Did they have plastic in those days?" he asked. Hughes arched his eyebrows, the uncertainty evident. Griffiths shook the oblong box with its snap-fit cover and a metal strip that secured it. "Pilot's, do you reckon?"

Hughes again shook his head. "Don't know; better bring it with us." There was a barely audible sound behind them and

204

Griffiths smiled at Swee Poe. "Well, Elvis, here comes Perry Como." They turned to face Tucker... only it wasn't Tucker.

David Spano seemed to glide into the clearing, the Colt automatic held, textbook fashion, in his outstretched hands. For several very long seconds there was complete silence, broken only by Hughes. "Who the bloody hell are you?"

Spano gave no answer, his eyes scrutinising the men in front of him. "You're former British soldiers – you two." The Colt pointed first Hughes, then Griffiths. "Who's he?"

Griffiths found himself answering, forcing some credulity into a voice that seemed for the moment not to belong to him. "He's a friend, from way back – twenty-five years, actually. More importantly, you've not answered our question. I'll put it to you again. Just who are you?" His right hand was easing its way into his trouser pocket, fingers gently seeking the gun he'd confiscated from Swee Poe.

Spano indicated to the gold. "Not that, it doesn't interest me, but I do want *that*," and he flipped the Colt towards the box. Hughes expelled a long breath, his voice composed. "Tell us who you are, or we give you nothing."

Spano took two paces forward. "I could kill all three of you and take what I wanted. I've killed before; it wouldn't bother me."

Griffith's fingers slid around the butt of the gun. He was very frightened as he moved to his right imperceptibly, trying to shield his hand withdrawing the weapon.

"You could kill us," said Hughes, "but you must have heard the choppers. There are people looking for us. Shoot and they'll pinpoint your position. And, for your benefit, Yank, we've killed as well."

Spano removed his left hand from the Colt and reached up

slowly to his breast pocket. With a flourish, he produced an ID card, complete with photograph and the words – FIELD AGENT DAVID SPANO – CENTRAL INTELLIGENCE AGENCY. "David Spano, CIA." In a flawed, British upper crust accent, he continued theatrically, "At your service, gentlemen." He smiled. "We're on the same side. All I want is that. I have my orders, and it's an American plane."

Hughes spoke slowly. "Are you related to him?" He jerked his head to the plane.

Spano took another pace forward, his gun level with Gethin's chest. "What do you mean?"

"The pilot, his name was Spano."

The American's eyes widened with disbelief. "How do you know?" he demanded.

Hughes placed his left hand palm outwards. "Easy, take it easy. I've got his dog tags." He produced the metal disc from his pocket and read it aloud: "J. Spano, RC USMC," and held it out.

"Give it to me," Spano reached out and took it, and the muzzle of his gun dipped.

Griffiths and Hughes moved as one; their bodies cannoned into the American. Griffiths found himself screaming, "Drop the gun, drop the gun," as his automatic sank into the throat of the violently struggling Spano. But he felt himself being turned over and in a move born out of desperation he pulled his weapon free and fired. The noise was deafening, the flash near blinding. Spano froze as Griffiths pointed the weapon towards his face.

"The next one blows your brains out!"

Spano's immediate reaction was to snarl and grab for the weapon in Griffith's hand, but just at that moment, Tucker entered the clearing and he brought his Parang down on the

American's skull, the heavy wooden handle thudding into Spano's head. He collapsed on his side, his right hand falling across Griffiths' legs. Hughes was gasping for breath; the struggle had taken virtually all of his strength. His words rasping, coming in spurts, he urged, "Get his gun, Tuck. Search him for weapons. Are you alright, Griff?"

Griffiths scrambled to his feet. "I think so. I don't know who taught him to fight, but he's a tough bastard."

Tucker was more pragmatic. "Is he dead?" As if in answer, Spano groaned and his eyelids flickered.

"Sit up, if you can." Hughes held the Colt. "Now that the boots on the other foot, tell me, just who *are* you?"

Spano eased himself up into a sitting position. "I am who I say I am, and that plane there was my father's. He was posted 'Missing in Action' in 1941. I have orders to obey, just like you had, when you were in the British Army. I was told to recover anything in the plane other than the bullion. That's why I asked for the dispatch box. Is there anything else there?"

"Not as far as we know. Is the box your father's property?"

Spano took a long time to answer. "I don't know. I hope it is. In fact, I pray it is. I never knew him. I was a very young child when he went away." His voice faded as he placed both hands on his head, his voice muffled. "Who hit me?"

Tucker raised his hand and Hughes nodded, "Just as well he did; we were losing the fight. Look, Spano, that plane is a war grave. It's pilot is still inside, but the pilot was your father, so, as far as I'm concerned, if you want the box, then take it. That okay by you two?"

Both men agreed. "Let him have it."

"Okay, here it is. Let's go, Elvis. Let's go," said Hughes. There was no reply – no Elvis. "He's gone. He's done a runner, the daft sod. He'll never find his way out on his own."

Griffiths shrugged. "Well, that's Elvis's problem. Let's go."

Hughes held up his hand. "Those helicopters are almost certainly looking for us. On reflection, it might not be a good idea to take a gold bar each. We could be charged with stealing, so we'll take just the one. I'll take responsibility for it, okay?" He received affirmative nods.

Spano stood up and accepted the dispatch case. "Can you just wait a few seconds?" he asked and walked over to the smashed cockpit. He looked inside, paused for a long moment, stepped back and saluted, turned on his heel and rejoined the men. Without a word, he just nodded, and they filed out of the clearing.

It had taken just twenty minutes to step out from the jungle into the rubber. They were only marginally surprised when ghost-like shapes rose out of the ground all around them. They saw the olive faces, and self-loading rifles with fixed bayonets. The Ghurkhas, impeccably trained, had laid a classic ambush.

The officer's voice was clear, unambiguous. "Stand still. Do not move. I repeat, do not move." Someone was coming straight for them: mid-twenties, white and armed with a Browning automatic pistol. "Put that object down." His words were addressed to Spano. The American made no movement. The officer stood six paces from the little group, snapped out a sharp word of command, and two of the Ghurkha riflemen raised their weapons and pointed them at Spano. "Put the case down, or I'll kill you." The words were softly spoken and they seemed to hang in the air over the little group.

Gethin Hughes interjected. "The plane, it was piloted by his father; he can rightfully claim that the case is his."

The officer's reply was exacting, "He cannot. I have my orders, very specific orders. The case is the property of Her

Britannic Majesty's Government."

Spano looked at the Browning held rock steady and the two inscrutable Nepalese faces and recognised defeat. He slowly placed the case at his feet, turned to Hughes and said simply, "Thanks."

One of the riflemen moved dart-like and picked up the case.

"Give that to the corporal," offered Hughes and he handed over the gleaming bar.

"This way." The Ghurkhas closed around them. One hour and twenty minutes later, they were put in separate cells in the Seremban police station.

It had not been a good day. Police and civilians wandered in and out of the station. There was constant activity and, at noon, they were offered tea and fried rice but none of them had any appetite. There was a glimpse of the American agent, Spano, as he was brought out of his cell. Four other men stood around him; one was chain-smoking; they all had American accents. There was a burst of loud conversation between the chain-smoker and a police superintendent and, with some surprise, they saw the policeman turn to a large safe, unlock it and withdraw a weapon. It was the Colt. Spano scribbled a signature, moved towards the door, paused, turned and saluted his imprisoned assailants. Then, he was gone out into the sunshine and freedom.

Shortly afterwards, a police constable approached, his many keys jangling. Unsmiling and silent, he unlocked each cell and indicated to the three men to step outside. Two civilians approached them. If they had a sign that said, 'BRITISH' they could not have been more transparent.

"Are you well?" Without waiting for an answer, the spokesman continued, "We'd like a word with you."

Outside stood three cars, their engines idling. "One in each, please."

Each car had an escort and a driver, but the journey to Kuala Lumpur was undertaken in total silence. They were driven to what looked like a deserted school, where they were offered a cold drink, which was accepted. The questioning was exhaustive; minor remarks and details endlessly re-worked and discussed. Their replies were virtually identical when they were asked about the terrorist contact twenty-five years ago: Gethin Hughes's amnesia, his operation, his total recall of those events, the decision to return to Malaya. The emphasis was on the fact that the bullion was not their concern, the trip was just a way for Hughes to defeat his demons. They were friends, mates, they came out of loyalty to one another. If they really were gold looters, why had they retrieved only one ingot?

Eventually, they were served with food and then escorted back to their hotel.

"Enjoy a drink at the bar, but do not, repeat do not, set foot on the streets of Kuala Lumpur."

They were happy to oblige.

Nineteen

London

11 a.m., Monday 4 October 1982

Via separate doors, the two men entered the room. They moved towards the table and formally laid out chairs, and Scott sat down. He placed his folder on the shiny table-top.

"You could shave in this," he commented, his reflection perfectly mirrored in the gleaming surface.

Michael eased himself into the chair beside him. "Well, today's the day, 'D Day', so to speak. What time do our errant fusiliers arrive back?"

Scott glanced at his wristwatch. "They're back; they landed at Heathrow at 9 o'clock. Allowing for customs, they and our Ghurkha officer friend should be here in about thirty minutes."

"Do you know the gory details yet?" Michael asked. His voice sounded edgy, the uncertainty evident.

"I do. I'm struggling to remember forty-eight hours of such intense phone, fax and radio traffic. The cipher clerks have had a real pasting. MI6, the CIA and we have had an exchange of opinions, as I like to call it."

"You mean, sorting out who's going to take the blame, if there is blame?"

"Correct. We'll know in thirty minutes or so. You know that a box, dispatch case – call it what you may - was found?"

"I do." Michael leant forward. "It was found, recovered and is now on its way here – not destroyed, as 'Laughing Boy' wanted."

"Was that down to you?" Scott had wondered about that, once the reports had started to come in.

"Yes." Michael gave what could be accurately described as a Gallic shrug. "When that box is opened, my friends in high places, very high, some of them, we - that is Her Britannic Majesty's Government – will finally have the answer to what has frightened seven bells out of successive Prime Ministers. If you…" He corrected himself, "If we are right, all well and good. If not, considering the expense, diplomatic overdrive, not to say embroiling our American cousins in some exceptionally murky activities, then, at best, the rest of our employed lives will be as paper clip and typing paper procurers!"

Scott stretched out his legs. He'd quit smoking several years ago, but would have given £20 for a small cigar, there and then. He added, "Spano was not what he seemed to be."

Michael leant forward again, "What happened about him?"

Scott was quietly undoing the sealing strings on his folder. "There are something like fifteen agencies in America, apart from the CIA and the FBI. Like us, they rarely share information. Spano was a field agent of the CIA, a legitimate member, but, unbeknown to the CIA, he was an active operative in one of the considerably more shadowy outfits: the 'Twenty Executive'. It's something the Americans borrowed or stole, use whatever word you like, from us. The name is self-explanatory. Twenty in Roman numerals is two crosses; i.e. double-cross. He was, to be blunt, embedded into the CIA. His real task was to infiltrate and extract information from the Soviets, KGB and Starsi. My man in Langley says he did just that. He obtained some information about the M-14 Hind, the main Soviet attack helicopter. He was lucky. The CIA were going to take him out, to use their delightful phrase, but someone, a Brigadier General in the US Air Force, managed to relay a message via Washington. It was, 'Hands off. Do not use extreme force'. Spano's a very lucky man. My little mole says another ten minutes and our Ghurkha friend would have 'deflected' him. It turns out that the pilot of the plane was his father. There can't be too many men who finally find their fathers' graves after forty years."

"What will happen to him?"

"No idea. That's up to the Americans. Spies trade secrets when it suits them," continued Scott, "and we're no different from the Americans, Russians and Israelis. No doubt, the Americans will tell the Soviets that one of their agents has been gullible: sort of a penalty try."

Michael smiled. "You'll be learning the rugby ethos; you'll fall in love with the game. I can see you at Twickenham yet!"

There was a loud knock on one of the doors and Mrs Mann entered, pushing a trolley on which she had a note-pad and tape recorder.

"Sir Garfield will be along directly, gentlemen," she said, and busied herself with plugging in the recorder and positioning the microphone.

Scott lowered his voice. "There is one thing: the manifest for the plane recorded one hundred and forty gold ingots, the bars weighing exactly fourteen pounds each, giving a total of 1,960 pounds; very, very close to maximum take-off weight. This could only have been achieved by forfeiting the ordnance, machine-gun, ammunition and crew man, and with fuel tanks half full on take-off, just enough for the trip from Seletar to Palembang, with a little to spare. Anyway, back to the gold; only one hundred and thirty-eight bars have been recovered.

Twenty-eight pounds of pure gold is missing, unaccounted for. Finance is going ballistic. The three fusiliers have repeatedly denied any involvement, and, not unnaturally, they told our people to piss up their legs and play with the steam, or something very similar. They maintain they haven't got any of the bullion and, furthermore, if it wasn't for them, none of the yellow stuff would have been found at all!"

"Well," Michael interjected, "that's true. By and large, they made us look amateurs. Three men, past their prime, and what do they do? One: they gave us the slip and we took ages to find them; two: they knew exactly where to find the plane and managed successfully to set us on a dead-end course. Regardless of this outcome, there will be some hard questions to answer."

Scott merely nodded and said, "So be it."

Sir Garfield made an unobtrusive entrance. He ushered in a man in his mid-twenties, by his bearing, a soldier. "Put it on the table, please".

The soldier placed a large case before them.

"You may leave now."

The soldier closed the door behind him. Sir Garfield polished his glasses.

"That was a lieutenant from the Royal Ghurkha Rifles. He was in charge of the platoon that 'apprehended' the party in Negri Sembilan. He escorted, with his entire platoon, I may add, the object you now see in front of you, from Kuala Lumpur to Heathrow and thence to here. A British Airway's flight was diverted from its normal route over the Middle East, including Pakistan and Afghanistan. Instead, it flew over the Indian Ocean and then north over Africa. Armoured cars and light tanks from the Household Division were at Heathrow to meet the flight. The press were told it was an exercise. Any questions? No? Then, gentlemen, I suggest we get on with it."

"Where are the three ex-soldiers?" Michael's voice was in no way deferential.

"Officially, helping the authorities with their enquiries, but in reality, they are having breakfast in the private staff canteen. We believe their version of events. It all checks out. As for the missing bullion, I don't know, but, perhaps, in 1941, somebody couldn't count. What does count is what's in there." Sir Garfield pointed his spectacle case at the box.

The bakelite container was surprisingly hard to break into. "It's been x-rayed," Sir Garfield offered, as Scott wrestled with the holding bands. It had occurred to him to wonder whether the case had been booby-trapped.

"Where was this?"

"In Kuala Lumpur. We couldn't have taken it on the plane, otherwise." Sir Garfield had taken his pipe out of his pocket, and the tobacco tin came next. "Give it a clout," he suggested impatiently, then, to everyone's surprise, he took off his size nine, patent leather shoe, highly polished by his valet, and thwacked the fastenings hard. Scott and Michael exchanged glances, but the bakelite remained intact. "Mrs Mann, ring down to maintenance and have them send up a man with a hammer and chisel," said Sir Garfield, somewhat frustrated at the situation.

★ ★ ★

The private dining-room was a wood-panelled bastion of good food, and cheerful quietness. The three friends had enjoyed bacon, scrambled eggs, sausage, mushrooms, toast and real coffee.

"That tasted good," said Griffiths, as he used his napkin to wipe his mouth. "What happens next?"

Tucker was looking at Gethin Hughes when he said, "I hope that wasn't the condemned man's last meal."

Gethin shook his head. "Not at all. We will probably be visited by more spooks, and civil servants tying up loose ends, but that's it. We should be on the 5.55 from Euston."

"What were all those questions about the two ingots of gold going missing? And why did the Ghurkha take the case off Spano?" asked Tucker expectantly.

"I don't know about the gold, but I'd bet a fiver, if it has disappeared, Elvis took it. And as for the case... that Ghurkha meant business."

"Would he have shot Spano?"

Griffiths pushed his plate away. "Without a doubt. Whatever is in that thing, I hope it was worth it."

"Your transport is waiting, gentlemen, to run you to Euston," said a smiling civil servant, who had been hovering in the background. They filed out past him and Gethin returned his smile and said, "If there is a reward, you know where to find us."

"We do now," the civil servant replied, somewhat sarcastically.

★ ★ ★

The barman was unenthusiastically polishing a glass. The man coming towards him looked weary, his only luggage two tourist carrier bags, but very heavy bags, to judge by the strain on his face. The barman's eyes asked the questions; his lips stayed closed.

"I've had trouble parking. Closest I can get to here is three hundred yards." The man breathed heavily as he took out a wallet and laid a $50 Singapore note on the bar. "A Chivas

Regal. Oh, make that a double, and one for yourself. Today, I've earned it."

"Certainly, sir, thank you. Are you requiring accommodation? This hotel is one of the finest in Singapore, only built two years ago."

"I know it wasn't here when I was last in Singapore."

The barman noticed the visitor's fat wallet, commenting to himself that that was the trouble with the world today: the wealthy looked just like everybody else. He registered the drinks at the till and slid the money for his drink out of the change.

"No, I do not require a room, but you can order a taxi for me. There's some business I have to attend to. I'll leave the car where it is and come back for it later." The whisky tasted so smooth. "I'll have another – a double. Keep the change but don't forget my taxi."

He declined the taxi driver's eager offer to carry his bags, preferring to struggle back to the foyer with them.

"You just come from Penang, sir?" The driver nodded at the bag's logo – 'Penang the Golden Island'.

"No," the man answered, "I bought that years ago. Now, my man, take me to Singapore International – Terminal Two – Swiss Air reception desk."

The driver, sensing a large tip, gave a wide grin. "Yes, sir."

He wasn't disappointed.

★ ★ ★

There was a business-like knock at the door, and a man wearing an old-fashioned bib and braces overalls and carrying a neat, green canvas holdall, entered the room and headed for the despatch case.

"Leave the tools, they'll be returned to you" he was told.

"Shall I be mother?" suggested Michael, as he rose from his chair.

Sir Garfield grunted approval and requested the return of his shoe. Michael slid it across the carpet and Sir Garfield put it back on his foot.

The case did not surrender itself easily; the brass band holding the two halves was ten gauge and tough. It broke only after repeated crushing by a large pair of heavy duty metal-cutters. There was complete silence in the room because, despite strenuous efforts to part them, the two sections remained stubbornly wedded to each other. Michael brought the claw hammer down hard on the protective shell, but there was no sign of it cracking.

"Wait a minute!" Sir Garfield said, and held out his glasses. "Put these on. They'll protect your eyes if it shatters."

Michael gladly accepted. He gave another, much harder, blow, resulting in a splintering crack. He struck again and a spray of tiny plastic pieces flew around his head. One further blow and the case finally split open. As gently as he could, Michael broke away the remaining pieces, revealing the contents within. With help from Scott, several typewritten sheets, some printed pages and sealed dockets were carefully removed. All the papers were collected and counted; there were fourteen in total. There were, in addition, seven thick, sealed dockets and three letters, all addressed to senior generals who had served in the British Army during the Second World War and immediately afterwards. Sir Garfield was sitting at the head of the table – poised would have been a better word - his back straight, his erect figure strangely imposing, but without his glasses his face looked younger.

"Gentlemen, please continue," he instructed. "Let us investigate our finds."

Scott took the first page, noticing immediately that the paper was of a very good quality, the typing not so. He read from it slowly, taking care when handling the sheet. When he had finished reading, he passed each page to Michael, who also read every one equally painstakingly, and Mrs Mann was asked to place them in front of Sir Garfield. He also read each one, on three occasions returning to a page he had perused already, as if checking anew, and then he laid them down again. When Sir Garfield looked up, Scott's eyes went to the unopened dockets and envelopes. Sir Garfield shook his head.

"We'll deal with those later. What are your deductions about what you have just read?"

Michael said to Scott, "It's your ball, go for the line."

"Before I start, sir, may I give a potted version of military doctrine? Every army that has ever existed has been haunted, terrified in most cases, by the fear of being led into a trap, when plunging headlong after an apparently beaten enemy in a shambling rout of retreat. Every commander of every army has had to face the consequence of over-extending his forces in order to capture that military cup of gold: a quick, decisive, victory. Many generals have seen that cup snatched from their fingers, many millions of their soldiers have died because of that dream. Some historians believe that the Germans actually lost the war on 24 May 1940. As the German Panzers and the Wehrmacht swept all before them, Belgian, French and British soldiers retreated for their lives. The British staged a counter-attack at Arras, and this caused extreme consternation and outright panic at German High Command. Rommel, no less, halted his Panzer division and others for forty-eight hours. This limited counter-attack by a small Allied force convinced Hitler and his minions, at least for a merciful two days that more powerful French and British forces were poised to encircle his over-extended German Army. The German delay caused by this mistaken belief saved umpteen thousands of British and French troops. Incidentally, if the British Expeditionary Force had not been lifted from the beaches at Dunkirk, without a doubt and notwithstanding the Battle of Britain in the air, we should have been unable to resist a German invasion of these shores. The regular British Army was to have been evacuated to Canada, the conscripts told to return to their homes and," Scott cleared his throat, "we would not be sitting here now."

He pointed to the papers in front of Sir Garfield. "Those papers reveal that massive reinforcements of soldiers, trained men, the Australian 9th Division, the New Zealand Second Division, the Fourth Indian Division, all crack infantry fighting in North Africa, would be shipped to the Andaman Islands and ordered to invade Thailand. The much vaunted 'Operation Matador' was intended to cut off the Japanese forces in Malaya. Also, a huge deployment of Royal Navy capital ships would sweep down from East Africa and Ceylon – these papers refer to aircraft carriers such as *Victorious, Formidable, Implacable*; battleship *King George V,* and the battle-cruiser *Renown,* as well as three cruiser squadrons, over seventy destroyers, and sixteen submarines. The carriers would ferry Hurricanes and Spitfires for the air cover needed to hold, drive back and defeat the Japanese forces.

"The Japanese were very wary of the few existing Hurricanes operating out of Singapore. They were infinitely more dangerous than the Brewster Buffalo. The dispatches ask for the resistance to the Japanese to last for a maximum of one hundred days. Then, like some avenging angel, the full might of the British Empire would descend on Japan. On page nine, the War Office directive is quite clear. It says, '*Continue to give ground to the Japanese – retreat to Singapore – let the Japanese divisions over-extend themselves. Once in Singapore, stiffen resistance and await reinforcements*'. Page ten is the crunch page. It lists the removal, on Stalin's orders, of the entire Soviet armies from the Russian eastern borders, borders violently disputed with Japan over recent years. In April 1941, Japan and

Russia signed a neutrality pact. The German's attack on Russia in 'Operation Barbarossa', in June 1941, was a massive surprise to the Japanese, as it was to the Russians. For that reason, Japan omitted to inform Nazi Germany of her plans to attack America at Pearl Harbour. The Russians were caught catastrophically off guard by the German Panzer offensive, and lost troops on a gigantic scale. On 7th October 1941, a whole Soviet Army was caught. Six hundred and sixty thousand Russian soldiers were captured, and thousands of guns and artillery pieces and over one thousand Soviet tanks passed into a brutal and, for many thousands of Russian men, a deadly captivity."

Scott cleared his throat. Sir Garfield signalled to Scott to stop his exegesis.

"The sun's over the yardarm. Who's for a drink?"

Michael and Scott were in favour. A bell was rung and, just a minute later, there was a knock at the door, a drinks' cabinet was wheeled silently across the pine-block floor, and the doors of the drinks cabinet were opened with a minor flourish.

"Help yourselves. Mine's a gin and tonic, a large one, and please don't drown it!"

Michael served Sir Garfield's drink and poured gin and tonics for himself and Scott. It tasted marvellous.

"Carry on," said Sir Garfield.

"The next day, 8th October, another six hundred and fifty thousand Soviet soldiers were isolated, and whole armies went into captivity together, again with many thousands of tanks and guns. Stalin appointed a new general, Zhukov, who told Stalin that he needed one hundred divisions and two hundred of the new and highly impressive T34 tanks, to hold onto Moscow and stay in the war,. Stalin had a spy in Tokyo, the correspondent of the *Frankfurter Allgemeine* newspaper, a man called Doctor Richard Sorge, a German national, who was also a dedicated

Communist. Sorge established that Japan would not renege on the non-aggression pact, at least, not for several months. Stalin, armed with that information, stripped the Far East Russian border of all defences, artillery, armour and infantry, leaving a skeleton force in the garrisons along the borders with China, Siberia and Mongolia. So far, we've had dispatches that are upbeat, highly optimistic and, frankly, to British insiders, completely unrealistic. The War Cabinet would never have sanctioned the removal of crack divisions from North Africa. The battleships were essential to patrol home waters, to counter the threat of the *Tirpitz*, *Prinz Eugen* and other very powerful surface raiders. Every destroyer the Royal Navy could lay its hands on was deployed on convoy escort duty in the Battle of the Atlantic. Some of the aircraft carriers were not even in commission in 1941. I have to say," continued Scott, "it is the last four pages that are critical; they emphasise the complete absence of Russian defences in the Far East, the vulnerability of the Russian ports pinpointing possible landing areas for a sea borne invasion. The papers point out that, if the Japanese did invade the Soviet Union, no reinforcements could be sent to stiffen Russian resistance. All of the Allied military might would be needed to defeat and then mop up the Japanese in Malaya. In essence, the War Cabinet papers are a transparent attempt to divert Japanese offensive action away from Malaya and Singapore, and point their military ambition in another direction – Russia. Russia, at that time, was in a life or death struggle with Germany, and an ally of Britain and America. It would be regarded as one of the most cynical acts of treachery ever seen."

Scott paused. Sir Garfield was looking straight at him. Mrs Mann had her face lowered, eyes on the shorthand pad, the tape recorder emitting a quiet hiss. The room seemed unusually cool, bordering on cold. Sir Garfield took a tentative sip of his gin and tonic.

"Please continue."

Scott, ignoring his drink with some reluctance, continued his analysis.

"In 1941, the British war effort was finally getting up some steam, and many British Trade Unions were Communist led and Communist dominated. Can you imagine the complete, volcanic response if the content of these papers had been released by the Japanese? Britain, prepared to stab Russia in the back, all to save a bastion of the British Empire! What would the United States of America's reaction be? They distrusted Britain's Empire-building ambitions, anyway, as much as the Russians. What if they had cut off economic and military aid to Britain, retreated back into fortress America, and had opted to prosecute the war solely against the Japanese? The British Communist Party had MPs, but not many. Their power base was the unions. The other side of the coin was British disdain of Soviet Russia, from the majority of MPs, high ranking officers of all three services, right throughout the British Aristocracy and, it was widely rumoured, British Royalty. There would be many people, people in positions of high authority, who would delight in the defeat of the Russian Bear and who regarded the Soviet Union as far more of a threat than Hitler's Germany. I'll stop now. I'll take any questions."

Although he spoke to the room, it was to Sir Garfield he was looking.

Twenty

London

12 noon, Monday 4 October 1982

Sir Garfield had his hands together, as if in prayer. "Carry on, Scott."

"It's the last four pages, as I said before, that do the damage. They point out that there was growing belief in London and Washington that the Russians and Comrade Stalin were in imminent danger of losing the war against Hitler and his armies. It repeats that, if Japan invades through Manchuria, the Russians will be at their mercy; all the land, coal and natural resources of eastern Russia and Siberia could end up by being seized. With a further right hook deep into northern China, Japan would become self-sufficient in all the raw materials she craved. The invasion of Russia northwards and not southwards towards Malaya, the Philippines, the Dutch-East Indies, New Guinea and eventually Australia, made huge military sense. There was no long, risk-infected sea journey for troop transports. Over half of the Imperial Japanese Army was already in Manchuria, where there was no Red Army guarding their far-eastern borders. The Japanese could stroll in. In 1959, a Canadian military analysis concluded that, had Japan invaded Russia in January 1942, Stalin's Russia would have been destroyed, with all the consequences that would have had for the world that we live in today. STAVKA, the Soviet Supreme Headquarters, headed by Stalin, would have had the nightmare prospect of Communism fighting on two fronts, against the wildly jubilant German Army in the west, and a rampaging, pitiless Japanese Army in the east."

Scott took a sip of his drink before he continued.

"The other, unmentioned, point is that the Japanese Army would be enthusiastic about any plan to invade Mother Russia. In 1941, there was huge rivalry, often open hostility, between the Imperial Japanese Navy and Army. The Navy had grabbed all the glory by attacking the American fleet at Peal Harbour, but was quick to realise that the main prize – the destruction of the three fleet aircraft carriers of the United States Navy – had eluded them. General Yamashita, 'The Tiger of Malaya', would have been beset with worry and fear if these papers had fallen into his hands. He had at his command some thirty thousand Japanese infantry, not jungle-trained, as the British High Command had tried to paint them, but tough, brutal, battle-hardened troops, whose experience was gained fighting in Manchuria, where there was no jungle. Some of Yamashita's fears would be compounded by the actions of a few British General Officers, strong defensive positions with fire lanes cut, adequate ammunition, huge stores of weapons, and petrol and motor transport, all abandoned, sometimes with only the briefest of gesture defence. The British, retreating all the time, with only isolated counter attacks, such as that at Gemas by the Australians, which stopped the Japanese advance dead in its tracks. Would these be the soldiers that would land behind the Japanese in Thailand and sweep down on them from the north? Yamashita must have had agonising nights. He had thirty-two thousand soldiers, the British had one hundred and thirty thousand, and thousands more to invade behind him. The whole strategic and tactical scenario was one that screamed 'trap': advance. At Singapore, the impregnable island fortress, he could be attacked by having British forces landed behind him, harried by the Spitfires and Hurricanes, the planes and pilots a match for the Japanese Zeros. Further, with the massive

Royal Navy presence promised, he would have no sea lifeline to sustain his forces. Incidentally, that is exactly what did happen, eight years later, to an invading army in Asia. The Communist North Korean Army invaded South Korea in June 1950, and swept all before them. They left the South Korean Army and the United Nations Forces clinging to a tiny foothold of South Korea, around the port of Pusan. Field Marshall Macarthur launched a seaborne attack at Inchon, three hundred miles above the North Koreans, which was a master stroke. Cut off from supplies, food and ammunition, the North Korean Army were in full retreat, only halting when they reached the Yalu River, which was the Korean border with China, where they had to be massively supported by hundreds of thousands of the Chinese Liberation Army."

Scott leant forward, the intensity of his voice all the more evident because of the stillness of the room. "I'm not a military man, but I would be as certain as could be that, if the Japanese High Command, through the capture of these papers, had known that Russia's borders were completely undefended, they most certainly *would* have invaded eastern Russia. Their invasion fleets would have sailed straight up through the sea of Okhotsk, cutting off and isolating the Kamchatka Peninsula, and then spread to west and north. West would have taken them deep into Siberia; north would have led to the Bering Sea, the Aleutian Islands and Alaska, and right through America's back door. It was a fabulous, once in a thousand years opportunity. What would have been the outcome of the Second World War? I don't know. It didn't happen. I can only be sure that, if the Japanese High Command had had these papers, they would have invaded the Soviet Union, and there was *nothing* that Stalin, or STAVKA, could have done about it. At that stage of the war, they were completely extended. The Soviet Far East Fleet had ships, but no sailors; they had been formed into Infantry Divisions and sent west. It would have spelt the virtual end of Communism, at least in Europe. With the Russians out of the war, Germany would have only one war to fight, against Britain and America."

Mrs Mann was hunched over the tape recorder, her right hand moving furiously across her shorthand pad. Sir Garfield sipped his drink. Michael sat motionless, his drink untouched on the table.

Scott continued. "What I'm going to say now is pure conjecture, but think about it. The Canadian First Army, stationed in southern England in 1942, would have been immediately recalled to defend Canada's western seaboard. The Wehrmacht would implement 'Operation Sea Lion', the invasion of Britain. Could we have stopped them? Almost certainly not. The British Royal Family would have been removed to Canada. With Britain subjugated and the Mediterranean lost, Australian and New Zealand forces would have been recalled home, if they could have extricated themselves from North Africa. No British Commandos would be there to help sabotage the German's Norwegian heavy water production, necessary for the manufacture of atomic weapons. It would, I suspect, have developed into a race between America and Germany as to who would be first to build the atom bomb. And who would have won? I don't know."

Michael now chose to speak. "I've done a little digging, discreetly, not approaching people, but reading records, particularly, Hansard from 1937 through to January 1942, and very illuminating it was, too. I've also read selectively all the war-time broadsheets, the heavyweights of the British press. There was a discernible anti-Soviet sentiment evident in their columns. Many in the British establishment regarded the Soviets as blood-soaked gangsters. Incidentally, General Percival, the General Officer commanding British Forces in Malaya, was awarded his DSO fighting the Russians in 1919, when, as you know,

British army units were sent to north Russia to fight alongside the White Russians against the Red Army. It's something Stalin never forgave. After Berlin fell, in May 1945, a large part of the Red Army was gradually moved thousands of miles east and, at midnight on 8th August, Russia declared war on Japan and kept on fighting the Japanese until the September, when they invaded and took Japanese territories and islands. They were brutal in their conquests. All this was weeks after Japan had unconditionally surrendered. The Japanese have been bitter about this ever since. Right wing politicians have long bemoaned the loss of part of Imperial Japan to the Soviets, and rued the lost opportunity to invade and conquer the Soviet Union when they had the chance, i.e. in late 1941 and early 1942, when the Soviets were on their knees and the Red Army was at its most demoralised.

"You must remember that, in 1930s Britain, and well into the war, there was a large and violent Fascist faction, led by Sir Oswald Mosley, who claimed that he could bring out thousands of his black shirts onto the streets of London. They were open in their admiration of Hitler and loathing of Communists and Jews. So were, incidentally, several General Officers of the British High Command. Hore-Belisha, of Zebra crossing fame, when serving as Secretary of War, was repeatedly snubbed and ridiculed simply because he was a Jew." Michael looked up at Sir Garfield and said, "I'd like to ask you a question, sir. Where is our friend, the MP, the one we've nicknamed 'Laughing Boy'?"

Scott immediately realised they were on very thin ice, and political ice was notoriously thin. A step too far and you went through, never to resurface. He gave Michael a quick glance, his eyes signalling the message: 'Ease up, we're on dangerous ground'.

Sir Garfield nodded, as if pondering the questions. Turning to Mrs Mann, he enquired, "Tape still going?" The reply was an affirmative nod. "Good, let it run." He raised his glass and the level within it dropped sharply. "'Laughing Boy' is otherwise engaged. You need to know no more, other than that this operation will now be under *my* scrutiny - understood?" The words were matter of fact, but the implication was clear.

"Thank you, sir," Michael said. "I'll continue, then, if I may. The last question is the obvious one. Who was behind this? These documents, if they had been discovered by the Japs, would have changed the course of the Second World War and history. Scott and I have presented you with all the relevant facts, as we know them. It now goes out of our hands and into yours. It's become 'political'. What are *you* going to do?" There was no 'sir' at the end of this sentence.

Sir Garfield turned to Mrs Mann. "I think you can turn the tape off now, my dear, and then avail yourself of a cup of tea. Thank you."

Effectively but courteously dismissed, Mrs Mann left the room.

"I'd like another," Sir Garfield said, and he held up his now empty glass, adding, "Will you join me?" Scott did the honours. The gin was chilled and expensive, the tonic a superb mixer.

Sir Garfield took an appreciative sip.

"I'll tell you what *I'll* do about it. A thorough investigation will take place. All aspects of this matter will be subjected to the most rigorous, in depth examination – along with military, civil and political persons, whoever they are, or were, as is more likely the case. We are talking about events forty years ago, but, nevertheless, they will be scrutinised. Something this ambitious had to have had political input as well as military. Those dockets look as if they might contain new naval codes. The original ones were, incredibly, sent by merchant vessel from Southampton to Singapore. The ship was crippled and boarded by German submariners, who, in turn, handed the codes over to the Japanese, who knew exactly where and when all Allied shipping was bound for, its course and tonnage etc. It led to terrible slaughter. The letters addressed to the generals will be opened in the presence of any surviving relatives. Whoever was implicated in this monstrous act will be identified. On that point, gentlemen, you have my word." He raised his glass. "Cheers!"

Scott and Michael raised their glasses. When Scott spoke, it was with some hesitancy.

"I think the Singapore part is not the complete story. I suspect there was a larger, darker side to this, an ulterior motive, so to speak."

Sir Garfield surprised them both by saying, "I'm inclined to agree with you. When I was asked to take over this case, I did some digging, as well. It was very surprising and very frightening. This I will tell you. There should be copy records of the War Cabinet's decisions, and implementation of those decisions, that were sent out in December 1941. With all other 'top secret' classification, the copies should be in the records at Kew, but they cannot be found. This, on the table before us, is the only known record." Sir Garfield paused, took another sip of his drink, and then pushed the glass away. "We meet again in fourteen days from now. That's all, gentlemen." He stood up and immediately left the room.

Scott and Michael sat and thought about what they had just heard.

"What do you think we'll uncover, or rather, he'll uncover?" Michael asked. Scott answered, speaking for nearly twenty minutes. When he had finished, they emptied their glasses. When Michael finally spoke again, it was to say, "Bloody Hell!"

Twenty-one

Aberystwyth

9 a.m., Tuesday 5 October 1982

Every one of them was hung over, for they had been drinking steadily, on the Inter-City Euston to Birmingham train, and on the train to Aberystwyth. Aberystwyth seemed a million miles away from the warmth and humidity of Malaysia. The events of the past days, crowding crazily on top of each other, had sent the companions on a wild roller coaster of emotions: exhilaration, fear, jubilation, speculation and then, lastly, a deep sense of emptiness. What had been done was done. What more was left? Individually, each man felt an almost bursting pride in his two friends. Griffiths refilled the coffee percolator and held out his right hand, straight and level, Hughes and Tucker immediately responded, their hands smacking onto the outstretched palm.

"Once a Fusilier, always a Fusilier." There was genuine pride in the voices.

"Look at the state of us." Tucker was nonchalant, his face creased in a smile. "We'd never pass muster on parade."

"We don't have to." Gethin's contentment was obvious, his mind clear and clean. "I've never felt better in my life."

Griffiths and Tucker nodded agreement. It was transparently obvious.

"The point is now: what do we do today?"

Tucker had drunk as much as the other two, and was

beginning to feel regret and a little embarrassment.

Gethin Hughes was again a platoon commander, his words decisive.

"Nothing! We do nothing. I've defended enough over the limit drivers to know how long it takes alcohol to leave a man's system. We stay put till five o'clock. In the meantime, I'll phone Ruby. Griff, will you take Tuck back to South Wales?"

Griffiths nodded. "It'll cost him."

Tucker broke into one of his laughs. "No, it won't. I'm skint."

"Talking about skint, what will happen to the bullion? Do you think we might get a reward?" Griffiths asked, his eyes bright with anticipation.

Hughes, who was sipping gently from his coffee mug, answered, "I believe we will. I'll compose a letter; something along the lines of: three ex-soldiers on a pilgrimage, wrongful arrest, solely responsible for finding and reporting umpteen million pounds' worth of gold bars. What is Her Majesty's Government going to do about it? I'll add a rider saying that at least three quality broadsheet newspapers are in contact with me. We'll get our reward. Trust me."

"Trust a solicitor. In the popularity league they're only once place from the bottom, just above grave robbers," Griffiths said, smiling broadly. They all laughed.

Tucker was beginning to shrug off his embarrassment at having had a share in the drinking binge. After all, what were mates for!

"I wonder if that fellow Elvis did nick any of the gold."

"Of course he did; it's got to be him, crafty sod. I wonder where he is now. Is he still milling around in the jungle, or living the life of Riley?"

Griffiths moved his mug onto the draining-board. "Living the life of Riley; I'd bet on it."

★ ★ ★

Swee Poe was not in any way discomforted by the cold. Compared to the Alaskan tundra, Geneva was the French Riviera. He was ushered into a large, spotlessly clean office. Germs and dirt would not have been tolerated. The senior manager was courtesy and charm itself. The scales were wheeled in with immaculate efficiency. The two bullion bars were weighed, checked and weighed again. Swee Poe was invited to watch. The calculators whirred and the value, in red neon buttons, appeared on a large screen, in Swiss francs, American dollars and British sterling. Swee Poe felt powerful, akin to putting Sammy automatic in his waistband.

"Which currency would you prefer?" the manager asked. Swee Poe indicated American dollars. There was a barely perceptible pause. "The amount is now in your account, sir." It was a very deeply courteous 'sir'.

★ ★ ★

In the office in Soho, the young man had confirmed the 11am appointment. Mr Jones had come to see his grandfather and was there at exactly 11am. The entry-phone buzzer sounded. The young man left his desk and checked the monitor of the newly-installed closed circuit television. It revealed Mr Jones, dark suit, large briefcase, smiling benignly at the camera. He had ostensibly come to discuss some investments. The young man pressed the entry button.

Then, everything seemed to explode. A surge of men and women, some in police uniform, erupted into the foyer. They rushed past and around him. He was deeply shocked to notice that some were armed with sub-machine guns. Everywhere there was noise, shouting and screamed orders. He was manhandled, pushed violently to the carpeted floor and, from an ant's eye view he saw his grandfather being frogmarched into the room. He squirmed, anxious to shout encouragement to his grandfather, but a large shoe descended on his neck, and it hurt. The noise was subsiding and Mr Jones was speaking. The word *arrest* was featured as Mr Jones issued the standard caution and proceeded to read from a charge sheet. It covered extortion, money laundering, VAT evasion, illegal gambling, illegal immigrants, corruption – the allegations seemed endless. His grandfather stood silent, his gaunt, finely honed face expressionless.

The pressure on the young man's neck was eased, marginally, allowing him to gasp, "Grandfather, are you alright?"

Grandfather's voice sounded resigned. "No, my grandson, I'm afraid not. We are finished. It's over. Save yourself."

The words, spoken in Cantonese, were immediately copied into a notebook held by one of the policewomen. She spoke slowly.

"I've a degree in the Cantonese language, four dialects actually. Would you care to make any comment, sir? Please remember that you have been cautioned." The sir was a pantomime. The young man started to sob with rage and impotence. In English, he screamed, "Go to Hell!"

The policewoman's lips were pursed in smile. "Do I catch a number 29 bus, sir?"

★ ★ ★

Swee Poe headed for a large, expensive restaurant in the square, two hundred metres from the bank. From the communications centre at Singapore International he had sent a long, detailed fax to the Serious Crime Squad at New Scotland Yard. He divulged full details of the organised crime syndicate headed by the old man in his Soho office. He gave details, phone numbers and, where possible, names. The fax was on its way before he boarded his flight to Geneva. He was well satisfied. From a gift shop carrier bag he withdrew three expensive greetings cards. Everything in Geneva seemed to be expensive. He wrote briefly on each one, affixed a Swiss stamp and caught the eye of a hovering waiter. "Do you speak English?"

"Yes, sir."

"Post these for me and bring me a large Chivas Regal."

"Certainly, sir."

"Oh," Swee Poe called after the retreating back, "and book me a taxi for ten minutes from now."

"Where do wish it to take you, sir?"

"Geneva International."

"Going somewhere nice?"

"Yes, Brazil." He settled back, life was good, very good.

★ ★ ★

They all left together, Gethin to go back home to Ruby in Welshpool; Griffiths and Tucker to drive home, too. They had spent the day reminiscing, and enjoyed a fish and chip lunch from the chip shop by the roundabout. Griffiths was quieter than the other two. Only as they went through the front door was the subject voiced.

"Are you still going to do it?" Gethin's voice was low, the concern obvious.

Aware that both men were waiting for an answer, Griffiths nodded and said, "I have to. It's eating into me. If I don't, I'll never be a full man again."

"If you're caught, I'll defend you."

Tucker put his arm around Griffiths' shoulder. "I'll pray for you, and for the man who killed Bethan. The Lord will judge you, Griff, and him." He squeezed his friend's shoulders. "God Bless you."

It was a gloomy, dark evening, Cardigan Bay a murky grey, the waves making a white, rolling pattern as they crashed ashore. Strangely, there were no birds to be seen, no seagulls, pigeons or starlings. They seemed to have abandoned the night to the humans.

Griffiths' car had slid to a halt outside Tucker's little flat.

"Cup of tea?"

Griffiths declined. "I'll be on my way. Look after yourself, Tuck."

"You too." They had said all there as to say.

* * *

Swansea was a big town and the council thought it deserved city status. Griffiths eased his car to within twenty metres of the 'The Brigands Inn' public house. The poster outside was in bold redletters: "LIVE MUSIC EVERY TUESDAY, 9 – 11.30. THE GOWER CRABS, with RITCHIE 'DUKE' JENKINGS".

Griffiths pulled the handle to spring the boot lock. The cricket bat was over thirty years old, its face pockmarked by thousands of rock hard cricket balls. He slid it out of the plastic sheet, took a large, dark blue balaclava out of a polythene bag, and checked his watch. It showed 8.14. Bands, and particularly rock bands, usually took half an hour to set up their sound equipment. He sat and waited. He felt cold, his mind focused narrowly on what he had to do.

* * *

A uniformed man had knocked loudly on his office door and asked, "Lieutenant Colonel Gerhard Elias, would you accompany me to Brigade HQ? I have transport waiting."

Elias was surprised. His voice was vexed and impatient. "Don't they have one of these in Brigade?" His finger jabbed at the telephone.

"I follow orders, sir." The unemotional voice was disturbing.

Elias felt a frisson of unease. "Very well." He dropped his pen onto the desk. "The *General's* report will have to wait." He took his overcoat off the rack. Berlin in October was as cold as January in the South of France. He picked up his briefcase and said, "Okay, let's go."

The room into which he was taken was medium sized. The spacious apartment had once been the home of a middle-class family, whose grandfather had invested in the giant Krupps steel and engineering corporation. He had made his money in the First World War, when the price of armaments reached a premium. Then followed the German army's defeat, hyperinflation, civil unrest, and the grandfather had died, his fortune largely, but not entirely gone. The property had been altered to make two apartments, one for the family's use and one to rent. The German Democratic Republic now owned both flats.

Elias entered and immediately accepted that this was no usual briefing. The three men present all outranked him by several levels of seniority. The man on his left was curt.

"What is the current status of the file on Spano, the Central Intelligence Agency operative?"

Elias fielded the question. "As of last month, he has not defected, but he will. He is on the point of taking the hook." Elias's right arm came over in a lazy arc, simulating a fly fishing cast.

The man in the centre chair leant forward. "I don't think you'll have fish for supper, Colonel Elias. Spano won't be in touch with you again. Apparently, he wasn't what he seemed to be."

Elias stood up, head held high. "He was an agent of the American Central Intelligence Agency; that is irrefutable!"

"True, he was a member of the CIA but we are now very reliably informed that his real paymasters were the Twenty Executive. You know of them, their two crosses – double-cross – a very much smaller department than the CIA or FBI. Their task is to subvert our people and extract information from us, and the Starsi. Our agents are their target. Apparently, Mr Spano had some success."

Elias was thinking furiously, but he asked calmly, "What do you mean?"

The man on his right, who had not yet spoken, removed a cigarette case from his jacket pocket. It was silver, small and neat, much like the man himself. He withdrew a cigarette and lit it. He inhaled, at the same time flourishing the lighter.

"Zippo. One of the best in the world. American." The tone of his voice did not alter, when he added, "The Hind M-14, our Russian Air Force's love baby, is better than anything that the Americans currently have. How do the Americans know so much about it?"

Elias saw the light at the end of his tunnel. "We lost one in Afghanistan - the Mujahideen downed one - they sold it. The Americans are probably gloating over it right now." He tried to keep the vindication out of his voice, but only partially succeeded.

His inquisitor puffed a haze of blue around his face.

"True, true, the Mujahideen did bring one down and,

Colonel, you are right, they did sell it on, complete with the manuals."

Elias found himself nodding, aware of a warm sensation, like a very large brandy, moving up from his stomach into his chest.

"However, the Mujahideen did not sell it to the Americans; they sold it back to us! So, Colonel, can you now explain how the Americans know so much about our now not-so- secret helicopter, its weapons capability, range and attack angles?"

Elias felt the brandy burst, evaporate and a sour, foul smell spreading into his throat.

The first man took his time before speaking.

"We have to find out exactly what you told this man Spano. It might take some time." The door behind Elias was opened and two soldiers of the German Democratic Army stood on the threshold. "Colonel Elias is to accompany you to Divisional HQ."

Elias turned. There seemed no point in saluting now.

★ ★ ★

David Spano was flown from Kuala Lumpur to Frankfurt, and then to New York. The service and food on both Jumbos were first-class, but it was possibly *the* most uncomfortable journey of his life. He was accompanied by the CIA Head of Station in Malaysia, another agent and two plain clothes USMC NCOs. The complete absence of conversation was, he found, reminiscent of his time as a POW. He occupied a window seat. Immediately behind him sat one of the NCOs; the other sat at the rear, by one of the toilets. The CIA agent sat in front of him and, distancing himself from the others; the Head of Station had an aisle seat, the empty seat between them a *cordon sanitaire,* as if to keep any vile infections at a distance. The Head of Station spoke only once, on disembarking at New York, where they were met by three CIA agents.

"He's all yours, and good riddance!"

The silent treatment continued on the commuter plane to Langley.

"I'd like to wash and freshen up," suggested Spano.

The agent looked up from the sports page of the *New York Herald Tribune*. You're going nowhere, Spano. Sit down!"

Conversation closed. At Langley, the person at the reception desk was icily correct; there were no greetings, no smiles, and no pats on the shoulder. If the three agents were experts at dumb insolence, the interview with his director was worse. Clearing his throat, the director sniffed at what was a bad smell coming from the air conditioning. He ran through the dossier in front of him, frowning frequently, and finally, he looked up. "I'm a director of the CIA. I hire and fire. Spano, you're fired!"

Spano wasn't going to go without a fight; it had never been in his nature.

"We're supposed to be on the same side. The Twenty Executive is a sister organisation. The American taxpayer funds us both."

The director's face betrayed his rage. "Sister organisation! Prostitute organisation, more like! Every dollar spent on that pansy outfit ought to come here."

Spano's left hand thudded onto the desktop. "Tell that to my bosses and, when you've told *them*, tell the President. He personally authorised the Twenty Executive. How many times has the CIA been found wanting? Have you ever delivered intelligence, on budget, on time? If so, name them!"

The aggression in Spano's voice shocked the director, but he recovered quickly. "Spano you're out – finished – your cover's been blown. The KGB, the GRU and the Starsi, not counting the Brits and Israelis, know who and what you are. You'll never operate as an agent again. Damned right you won't. I'll personally guarantee it. Now, get out of my sight!"

Outside, the Brigadier General was waiting for him, his tanned face untroubled.

"Lynch party?"

Spano nodded, "I've had worse bollockings, but not often."

The General opened the Buick door. "First, a holiday, and then we'll find you some sort of job. I'm sorry about your father."

The car moved away into the lush Virginian countryside. Spano barely spoke, his mind too full of recent events.

★ ★ ★

Choi's secretary was plainly flustered. "I'm sorry, I cannot trace Mr Choi. He was due at a meeting here at nine thirty. I've rung his home number, and asked around the departments, but I can't find him. Who shall I say wants him?"

The taller of the two men was laconic. "The United States Government. Thank you, Ma'am."

At that precise moment, Choi was thirty-three thousand feet above the North Atlantic, en route to Ho Chi Min City, via Paris and Kuala Lumpur. He felt as if he was already home. It had been a long time since he had had a real Vietnamese meal and some Bourbon whiskey. He was well content. There would be sharp words and threats from the Russians, but that was their problem. If one of their agents had been too trusting, he was sure the error of his ways would be pointed out to him. The thought of Bourbon made his taste buds tingle. He pressed the button for the flight attendant.

"A Wild Turkey Bourbon, if you please, and make it a large one."

Twenty-two

London

18 October 1982

Outwardly composed and calm, both men were inwardly excited and nervous. Three days after their last meeting with Sir Garfield, each had received instructions that their folders, in their entirety, were to be presented to his secretary as soon as possible. This had been done, without mention of the fact that they had photocopied every entry. They were exactly on time for the next meeting. The unwritten code of senior civil servants was: 'Always be there. Always be on time and never lose your temper, unless you want to.'

The minutes ticked by. Sir Garfield was late, which was unusual. Twelve minutes after the appointed time, he entered, without Mrs Mann or any of the usual retinue, and he sat down. He did not apologise for keeping them waiting.

"Thank you for coming. We'll get straight on with the business."

He had a minor hiatus while extricating his glasses from his briefcase. His first words were electrifying.

"This gives me no pleasure whatsoever. What has been unravelled is one of the nastiest and most heinous examples of treachery anyone could possibly imagine. Before I continue, I would like to thank you and commend you both for your diligence and expertise. Without your participation, this could have gone very wrong. If these papers had fallen into hands other than ours, there would have been a seismic fissure in both British politics and British society. That stated, I'll proceed."

The pen was arrow-straight as he pointed it at Scott. "Your theory was, with very little error, uncannily accurate. The plane, with papers and gold, was ordered north and not south-west, straight into the advancing Japanese and their Zeros. The two Buffaloes that were scrambled to escort the Vindicator were extra bait. The sacrifice, for that's what it was, was meant to be a large enough target for the rampaging Zeros not to miss, but they did! The Buffaloes were shot down and the Vindicator crashed, God knows why. It lay undiscovered, rotting away for fifteen years, before it was found by a British Army patrol."

Scott had raised his hand but Sir Garfield made a quick dismissive gesture.

"Later, Scott. Let me continue. If the capture of the orders by the Japanese was, on the face of it, an attempt to halt the drive on Singapore, that was the first, rather obvious directive. The other was more complex. With the folders you have presented, and with what I have assembled, it gives us, as the Americans say, 'a whole new ballgame'. Firstly, the papers, purporting to be War Cabinet Minutes, dated 11th December 1941, from the London office were, in fact, counterfeit."

Scott's and Michael's expressions mirrored the shock they felt.

Sir Garfield leant forward, his glasses glinting from the lights above.

"The paper they were typed on was not manufactured in Britain, nor were the pages typed here. The paper was of local manufacture, i.e. Singaporean. Also, one set of initials is certainly not authentic. I've checked, and one initial has been reversed – forename before Christian name. Those papers were typed in Singapore, not London. That said; the origin of the papers was unquestionably British. The plan was conceived here and, via telephone and cable, implemented in Singapore."

Sir Garfield looked hard at Michael and Scott. "The question is, by whom? There were just eleven people involved — six here and five in Singapore. There were, incidentally, thirty-one people, as far as I can establish, who knew, approved and, in six cases, sanctioned the papers. Those people were playing a dangerous and deadly game, because treason was a capital offence." He sniffed contemptuously. "Read through this list." He slid a typewritten sheet along the gleaming smoothness of the table towards Scott, who read it first. He passed the sheet over to Michael to read.

"Give it back, please."

Michael returned the paper to Sir Garfield, who asked, "Any guesses?"

Scott's voice was neutral. "A government in waiting?"

"Correct. Do you recognise any of these?" A polythene folder of photographs was produced and again sent down the table. The photographs were grainy and looked old. The first was of a civilian, wearing a dark suit and white shirt and giving a Heil Hitler salute.

Scott did a double take. "'Laughing Boy!'"

"No, but a close relation."

The other photos were all in a similar vein. Two of the men and two of the women wore arm bands with swastikas on them.

"These photographs were taken surreptitiously in the late 1930s, some in 1940. Because Britain was at war, wearing the swastika was a treasonable act. The gist of what I am trying to say is that there existed in Britain a cell of people who wanted Britain allied, not to America or Russia, but to Germany.

That cell included industrialists who saw the unions becoming increasingly militant; high churchmen who admired the order and religious fervour of Germany; aristocrats, who saw no future for themselves after the war, and politicians who were convinced that Britain was already beaten. This view of the situation wasn't confined to British politicians; a lot of American politicians thought so as well, and told everyone who would listen. Also, there were military men of high rank. The story of how they, the traitors, found out that Stalin had stripped eastern Russia of all his troops is like something out of an old fashioned comic, full of lurid and basically untrue articles. A bit like today's press, actually."

Scott and Michael smiled and privately agreed.

"In 1935, a grand review of the Royal Navy Fleet was held at Portsmouth. Among the navies of the world to attend was the Imperial Navy of Japan, which had fought alongside Britain, France and America in the First World War. A large party of Japanese sailors had spent seven months in Portsmouth. One Japanese Petty Officer stayed for a further 2 years, on a training course; he had formed an attachment, or liaison, with a local pub landlady. He apparently became enamoured not only with her but also the English way of life. When he finally left for Japan, he promised to write and to return. When Agent Sorge sent his coded message to Stalin on 4th October 1941, he was almost immediately arrested. The Chief Petty Officer was at that time in Manchuria, delivering naval guns to the Japanese Army, and a member of the organising cadre of the Manchurian railway was with him. The two men had become friends. The man whose job it was to oversee repairs to the Manchurian railway, which would have been the vital supply line for any invasion of Russia, suddenly collapsed. He struggled for words, but, apparently, with the lucidity of near death, revealed to the Petty Officer that the Soviets had left no effective forces in eastern Russia. They had *all* been entrained and sent west, to repel Hitler's forces. He had only just found out. Only one man in Tokyo knew. That man was Sorge. Actually, to be truthful, there were two men who knew: Sorge and his radio operator, Max Clausen. The railway man died.

"The Petty Officer was in a quandary. He'd seen enough of the war in Manchuria to be sickened. He couldn't tell the Russians, he quite simply didn't know anything of their language, but Russia was an ally of England, and he liked England and the English, so he wrote a completely open letter, in English, to his lady friend in Portsmouth. He had no skill with codes. Thanks to the Japanese postal service (airmails department) and the General Post Office in the UK, the letter was delivered on 1st November 1941, five weeks and three days before the Japanese attacked Pearl Harbour and overran Malaya."

Sir Garfield paused, his eyes scanning both men's faces.

"Do you follow it? Right. I'll take questions, when I've finished. The landlady was nonplussed. Usually, the Petty Officer's letters were full of endearments, gossip, and messages of goodwill to be passed onto people he had formed friendships with in Portsmouth. This was different, however, so she confided in one of her regulars, a detective inspector. He read the letter and promised he'd take it to a higher authority, which he did. But the letter ended up with that group, actually, with that man, seventh down on the list. It is never safe to assume anything, but no other conclusion can be reached than that this was the time when the plan was hatched.

"When the Japanese landed at Kota Baru on 8th December 1941, all that was needed was to find a way to let the Japanese War Cabinet know that Russia was there for the taking. The counterfeit order, the gold, the sacrifice of the Vindicator, Buffaloes and crews had been meticulously planned – planned, incidentally, with far more care and skill than a lot of plans in that conflict. There are now only two people left alive out of the original group; one is in his nineties and has dementia, the other is a widow, who claims she remembers nothing of her husband's activities. She, apparently, never really liked him, certainly never loved him, and she asks simply that we go away and let her enjoy the Spanish sun."

Sir Garfield laid down his glasses. He looked exhausted, the weariness around his eyes noticeable.

"Well, what are your observations?"

Scott and Michael thought he'd fought a battle and lost.

"What are you – we – to do now? Where do we go from here?" asked Michael.

Sir Garfield was massaging his temples, trying to erase the tiredness that enveloped him. "Where do we go? We go into the sidings. There is nowhere else to go."

Scott and Michael remained silent. Sir Garfield looked again at the sheet in front of him.

"The fall of Singapore was the worst defeat of the British Army in the history of our country. It was as catastrophic as it was unexpected, at least to the British public. The people who planned this are gone from this mortal world. What would good would it do, to break news like this? What would the Russian reaction be? Massive, violent, fury. The Americans would be utterly appalled to discover that a country that they had famously aided with supplies, war materials, and food, would have been prepared to betray them and side with the blackness of Nazi Germany. No, we do nothing. I fought my corner for further, deeper investigations to be undertaken, but have been told no. Not just told, but ordered to do nothing further." Sir Garfield sighed and it was as if the fire had finally gone out.

"What happens to 'Laughing Boy'?" Scott asked Sir Garfield.

"I'm led to believe that he is not standing at the next election. Some reason given, the usual thing: wants to spend more time with his family, blah blah.' He won't be missed."

"Was that why he wanted the box completely destroyed? He was terrified that the secrets that it held would be revealed, including whoever it was whose identity he was shielding?" Scott asked, twisting his pen between his fingers.

"Correct."

"Where are the War Cabinet papers now?"

Sir Garfield raised his hands in a gesture of surrender. "Shredded and incinerated."

"What was in the private letters to the British generals?" asked Michael, as he leant back in his chair, hands clasped behind his head.

"Nothing of any military importance whatsoever, just letters from concerned wives. They were really a master stroke, they were so convincing; one letter even urged the general to avoid dampness as it would bring on his rheumatics."

No-one spoke. The silence was total, as if each one of them was lost in his thoughts.

"It was all for nothing, then?" Michael was looking at Sir Garfield, and it was as if he were talking to himself.

"No, Michael, it was not for nothing. A potentially huge political explosion and fallout have been averted. Her Britannic Majesty's Government is the beneficiary of a very substantial bullion windfall. In another twenty years' time, when the horrors of the Second World War have slipped from the world's conscience, I have no doubt that words and names will be fed to the media. The people who were involved in this will be gradually exposed, but not now, and they are either dead already, or have a limited time left to them. They say time is a great healer, but the scars of the last war have still not healed."

Sir Garfield paused, thoughtfully, before he asked, "Do either of you realise the extent of Japanese investment in Britain today? The cars, television sets, motor cycles, music centres, radios, and other electrical goods: that trade with Japan runs into billions of pounds. No, now is not the time to release anything of this incident."

Scott restrained his tone. "So, the men who fought in Malaya and Singapore and the ones who died there get no satisfaction, no long overdue credit for what they did? Poor, undervalued foot soldiers in a poorly trained, poorly led army that people simply do not want to know about. Singapore will always to be associated with defeat and abject failure; whereas the truth is that the enemies were not only in front of them, but *amongst* them and *behind* them. Those people," and he nodded to the sheet of paper on the table in front of Sir Garfield, "cared not a tuppenny damn about Singapore or its people. They saw it merely as a convenient stepping stone to their perverted dream. All those servicemen left to rot. There was no Dunkirk from Singapore; only a handful escaped the clutches of the Japanese. It could all have been so different. There is not one of the really guilty people on that list, no one that supplied aircraft that were not up to the job. No mention of those responsible for men given ten weeks basic training before being sent into the jungle to face a fanatical enemy. No real leadership, too much political interference, simply to keep up the appearance of a huge empire. Reinforcements, a whole division of troops sent to Singapore, when all the signs were of its imminent collapse, and they stepped off the boats and straight into captivity. Singapore was described as 'the naked island', and that, effectively, was what it was. A political pawn sacrificed."

Scott turned his head away, the disgust obvious.

"There is nothing more to be said."

Sir Garfield was gathering up his folder. "I have no doubt that a new set of papers from the War Cabinet, giving a very different picture, more in line with what was originally agreed, will find its way, suitably dated, into the Public Record Office. Good day, gentlemen."

Scott and Michael remained seated after Sir Garfield had left the room. Neither felt the need to speak. Eventually, Michael rose and went to the window. Autumn was settling its chilly hand over London, little swirls of golden leaves went skipping over the pavements.

"Ever since we started into this thing, I always suspected it would end in disarray. What have we achieved? We have unveiled a collection of loathsome people who, in today's climate, would be regarded as deranged fools, dangerous individuals, needing to be locked up. Yet, in their day, they enjoyed immense power and the best privileges that money could buy. What sort of country were we? What can we say about the others, principally military men and their political masters, almost without exception totally inept, and thousands of men paid with their lives for that ineptitude? Commanding officers running away, leaving their men to die, often in the most appalling manner – they disgust me." Michael shook his head

Scott stood, made for the door, paused and turned.

"Sir Garfield said that, in twenty years or so, names would be leaked, facts given, drip-fed to a by then largely disinterested British public. I think my only brief is to bring that time forward to now. It's what I'm going to do. I feel I owe it to the men that didn't come back from the Far East. You must make up your own mind, but that is what I am intent on.

Michael raised his eyebrows. "I'm with you. It's going to be an early pension, that is, if we get one at all, but I'm with you."

* * *

Griffiths switched on the electric kettle, to boil water to make his breakfast coffee. It's hissing was noisy but it did not mask the sound of the post coming through the letter-box. Three envelopes lay on the doormat: one a bill, the second a payment cheque and the last a larger envelope, the handwriting on which he recognised as Tucker's. It contained no note, just a cutting, neatly folded, from *The Swansea Evening Post*.

It was fourteen days since he'd lain in wait for Richie Jenkings. The scene was still vivid in his mind. The van pulled in, the doors opened, and three men got out. Two of them went to the back of the van and started to unload some amplifiers. Griffiths saw the man he had last seen in the Aberystwyth courtroom, and heard the same loud, Swansea accent. Jenkings carried his load into the pool of light that spilled from the open doorway of the pub, and disappeared inside. Griffiths felt for the balaclava on his passenger seat, and pulled it on. There was no fumbling; his hand was steady and sure. Two figures reappeared, but neither was Jenkings, and more equipment was carried into the pub. Then, a lone figure emerged and walked towards the van. This time, it was Jenkings. Griffiths eased the car door open and silently stepped out. He was in shadow, the early moon giving only a weak light. He strode up to the man, uttered no sound, but swung the cricket bat straight into Jenkings's face. He emitted a strangled scream. Griffiths hit Jenkings again. As he fell, the box of electrical components spilled from the van. Griffiths struck home with the bat again, not into Jenkings's face this time, but onto his outstretched hands on the road. Griffiths returned to the car, started the ignition, and swerved out into the road. He had no lights showing. He saw two men emerge from the doorway. Griffiths accelerated past them, their faces looking pale and ghostly in the moonlight. Forty yards down the road, he put on his lights, and then he trembled for what seemed an age. Finally clear of Swansea, he pulled into a lay-by and relieved himself. The shaking eased and he drove home, carefully obeying the speed restrictions. Eleven miles from Aberystwyth, he passed the spot where his wife Bethan had been killed. It was as if a deep, troubling weight went from his chest and head.

"I'm sorry, Bethan," he said, "but I had to do it. God Bless."

He let himself into the house and waited for the police to come, but they didn't. He read the extract from *The Swansea Evening Post* carefully. The report was a negative one:

Police are still hunting the person or persons who attacked a Mr Richie Jenkings, lead singer and guitarist of 'The Gower Crabs'. Several people have given statements to the police. Mr Jenkings is still in Morriston Hospital, and although out of the intensive care unit, he is not expected to be discharged for several days. In the meantime, police are investigating allegations of a turf war over drugs, allegations vehemently denied by sources close to Mr Jenkings.

Griffiths re-read the article and then burnt it in his garden, using some vegetable oil to ignite the paper, and an empty soup tin out of his refuse bin as an incinerator. He drank his coffee and went to work.

★ ★ ★

All police stations tend to smell the same, and the one in the Central Division in Swansea was no exception. The Detective Chief Inspector was an impatient man, constantly chasing and chivvying his team.

"What does the status board read?" he demanded of the Detective Sergeant. "Any joy on that counterfeit money?"

The answer was a gloomy shake of the head.

"What about that rape in Manselton?" The mood lightened immediately.

"We've got him, and he coughed for another rape in the town centre, last April."

"Anything else still outstanding from the last ten days?"

"Yes. No joy on Richie Jenkings."

"I know that name. What's the score with him?

"He was attacked outside The Brigands Inn — not so much attacked as demolished — hands and face smashed."

"Has he any form we don't know about?" The Chief Inspector was trying to fit a face to the name.

"Well, his nickname is 'arsehole face'. Ring a bell?"

"Yes, now. What's that long streak of tank water been up to?"

The Sergeant was expansive. "We don't know yet, but whoever worked him over did a real job. Left him with a fractured skull, broken jaw, broken nose and compound fractures of the cheekbones. Fingers look as if they've been through his granny's mangle!"

"Will he ever play the guitar again?"

The Sergeant shook his head. "Not unless he learns to play it with his toes."

"Has he any known enemies?"

"Hundred of 'em!"

The Chief Inspector shook his head. He refrained from obscenities, as befitting a senior member of Bethel Baptist Chapel choir. "Who have you got on it?"

"Prosser and Edwards."

"Let it run for one more week, then, if there's no breakthrough, switch them onto the counterfeit case. That's the one I'm getting flak about."

The Sergeant scribbled into the diary. "Fair enough."

"Who are the All Whites playing Saturday?" (Swansea had a football team known as The Swans and a rugby team always called The All Whites.)

The Sergeant put the diary into the cubby-hole and reached for his coat. "The South Wales Police."

The Chief Inspector grunted, "Oh! Those thugs!"

Twenty-three

Epilogue

After a long, painful illness, Ruby's mother died. Gethin and Ruby decided to leave Welshpool and move into her mother's house in Harrogate. They left the green of Powys for the equally green and pleasant Yorkshire Dales, where they led a semi-retired life and were marvellously happy. Gethin was a deeply contented man, Ruby everything a wife could be. It seemed to Gethin that life was sheer bliss, and he felt very lucky indeed. They kept in contact with Griffiths and Tucker, made regular phone calls and occasionally wrote letters. Both men had visited them in Harrogate, and both seemed to be enjoying life. Tucker had met a lady, a widow, who had started worshipping at the Salvation Army Citadel. She was neat, rather shy, but possessed a lovely singing voice. Tucker was protective towards her initially, then, realised that he was becoming romantically entwined. He was particularly worried if she missed any of the services, and tried to ignore his growing feelings towards her, but he was unable to do so. After a chance meeting in one of the local shops, he stammered about a wedding to which he'd been invited. The invitation card had clearly intended him to bring a partner.

To his delight, she agreed to accompany him. Things moved very quickly from then on. They became engaged, and then married. Tucker, from being the classic loner, found himself with a wife, a grown-up daughter, a son-in-law and a thirteen-month-old step-granddaughter, whom he adored. He was commissioned into the Salvation Army as an Acting Captain. He was very proud and felt completely fulfilled. He had been invited to visit Gethin and Ruby's new home and there, together with Griffiths, he had been shown a cheque for eighty-thousand pounds. Gethin had been noticeably surprised by the size of the payment and the alacrity with which it had been made.

He explained to his friends, "I wrote to the Cabinet Office, and laid out our case for some form of reward. Privately, I was hoping for fifty-thousand pounds, split four ways – one share going to Parry's family. I was girding up my loins, so to speak, for a bruising and long legal battle when, seven days later, this arrived," and he waved the cheque in the air. "It arrived with this letter. It contains the usual gobbledegook but also the sentence, '...full global reparations for the return of treasury and government assets'. No questions, no probing, no delaying tactics. I was delighted and I must say very surprised."

Griffiths was sipping his beer. "I wonder if the pay-out is anything to do with that dispatch case."

Gethin shrugged. "We'll never know but it must have been bloody important, if it was. Anyway, all in agreement – twenty thousand each – including Parry's family?" Both men signalled a yes. "In that case, we'll have a round of drinks. What'll it be, Tuck?"

"A large Horlicks, if you don't mind."

Griffiths made a half-hearted cuff to his shoulders. "You can take this religion thing too far!" Everybody laughed. It had turned out to be a magical night.

★ ★ ★

David Spano had worked for, or at least, he was on the payroll of, the Twenty Executive for a further two years. Then, the Brigadier General who, Spano admitted had rescued him from a lifetime of bitterness and anger against American society, was promoted to a two-star General and left. His successor was a highly-competent man, but a civilian, and had none of the camaraderie and warmth of his predecessor. Spano applied for release and it was granted. Amply funded by his service pension and, ironically, by the CIA pension as well as the Twenty Executive 'golden goodbye', he moved to Arizona and bought himself a Cessna single-engined, light aircraft. He spent hours flying in the dry, warm air. On the relatively short flights, he examined his life, the USMC, the Wild Weasels, the POW days, the CIA and, finally, the Twenty Executive. He concluded that he'd done his best and America had been served well. He grew less isolated and found himself joining in the social life of the flying club. Gradually, he felt at home, certainly in the air, and also in other people's company. But tragedy struck, and on the 3rd August 1984, a truck blew a tyre on the freeway out of Flagstaff. It careered into the oncoming traffic, and Spano, in his Volkswagen coupé, was killed instantly. He was given a full military funeral, the Marine Honour Guard resplendent in their dress uniform. It was an impressive and fitting end for an impressive man.

★ ★ ★

In Malaysia, in late November 1984, a public works survey team put up bollards and a mobile trailer on the Seremban Gemas road, and entered the jungle, to clear the way for a road widening scheme. There, barely into the undergrowth, they discovered the remains of a body. The jungle and animals had done their worst. The deceased was finally identified by dental records. It was Sammy. A coroner's court found that he had been unlawfully killed, but no arrests seemed likely. He was buried in a Kuala Lumpur cemetery. There were no mourners.

★ ★ ★

The room was very cold, with only a single radiator – some days cold, other days dangerously hot – as the sole means of heat. The room was nominally an office, but there was no phone, just a desk, chairs and several shelves of books. Major Gerhard Elias, only one rank lower than his previous rank of Lieutenant Colonel, but a submariners' depth in his actual command, faced the prospect of being permanently left out to rust in the freezing Arctic port of Murmansk. When he left his office, his home was a small, cramped, one bedroom flat in an austere, Stalin-era housing complex. There, the temptation was to drink himself nightly into oblivion, but he still retained the sharpness of mind, despite the reduction in rank. He was forming a plan to fulfil what originally had been no more than a tale to deceive the American, Spano. This time, he really was going to go over the wall. It just needed very diligent planning and a certain amount of luck. He sometimes awoke from a feverish sleep, thinking he was already in America. Firstly, there came the despair because it was only a dream, and then the planning would kick in, for he was determined to do it or die in the attempt.

★ ★ ★

Anna Magda Crumpet and her beloved cat, Tigger, made a home in Honolulu, where she spent her days gardening, travelling and entering TV game shows. One in particular was called 'Memory Lane', in which she identified a staggering twenty out of twenty people viewed from obtuse, high-angle camera shots. She won nearly four thousand dollars and a great deal of public acclaim over the seven weeks she was featured. She also received public recognition. She was stopped in the street by a native born Hawaiian.

"You're that lady with the phenomenal memory!" he exclaimed. He was tall and muscular and Anna replied immediately, "And you're an actor. I've seen you in 'Hawaii

Five-O'. You were on screen for a good twenty seconds." Visibly impressed by each other, they arranged a dinner date. He was a teetotaller, and they got along fine. So it was that at the age of fifty-five, Anna Magda Crumpet became a married woman. She wished it had happened years ago. Tigger, however, was unimpressed.

★ ★ ★

Swee Poe loved Brazil. The people were charming and the sun warm. He ran a small antiques business, more to keep himself occupied than as a money making enterprise. Every Christmas, he posted a card to Griffiths, Hughes and Tucker. To Griffiths he sent a little message: "Hi Frank. I did it my way. Love Elvis." Hughes's cards always read, "Hi, Dean. Memories are made of this. Love Elvis." To Tucker he wrote, "Hi, Perry. Magic Moments. Love Elvis."

Their collective reply, if he could have heard it, was always, "The Cheeky sod!"

When the sun went down over the golden beach, there was always a large glass of Chivas Regal for company, as well as some of the lovely ladies of his acquaintance. Life was very, very sweet indeed for Swee Poe.

★ ★ ★

The old man did not live to be sentenced, but seven Asian men, including the grandson, and two women, received hefty prison sentences. A long, costly appeal was mounted, but it failed. A rival Triad moved into the areas previously under the undisputed control of the old man. New faces came, old faces left. They moved quietly, realising that to antagonise the police would mean trouble. In less than two years, all the old rackets were up and running again and bringing in the money.

"The King is dead: Long Live the King!" The new man was born in China, but British educated and a qualified solicitor. He ran a very tight ship and was going to be a very influential and rich person.

* * *

Griffiths started to see, on an occasional basis, a nursing sister from Aberystwyth's Bronglais Hospital. Their evenings out became more frequent and there were two holidays abroad. But one night, he sensed that things were not right between them.

"You're on edge. Have you anything you want to tell me?"

She was on her third gin and tonic in forty minutes, far more than her usual consumption. She placed her glass down, her eyes seemed hard.

"I do. Are we going to get married?" The boldness of the question caught him completely off-guard. In truth, he had never given any serious thought to re-marrying.

"I don't know." His reply seemed weak.

"Well, Kevin, make your mind up. I see no point in going on like this. There's no commitment! I want to plan what's left of my life. There's more to life than a series of leg-overs, when you want it, incidentally. I want a husband, a home and, if not with you, then somebody else!" Her face looked defiant, her eyes focused on his.

He opened his hands. "I repeat, I don't know, it's all so sudden."

She drained the glass. "Well, in that case, I'm off. Don't bother seeing me home."

He could have sworn a chill breeze passed over him as she swept past.

Griffiths surveyed his pint. "Well, that came out of the blue," he said to himself, conscious of veiled stares from the other couples in the lounge bar. He dallied over his pint, and then left. He felt hurt, even humiliated, and he slept badly that night.

Still wrestling with his problem next day, he passed a travel agent. In large letters, the blurb declared: THE SUNNY ALGARVE: ONLY £99 FOR 14 DAYS. SELF-CATERING. He entered the office. "Where's the Algarve, love?"

"Portugal – it's fantastic. My sister was there last month. It's lovely and warm, even at this time of the year."

He booked the holiday, there and then, and phoned the builder he worked for, saying he was going to be on holiday for two weeks. The builders were not happy, but what builders are?

The ward sister grew increasingly annoyed at the silence, and finally wrote him a brief, bitter note, terminating their relationship.

Griffiths returned refreshed from his break; the warmth had reminded him of Malaya, but there was the bonus – no-one was shooting at him. He made a big decision. He put his house on the market and wrote to Gethin and Tucker, inviting them to come out to Portugal and visit him, when he was settled. He left Aberystwyth with only one regret: that Bethan wasn't with him to share the rest of his life. Tucker and Gethin wrote and phoned regularly,

★ ★ ★

In June 1985, Richard Jenkings was sentenced in Swansea Crown Court to seven years imprisonment for possession and intent to supply Class A drugs. His solicitor blamed his activities on an unprovoked assault three years earlier, but the jury disregarded that line of defence.

★ ★ ★

Michael and Scott asked for and were granted early retirement on health grounds. They met initial resistance but, in 1984, they were pensioned off, still bound by the Official Secrets Act, which strictly forbids any disclosures of classified information. Both of them sought election as Members of Parliament, at the next general election. Both were unsuccessful, but resolved to stand again.

'Laughing Boy' retired from politics, allegedly preferring a quiet rural life. Sir Garfield also retired and wrote and published his autobiography, which was completely devoid of any mention of, or reference to, what was whispered as The Negri Sembilan Incident. The book sold moderately well. Sir Garfield died in January 1992.

Four days before he died, Sir Garfield received a phone call: his housekeeper (he was a widower) admitted to his study two men, she later told police. They were obviously known to Sir Garfield. They talked for well over an hour.

It was a bitterly cold January day; the frost-ridden ground was the only witness to their conversation. Sir Garfield was suffering from advanced colon cancer. He disclosed that his house had been burgled two weeks previously. Some items and cash were taken, and his private papers comprehensively searched. He then produced a package containing typed letters and accompanying photographs. These he gave to his visitors.

He reminded them of a meeting held ten years earlier, when the dispatch box had revealed the counterfeit War office memorandum, he repeated what the consequences would have been if the Japanese had recovered the documents and, as certainly, would have invaded Russia.

Britain would have become Hitler Britain. The Royal Navy, the British Army and Royal Air Force would have been disbanded, as would have the police forces, to be replaced by German and British armed militia, and then the Jews would have been disposed of. Trade union leaders and dissenting politicians would have been arrested. Parliament would consist of Pro-Germans, and some appeasing politicians. Russia as a Communist state would have fought a losing war against the German Army in the West and the Imperial Japanese in the East. Hitler's Final Solution would be complete.

The men shook hands and left. The housekeeper remembered one of the men had a briefcase with combination locks. On the A12 the men stopped for petrol. The garage owner recognized one of the two as a former England Rugby International, in the Freemasonry that is rugby. They talked for several minutes, the garage owner recalling his seven season with Bury St Edmunds Rugby Club. South of the village of Farnham, their car was in collision with an oil tanker delivering central heating oil. Both men were killed. No briefcase was recovered from the car, or handed in to the Suffolk police.

Five weeks later an inquest was held, complicated by the fact that the driver of the tanker could not be located, and further complicated because the firm who owned the tanker said they were unaware of the accident, and said the tanker had been taken from their yard when the bona fide driver was on his lunch break.

A verdict of accidental death was recorded. The driver of the tanker was never apprehended.

For a full list of publications,
ask for your free copy of our catalogue
– or simply surf into our secure website,
www.ylolfa.com
and order online.

y Lolfa

TALYBONT, CEREDIGION, CYMRU (WALES), SY24 5AP
email ylolfa@ylolfa.com
website www.ylolfa.com
tel. (01970) 832 304
fax 832 782